MW00627702

FLOAT

A Novel by Mary Jane Nordgren

Cover by William A. Helwig
Graphic Ingenuity

ISBN 978-0-9703896-9-5

Copyright 2020
by Mary Jane Nordgren. D.O.
and William A. Helwig
All rights reserved

TAWK PRESS
47777 Ihrig Road, Forest Grove, OR 97116

FLOAT is dedicated to my incredibly loving and supportive family, including Bill Helwig, artist, who has created the extraordinary covers for the Nandria Series.

CHAPTER ONE

Dr. Ricartsen's Exam Room,
Boonetown, Missouri, May 1940

Will peered at Dr. Ricartsen, watching him bluster and redden like a high schooler at the mention of sex. Nandria watched as well, and a compassionate smile came to her lips. "Now, Will, darling, as I told you, it is undoubtedly too early for the doctor to be able to tell for sure."

Ricartsen glanced gratefully at his friend's young wife, relieved that this Negro woman was unexpectedly rescuing him from embarrassment. Who would have thought even six months ago that Nandria Minnick would change the minds of the whole of Boonetown about what a darky was capable of? How many times had he caught himself feeling a twinge of jealousy that Will had found such an insightful, educated woman, brown-skinned or not? He hawked quietly, then caught himself and swallowed. You didn't just spit in the presence of a woman. And Nandria Minnick was not only a woman, she was a lady. He swallowed awkwardly and gathered what little he could muster of what was left of a physician's bedside manner.

"This is rather soon after the birth of your first, Mrs. Minnick. How old is Rose now?"

"Very nearly eight months, Doctor," she answered in that cultivated, British voice. Nandria realized the doctor's pleasurable reaction was to her accent. Most of Boonetown's folks seemed to hear it as proof that Will Minnick's war bride was more than skin-deep "different."

Ricartsen felt that twinge of jealousy seep into him again at the rich, low sound. He swallowed again before he could ask, "And how far along do you reckon you may be?"

Nandria looked at Will. It couldn't be much more than two months.

"I came home in March," Will started, and then caught himself and grinned at Nandria over his own presumption, though he was as certain as he was that he had two feet that his thoughts were on the mark. She chuckled with him. They'd always been able to laugh together over the awkward moments, and, even in her beloved England, a married couple of white and Negro created those in abundance. The laughter was part of their strength; that, and the surety of their devotion to one another.

"Pretty fast work," the doctor murmured, and Nandria— bless her heart—blushed more than he would have thought her skin tone could have indicated. "Will, why in this world would you send your wife alone to this neck of the woods? You know what southwest Missouri thinks of darkies. And this gal is from another country. She don't even know what her 'place' is."

"Didn't mean to send her. We were to come together, but at the last minute…"

"Rose and I were literally standing on the dock in Liverpool…," Nandria murmured, remembering, "…waiting to board ship."

"No more warning then that?" Ricartsen clucked the roof of his mouth. "I guess the Army does own you body and soul. Sorry."

And then that gnawing of what he'd heard rumored gnashed at his gut. Will would know, if anyone in the whole of southwest Missouri did. He was with Army intelligence, whatever that might be.

Seeing his frown, Nandria sat forward to ask quietly, "Do you have a concern, Doctor?"

"Well, yeah," Ricartsen answered, only realizing when he saw the fear on Will's face that this couple thought it had to do with them. "Well, not about you two. Something I'd been meaning to ask Will here."

Nandria exhaled slowly.

"You had me going there, Doc," Will breathed. "About the war?"

"Funny story I heard rumors of," Ricartsen said, nodding his apology to the Minnicks. "Germany; but it can't be true."

They were looking at him, now curious rather than frightened.

"About some woman, a mother of a sixteen-year-old who'd sent her innocent daughter off to some summer camp for Nazi Youth. The lady gets a letter from her daughter about how thirty-five of the forty-nine girls in her camp are pregnant, and she's one of the thirty-five. 'What?' the mother screams and rants. And then the girl warns her own mother to stop making such a fuss or she'll report her to her camp commander and the SS will straighten her out." Doc looked incredulous, but the Minnicks were looking at each other, shaking their heads sadly.

Will stared at the floor. Nandria lifted her chin. "'Brides of the Fuhrer,'" she explained. "The young people in Germany are taught they are doing great service to the Fatherland to bring as many Arian offspring as possible to populate the Third Reich. An honor."

"'Strength through Joy,'" Will muttered, rolling his eyes. "And such heady joy that would be at that age."

Nandria gasped, her dark eyes wide with sorrow and hilarity. "Not only heady," she murmured, so low Doc wasn't sure he'd caught it, but Will's suppressed guffaw confirmed it. Then how quickly Nandria looked up at him, nodding demurely. "The Hitler Youth motto," she told the physician.

"No!" Ricartsen looked even more colt-like with his jaw dropped from his intake of the information and from his sudden realization of the unvarnished reality these two mitigated with humor between them. It was their magic weapon against the prejudice they faced. "Really?" he managed as he looked between them.

Will nodded. "Like Nandria says, an honor. And woe to anyone who tries to shame them with the old moral codes. It started about a year and half back, probably more, but that was when we first heard of it."

"Surely their parents…" Ricartsen argued, then stopped seeing Nandria's expression.

"You must remember, Doctor, that the Youth for the past eight years or so—most of their lives—have been drilled with state propaganda. They have been told, and believe, that their parents, indeed, all their family, are far less worthy of their attention and loyalty than are their Fuhrer and their nation."

"And those kids had seen what the state could and would do to people who tried to protest or disagree in any way," Will stated, his hands clenched into fists. "So they could have their sex and patriotism, too. Powerful combination."

"Especially when the alternative is fearful," Nandria added, dark eyes sad.

Doc stood, shaking his head.

Will rose and bent to help Nandria up in preparation for their leaving.

"Are you booked closely this morning, Dr. Ricartsen?" Nandria asked, leaning forward over his desk.

"Don't think so." He shrugged, indicating that it wouldn't matter if he were; if she had another question for him, he would take time to answer it.

"Would you talk then with my husband? I do not believe his wounds are healing properly."

"Really?" Ricartsen blurted, then grinned at his own stupidity. "Could be that he's worked like a hired hand on his father's farm these couple months. How could he heal, pushing himself like that?"

"Exactly," Nandria said, rising. "I shall leave you men to talk this over between you." She left the room, opening and closing the door quietly.

Ricartsen moved to the sideboard to pour himself a glass of water from the pitcher Sadie Bean, his nurse, kept there for him. His narrow features contracted in a frown, he raised a second glass, offering it to Will. But the Army captain shook his head.

"You weren't gonna say anything to me about this, were you, Will?"

"Shrapnel, Doc. You saw that when I first got in."

"Yeah, I saw, but you never told me what you were doing to get in the way of the stuff. Even where you were. Just got to dress the wounds again, and you never come back in. So, what's the story?"

"What's to say? Pa needed a hand. I wasn't a lot of help. The hip especially slowed me down more than I wanted, but there it is. You deal with what is."

Will looked at him with such drawn-in intensity of secrets that must not be told, that even Ricartsen did nothing more to press for information he did not need for medical reasons. "Gonna let me see?"

Will hesitated. "They've got good doctors in the Army. London. New York."

"Any close around here seen ya?"

Sighing, Will shook his head. "So, do I go to one of your exam rooms?"

"Nah, Sadie'd want to make a record and keep everything official. Why don't you just drop your drawers and let me look. Then we can decide how to go from here." When Will complied, Ricartsen came around the desk, swallowing again, this time to keep himself from scolding a man who should know to take better care of himself. "Don't imagine them Bratton brothers did you no favors, either," he managed, giving Will at least a partial out for his neglect of his own wound care.

"If Horace Bratton hadn't snuck an attack on my family, he wouldn't be dead," Will snapped.

Startled at the intensity again in Will, Ricartsen nodded in agreement and added, "Too bad those Bratton brothers couldn't leave your missus alone," and then changed the subject back to Will's hip. "At least it ain't festering."

Will drew up his trousers. "Even I know to take care of that right away."

They looked at each other, castigation seen and acknowledged without words needing to be said.

"So, where do we go from here, Doctor?"

Ricartsen raised his palms, shrugging. "You ready to just rest and let it heal?"

"I live on a farm," Will answered.

"How long?"

Ah, now there was the question.

Float

CHAPTER TWO

The day wore on, and wore on Dr. Ricartsen. He was both challenged and bored by his rural practice in southwestern Missouri. "Just you keep your eyes open, Doc," Sheriff Yakes reminded him, but Ricartsen stared at him blankly. "Fer stuff missin," Yakes added peevishly.

"Oh, oh, your thief." Startled into paying attention, Ricartsen stared at the pot-bellied lawman lying on the exam table.

"Ain't mine yet, but he'll be sorry when he is, that I kin tell ya." Yakes grasped either edge of the examination table as the doctor's hands explored his naked front.

"Yes, yes, I'm sure he will be, Sheriff," Ricartsen assured him almost absently. "And I'll have Sadie take inventory far more often, if you like."

"And tell her to keep her eyes open fer anythin' sus! – picious!" Yakes gasped as the doctor's hands pressed deep into his gut. He exhaled unevenly now that the doctor had finished pressing his belly up under his ribs.

"Oh, yes, you can depend on that from our Sadie Bean."

There wasn't much that Sadie missed, and the whole town knew it.

They chuckled together, Yakes with the difficulty of a man recovering from pain; Ricartsen with the pleasant feeling of being restored to good humor.

Dr. Ricartsen was a man nearing thirty, though he often looked more like a gawky colt, tall, lanky with a thick head of hair that escaped most attempts to tame it, light hazel eyes that seemed to look deep inside your being when he focused on you. With a frown which Yakes reflected in his own expression, Ricartsen donned a rubber glove and motioned with his other hand for Yakes to assume the dreaded, humiliating position.

"Don't blame me, Sheriff. It's your age and it's gotta be done."

"Yeah," Yakes breathed, submitting.

* * * * * * * * * * * * * * * * * * *

The sheriff pressed his gut and sat up with a groan and gas that Dr. Ricartsen ignored, though the man was red-faced with embarrassment. Yakes hadn't mentioned it, but finally the awkward young doctor realized that this farting— and the pain— were what had truly brought the wretched man in to see him.

Why don't patients just come right out and say what they wanted? But they almost never do until their allotted time is all but over and I have my hand on the doorknob of their exam room, fumbling to leave.

Ricartsen turned to watch as the middle-aged man reached to put on his collarless blue shirt and button it over his protruding belly.

"You do that tooting a lot, do you, Sheriff Yakes?"

Yakes squinted, angry with Ricartsen for having brought it up, yet relieved to be able to talk to someone who might— should— be able to help. "I...I gotta be in public a lot," he started, then stopped, new red re-suffusing his features.

The sheriff was so red-cheeked he looked to Ricartsen like the fat-cheeked tomatoes the Paislers had given him even though they were one of the few families who did not owe on their bill. That the tomatoes were just a gift was almost embarrassing to Ricartsen, though he did not know why, or how they'd managed to have the plump, red things this early. It wasn't even the end of May. But no matter how things were going this late spring of 1940, Ricartsen held little or no hope of the world getting any better off in June. Ricartsen realized he had not been listening to whatever it was the sheriff was telling him. Instead, he'd been thinking about getting back to the radio in his office to find out about what was transpiring in the hated European war.

"Sorry," Ricartsen murmured, and Yakes peered at him like a little boy who'd finally gathered his courage to confess a broken window to his father, only to find the man deaf-eared and goggle-eyed watching some woman sashay away from them down the sidewalk. How many times had Ricartsen felt just like that with his own father? He felt his face warming under a flush of guilt.

A light tap at the door startled both men.

"Sadie," Ricartsen blurted, feeling his face grow warmer.

"She keeps close tabs, don't she?" The sheriff's eyes were sympathetic, as though the two men needed to ban together against the close ministrations of women. "My Patsy Lynn was

11

the same way. Always keepin' things a'goin'. But at least I got to…"
He blushed bright scarlet.

"…to enjoy the fine meals she cooked for you," Ricartsen
finished for him, grinning.

"Yeah," he nodded. "My P.L. was a good cook, all right.
Ev'rybody give her that."

"Why don't you come back tomorrow early, Sheriff Yakes?
Come on into my office and we can have a cup of coffee and talk
over your…little problem. Maybe I can help, but I don't dare take
the time now."

"Not with the Sadie-dragon breathin' down yer neck." Yakes
grinned. *Man to man. That was the way to solve this. Just so long
as it was not the gut cancer that had taken Patsy Lynn.* And yet, he
frowned. *Mebbe that's what I deserve.*

He looked up into Ricartsen's pale eyes and saw the doctor
had picked up on a shift within him that the medical man neither
understood nor liked.

"Tomorrow, early, then, Doc?" Yakes rose to tuck in his blue
cotton shirt. The tinnish star his sons had fashioned for him—
how many years before? — glittered dully in the added light from
the hallway as Ricartsen opened the exam room door. How many
towns he'd served had offered Yakes official badges of office? But
he always merely tapped this one and told them, "This serves
the purpose." And, as always in small towns, they'd known of
the boys' deaths and let him have his way. Yakes touched the star
now, and Ricartsen nodded and headed out the door ahead of
him, steeling himself to face his nurse's directions.

"Sorry, Doctor, but you got a lineup of folks waitin'," Sadie Bean was telling him. Huge and homely, Sadie was beloved because she got things done, most often with a gentleness no one would have expected from a woman her size. "Mr. House…"

"House again?" Ricartsen snarled. "Dear Lord, not another ass boil?"

"Doctor, keep your voice down!" Sadie admonished.

Yakes could hear the horror in the nurse's voice. The sheriff couldn't resist an upcurling of the corners of his mouth at learning what it was that brought the snobby Mr. House who looked down his nose at everyone in town to consult the doc so often. That nose of his'n that seemingly couldn't smell the rest of him while the rest of the town was avoiding him if it could. Their noses worked fine, unencumbered as they were by ego and denial. Yakes sighed. *Poor doc. Wonder if any of the folks who envy him would keep that up if'n they knew what he really faces one day to the next? Stickin' his finger up where no man wants to. And no man wants done, that's fer sure.* Gathering his wide-brimmed hat and shoving it onto his head without bothering to comb back his straw-like hair, Yakes stepped into the hall. *Funny how things aren't the way you thought they was when you get right down to lookin' close to the inside. We all got achin' nobody else kin see.* He wiped at his eye with his balled fist. Patsy Lynn. The boys. Gone. All gone. What was belly pain compared with that?

Float

CHAPTER THREE

Despite the fact that Boonetown wanted nothing of the war in Europe, including knowledge of it, Dr. Ricartsen huddled over the radio on the desk in his office in the house he was buying on time in the center of town. What had been the parlor suited well as the waiting room. His office had at one time been the formal dining room of the old house. In their corner of the rolling hills of southwest Missouri, the radio reception was less than reliable. The doctor took out the frustrations he could scarcely vent on his patients on the dial of the table model radio, fine-tuning again—with accompanying blue cloud comments—to try to listen to the scratchy voice of Edward R. Murrow. The papers strewn across the marred oak surface of his desk and onto the floor gave ample testimony to his irritation as the news faded in and out.

Sadie opened his door quietly to find him listening to the news about the war across the pond again. She sighed. *That war. Such a waste, for them. Probably for us, too, once we get stirrin' about it. And definitely now for Doc. His face drawn like that makes him look like a starving horse.* She opened her mouth to tell him that their last scheduled patient had not shown up, but his drawn-out moan stopped her.

"Oh, Lord, no! No!"

"That don't sound like the best news we've heard all day," Sadie remarked, startling him.

His first reaction was to growl at his huge and homely nurse. But then he beckoned her into his office to join him and at the same time motioned for her to be still. "Quiet! I gotta hear this!" His voice was wracked with anguish.

The radio went to static. Despite his frantic tuning, the newscaster's voice whined and then went silent. Ricartsen flopped back in his chair, arms stretching above him as though in supplication. "Son of a…!" Ricartsen started, but then heeded the slight shake of Sadie's head and swallowed the rest of his comment.

"So that war in Europe is goin' bad again?" she asked as she bent to gather up some of the clinic note pages that had been hurled to the floor.

"Such incredibly stupid planning. A lot of men are dying because their leaders have no imagination. No insight into what's happening right around them. Even with the Germans right behind them, their orders are to go forward!"

Sighing, Sadie glanced to see most of the would-be discarded note pages were about Mr. House. She made an untidy pile of them on the corner of Ricartsen's desk, then turned to face him. "I thought you said that nobody believed tanks could go through them forests. Isn't that what you told me?"

"Everyone thought the Ardennes were impenetrable. Thick, dense, gorgeous growth…"

"You seen 'em, have you?"

He shook his head sadly. "Only wanting to from descriptions and pictures of them in books. So lovely. It's hard to conjure someone being willing to destroy them merely to pass through. But the Krauts are flattening them as they go, evidently. Beauty, just crushed." He lowered his arms to snatch up a couple sheets of Mr. House's notes before she could grab them away from him. He crumpled the papers and sat watching the mass intently as it gently unfolded itself until the potential energy he had given it was matched by the friction of the folds against the wood. It stopped. Ricartsen sighed and leaned his scrawny neck against the sharp edge of the back of his chair. He closed his eyes.

Lips tight, Sadie reached for the now-loose ball of paper and began flattening the sheets to add them to the stack, which she hauled away from his reach. She sat to lean down to pick up the folder they had been in and set the note pages inside. She rose to store the folder on the shelf above the bookcase on the far wall. Slowly, she made her way back to the chair across the desk from her physician. She sat, her dry, rough hands folding themselves in her lap.

"Curious how quick what you think couldn't possibly happen, suddenly does," she remarked. "But we ain't gonna solve the world's problems 'cept one poor soul at a time. Mr. House…"

Ricartsen rocked forward. "He's not back again, is he?"

"Nope. Just wanted you to know that he paid another four dollars on his bill."

"Does that make a dent?"

"Well, not much of one. But it is something, I guess."

Gathering forward as though readying himself, he peered at her and sighed.

"Never mind," she assured him. "Nobody waitin'. I guess we're done for the day. Doc, why don't you come on home with me? Ron said he might be able to get home early this night and he'd sure be glad to have you join us for supper. I am a good cook, you know, despite my Ron still lookin' like skin and bones."

"He says you are, and I've tasted enough of your pickled beets and fried chicken that I always search for 'em first off at any picnic or potluck, before they're all grabbed up. Now don't you go frettin' about that husband of yours. He's healthy as a horse. And on that small frame his momma gave him, even a few extra pounds might not be good for his heart. You two are doin' fine, Sadie Bean. Don't let anybody tell you different."

"But you won't come for supper with us?"

Ricartsen shook his head. "The sooner I get out to see Mrs. Zorn, the sooner I'll be able to crawl into that bed of mine upstairs."

Rising, Sadie shook her own head, this time in anger. "That woman. Chances are when you get out to her place, she won't have a thing wrong with her. I swear she listens to everybody's complaints on her party line and by the end of the day, she's plum sure she's got one foot in the grave."

"Thank goodness for modern communication devices," Ricartsen sighed. "Well, the sooner done, sooner over."

He stretched those long limbs, and she knew it was no use trying further to get him to come for even one decent meal this week. *I need to find this man a good wife.* For a startling moment, her own daughter Ronda came to mind, but she choked, shaking her head.

"You all right, Sadie?" He stared at her.

"Yeah, yeah, I'm fine," she managed, but her face was pink with the effort. She waved him off and turned to leave.

"What time tomorrow?" he wanted to know, although it really didn't matter. More than once she had climbed the back stairs to awaken him on a morning he'd slept in after having been out on call through the night. What he wanted was to hear her voice again to listen to her breathing before she left him entirely. *Stubborn, that woman. She wouldn't ask for help for herself no matter the cost to her. For a patient, yes. Not only ask, but demand. But for herself—never. Country folk take a whole lot of gettin' used to. Frankly, it was easier, I think, back in East St. Louis. Lord, to be able to get to a big city in less than a three-hour grueling ride. Me, surrounded by people in a hurry. People who read newspapers the day they come out. People willing and anxious to discuss world events—anything besides the condition of the soil or the weather and how it's gonna affect the crops. Museums, art galleries, theaters, enormous libraries...Ah.*

She had answered, but he hadn't heard. Not the time of tomorrow's first appointment. But he had picked up on her breathing, if only subconsciously. Her air passage was clear again, and that was what he'd wanted to know. He nodded, and she swept out of his office with every indication that she was furious with him. But with Sadie, if she didn't tell you so directly, face to face, she probably wasn't angry. Frustrated, probably, with your stupidity.

Float

He sat a long time fiddling again with the radio dial, until he heard her close the front door behind her. He rose, stretching again, to wander into the back kitchen to search for something to gnaw on as he drove out to Mrs. Zorn's place. Only as he was stirring the oil back into the peanut butter before spreading it on day-old bread did he remember that he'd wanted to tell Sadie about the thefts Sheriff Yakes had warned him about. *But she probably knows about them already. Sadie knows everything in this town.*

CHAPTER FOUR

Nodding and smiling to the tiny seamstress with the needles and pins stuck in her collar, Sadie Bean shifted the small burlap bag to her other hand to balance the weight of her groceries from Owens' store. "Hello, Mrs. Drangler. You look busy, my friend. Just comin' from the Freshstalks?"

Smiling, as always, Ella Mae Drangler rolled her eyes. "You won't believe what that little gal is ordering. It'll be some wedding, all right."

"Good for her," Sadie agreed, then, knowing the Freshstalks, added, "They aren't burdening you too much, are they?"

"Hopefully all that work will set me up for a cozy winter," Mrs. Drangler smiled. "But you are a dear for worrying yourself over the likes of me."

Sadie nearly blushed. How few people saw this mountain of womanhood as a being who was herself in need of the nourishment of a bit of praise? Nodding quickly, she bid Mrs. Drangler a quick farewell and, regathering the sacks, trod on to Mulberry. At the corner, she crossed the block and raised her eyes to view the narrow two-story frame house her Ron had built just the way she wanted it. Smiling at his continuing thoughtfulness, Sadie opened the freshly painted white picket fence gate and let herself into their front yard. A tiny squeal wailed from the upper hinge as the gate closed behind her. Sadie made a quiet bet with herself that her husband would notice it when he came home. *That squeak won't be there tomorrow.* She smiled, grateful for this man she'd married.

Still smiling, Sadie climbed the seven stairs to their front porch. She eyed the granny rocker Ron had made for her, but it was too late in the afternoon for a comfort time rocking and dreaming. Too close to supper time and her man getting home for his lovingly-made meal. Pork loin this night; Sadie hefted the bag in her hand, glad Mrs. Owens had saved three choice pieces for them. Pork, and the first tender carrots from Ron's vast garden in the back. Slipping in the front door, Sadie hurried into her kitchen at the back of the house to set down her sacks. Tying on her apron, she immediately began preparations. She was setting the last of the peeled potatoes on to simmer when she heard Ronda at the front.

"That you, sweet gal?" Sadie called.

Instead of coming to the kitchen to hug her mother and peek under the lids to see what was cooking, the girl clambered up the stairs and all but slammed her bedroom door.

"What, child?" Sadie frowned as she wiped her hands on her apron. Grabbing up the burlap sack from Doc's, she hurried to the bottom of the stairs. She paused with her hand on the terminal baluster, remembering their laughter when Ron had brought her home to this house he'd worked numerous extra jobs beside his regular milk delivery route to be able to afford for her. She'd carried him over the threshold and they'd tumbled onto this very foyer floor. Nine months later, almost to that very day, Ronda had graced their lives. But since then, how many had the Lord seen fit to take back unto Himself before they'd drawn breath in this world? Four miscarriages for certain. Undoubtedly one had been the son Ron wanted, but he'd never blamed Sadie. He'd always simply been there to comfort. Still, Ronda had lived. She was their blessing, and something was wrong for her up those stairs.

"Ronnie?" Sadie cried and climbed to the second floor. In a moment she was at the girl's door. She knocked as she entered.

The big-busted girl sat with her back to her door, her textbook open on the simple desk in the alcove to the single window. She did not turn.

"Glad to see you studying, Ronda."

She did turn, then. Her eyes were red and teary; her cheeks were bright pink with evident frustration and the anger it engenders. Sadie moved into the room to seat herself on the edge of her daughter's bed nearest the alcove.

"Your math again? It's only your second session. Would it have been easier with all the other subjects to distract you during the regular school year?" Sadie asked reasonably. But within herself she questioned their parental decision to set up this special summer lesson. Ronda had always feared and dreaded math. Perhaps if she had been taking it with the others, she could take heart that they were having as hard a time as she was. "Would it?" Sadie pressed.

Ronda had always been a pleasant child, fun-loving and as eager to help anyone as was her father. She was a fine combination of the best of each of her parents. Sadie was proud of her, although modesty demanded that she not say that out loud and burden the girl with a swelled head.

Realizing from long experience that her mother would not coddle her over this or anything else that might be bothering her, Ronda glanced at the half-hidden burlap bag on the floor and changed the subject.

"What's in the bag, Mama?"

Grinning, Sadie lifted the burlap and held it out. "They ain't new, but they're just your size and Doc didn't have any use for 'em."

"Doc takin' stuff instead of money on people's bills?"

"He does, if'n he's gonna get anything at all from many."

Ronda leaned to reach for the bag, but Sadie playfully drew it back.

"Hey," Ronda chirped, and lunged. Sadie drew it away again. Giggling, they tussled a moment on the bed until, laughing in triumph, Ronda grabbed the bag and twisted away to open it. "Oh," she cried, disappointed.

Straightening, Sadie sat up and smoothed her hair and her apron. "They ain't real purdy."

Ronda stamped her feet, one on the braided rug they'd made together years before and one on the bare wooden floor. Accusingly, she held out the rugged pair of brown shoes. "They're ugly! Clunky. I ain't gonna wear these. Somebody might see me in 'em."

Sadie's shoulders rolled back and she stood upright. Although the volume of her voice did not change, the tenor did. Cowering slightly, Ronda nevertheless did not sit down as her mother towered over her.

"Them are good, sturdy shoes," Sadie pointed out. "Your feet will thank you after a hard day standing and running."

"You should know," Ronda vented in angry response. Her tone surprised herself as well as her mother.

After a moment, Sadie answered, "I do know." Sadie stared at her daughter, questioning this uncharacteristic obstinacy.

"Workin' all day with Doc Ricartsen," Ronda ventured, seeing her mother's confusion. She lifted her chin an inch, maybe two.

Sadie rocked back, cocking her head so one graying wisp of hair fell loose at her temple. "Where are you going here, Missy?"

For the first time, Ronda glanced up to be able to read her mother's expression, but it was blank. Swallowing, the girl whispered, "Just wonderin' where I come from."

"Come from?"

The rebellious spirit took the girl farther than she'd ever dared venture before. "Did you ever stop standing and runnin' and lie down for…?"

The slap from her mother's open hand, Ronda never saw coming. The buxom girl was both surprised and not surprised to find herself on the floor beside her chair. The sting in her cheek rose along with the red hot feeling of shame. It was several minutes before she got to her feet, weeping.

"I—I'm sorry, Mama."

Standing rigid, Sadie nodded curtly. "As well you should be."

Overwhelmed with misery, Ronda, face lowered, stepped toward her mother. "It's just that…"

Sadie cocked her head again, an invitation to go on; that she was listening before passing judgment.

"Th- the kids say…" Ronda whimpered.

"Since when does a Bean listen to what some foul-mouthed fool says? Ain't I taught you better'n that?"

Ronda broke into sobs, jabbing at her well-developed breasts. "I'm so— big! Clunky. Ugly."

Sadie's shoulders fell and the steel in her eyes softened. "Like them shoes. And your ma."

Shivering, Ronda crouched, trying to run past her mother out the door of her room. But Sadie caught her in muscular arms and drew her close to her even more ample bosom.

"Ronnie, Ronnie, loved child, you are Ronald Bean's daughter, I am proud to say. Your pa was born smallish, but only on the outside. He is one of the finest men I've ever been privileged to know. Big inside, and that's what counts."

Sadie gathered a holey, soft hot pad from the pocket of her apron to wipe away the snot glistening on her daughter's upper lip. *How many times have I done that when you were a tot? Oh, my baby girl, you are loved so much, but that doesn't make your coming to your own in this world a whole lot easier, does it?* Hugging her close and swaying with Ronnie in her arms, Sadie hummed the off-key lullaby she'd sung to her as an infant. Gradually Ronda's sobs eased.

"You sing awful, Mama," she whispered.

"Don't I know it?" Sadie laughed, and danced with the girl in her arms. "Pastor before Mr. Kylie said I was good in the choir because I made all the rest of them sing louder." Swaying with her, Ronda tittered and then giggled, letting herself dance in this overwhelming maternal comfort.

"I kn-know, Mama. I love Papa, too."

Sadie held her away for a moment longer, staring into her eyes. "I will fight anybody who tries to hurt him." Her expression included her daughter in that threatening promise, and Ronda nodded in agreement.

"And right you should," she said, but Sadie overrode her acknowledgment.

"Lord knows he's taken enough crude, mean-spirited remarks in his life. He don't need such-like from his own kin."

"Oh?" Ronda questioned. She'd never considered that, although she'd heard jokes hurled at her dad more than once, often from men who had been drinking, like at the KKK picnic. But he'd always taken them good-naturedly, and she'd never thought about how much they must have hurt. She shook her head and stepped back. Her mother kept one hand lightly on her shoulder as though unwilling to sever the connection between them.

"What do them kids says, Ronnie-Girl?"

It was Ronda's turn to hem and haw. It was one thing to hear such things, but another entirely to say them aloud—especially to her mama. But at Sadie's lifting of her eyebrow Ronda knew she was one step from command. The girl hunkered her shoulders and looked down. Swallowing, she murmured, but Sadie lifted her chin, and finally she spoke.

"That— that he must hafta climb you like— like a mountain…" she whispered to the floor.

"And prob'ly take a roll of string with him in case he got lost inside." Sadie's hand dropped of itself to her side. "Yeah," she sighed, "I've heard that one. Somebody even sent us a brandy keg once. Just after our honeymoon." She turned away and sat wearily back down on the edge of the bed.

"A brandy keg?" Ronda moved to the end of the bed. She held onto the foot board with both hands.

"Said they couldn't find no St. Bernard."

"Oh, for mountain rescue. That's—that's almost funny."

"That's what your father said," Sadie nearly spat.

"Papa laughed?"

"What else was there for the man to do? I hope never to hear a laugh like that again. Like his insides was rippin' open."

Ronda swung herself around the far corner of the foot board and flopped to sit on the bed with her back to her mother's. They needed to twist to be able to see each other over their shoulders. *So you want your independence, little miss. Well, good for you. I'll respect that if that's what you want.* Sadie waited quietly so it was

Ronda who spoke, and her words were a question her mother had not anticipated.

"How come some people are so mean?"

Again, Sadie sighed and turned to gaze out the second story window at the elm whose upper branches were bowing and scraping in the sundown wind. As she watched, she convinced herself she'd seen the errant light of a firefly deep in the back yard.

"I guess most times they're hurt or maybe scared inside their own selves." She twisted back to face the girl-becoming-woman. "But don't you get used to bein' mean. Pretendin' that what you say and how you say it to a body don't matter. Mebbe even workin' to get in the first lick sometimes at somebody."

"Like I just done to you."

"Well, I'm guessin' you was just tryin' it out. But you saw how a good smack can handle that theory."

Ronda rubbed her cheek and giggled. As she looked over and up at her mother, she burst into laughter at Sadie's expression. The huge-hearted nurse guffawed, and the two tangled awkwardly in each other's arms, laughing.

"Oh, Mama, I'm so sorry."

"There, there, Gal, no more to be said. So when's your math test comin'? That's what you're worried about already, ain't it?"

"Never, I wish. I just don't get it. I'm sure to flunk. And Professor Willis can't seem to understand how anybody could not understand it the way he does—like through his skin."

"Is that what you was asking Doc Ricartsen about the other day? Could he help you?"

"Said he was too long away from such. Could only remember how bad it scared him, and how glad he was to pass and be done."

"Did he have any idea who to send you to?" Sadie reach to turn the girl's face toward her. "What? What's eatin' ya?"

"He—he said the only one he could think of who might be a help was Will Minnick's, er, wife."

"Why, yeah! Miz Minnick's the very one. She's got college, and her mama taught stuff like that in London, I think. What? Are you afraid of her? She'll help you, I'm sure she will."

Squirming away, Ronda stood looking away. "But, Mama, she's—she's a nigger." She did not see Sadie's right hand lifting of itself as though to strike her daughter for only the fourth time in her entire life.

CHAPTER FIVE

In the wooden playpen set near the elm tree in the Minnicks' yard, Rose was busy pulling on the uprights, as though at seven-and-a-half months old she was determined to stand in the late morning sun.

"Will you look at him?" the biracial baby's white grandmother chattered. "Ain't he smart? And strong. My, my. He's gonna be quite the man."

"I hope not," Nandria whispered, nearly exasperated that she could not convince her befuddled mother-in-law that the child was a girl. Wiping her own cream-and-coffee forehead with her sleeve, Nandria looked over from her hoeing in the garden. Doris Minnick had set her yarn and needles on the ground beside the rocker and clucked and smiled to get the baby to try again. "She's your granddaughter, Mother Minnick," Nandria explained again as gently as she could, as tired as she was.

"Nah, this farm don't make girl children. I had the two boys. And the Pessolvers afore us had six boys. That's a passel."

"Indeed, a passel. But I brought Rose here with me. She was born in England."

"That solves it. He's cute, though. Goochie, little Goosebunny. Goochie."

Again Nandria wiped her brow and, although it was early yet, looked out for any sign of the men coming in from the field for their meal. As she was turning back to check on Rose she saw dust rising above the farm lane.

"Oh, it looks as though we may be getting company."

"Company?" Doris yelped, scrambling back to the rocker to sit down and smooth her hair and apron. "My dress, my hair. No, no company." But her eyes gleamed with anticipation. "Wonder who it is?"

Squinting, Nandria made out a figure on horseback. "It appears to be a young woman riding a mare. Alone. And she is carrying a satchel."

Doris grinned. "I wonder what she's selling."

* * * * * * * * * * * * * * * * * *

In the northwest field, Grover Minnick climbed down from his ancient Ford tractor and kicked half-heartedly at the monster back tire. "What'd it sound like to you this time, Willard?"

"I'm no mechanic, Pa," Will protested, but he knew his father was asking out of his own frustration. Pressing his injured side, Will tried to focus on what he'd heard to be able to answer with as much help as he could give. As father and son huddled next to the engine, their long-term farmhand Bodie limped to where young neighbor Greg Paisler stood a moment in the shade of a tree at the edge of the field. Greg passed the old handyman his jug of water. Warm though it was, it tasted good simply because it was wet.

"You sure ya wanna be here on Mr. Minnick's farm 'stead of yer own place with yer brothers, Greg?"

Greg looked out over the rolling acres. "My family put all our acreage into cotton. For the war, they said. But cotton's a thirsty crop. If'n we have a dry summer…" He shrugged broad shoulders and shook his head so the thatch of sun-bleached brown hair tumbled. From the looks, it was as near as the young man came to combing it. Bodie grinned, then went sober when Greg turned to him, anger in those chocolate brown eyes.

"So you'd'a left some acres in food?"

"I tried to tell 'em, people's gotta eat, war or no war."

Bodie nodded. *It makes sense to me, I reckon. No wonder the boy's upset, but why angry? And why's he spending the summer here?* "What if'n that cotton pays off?" he ventured quietly.

"Only hope it does." Greg bent to pick a long stem of meadow grass and stripped it to set the end between his teeth. "But they just overrode me. I can't work with people who won't even talk over an idea. Hell, they didn't even listen that I had one." He threw the long stem down, his lips pressed tight.

Ah, the boy's proud. He'd'a stood bein' out-voted, but not ignored. "Ya do know Minnicks can't pay you next to nothin'."

"We can settle come harvest for whatever they think I've been worth. Besides, I seen Will wincin'. He's hurting more from that war wound than he's lettin' on." Drawing back his shoulders, Greg let himself chuckle. "'Sides, I sure got a taste for his wife's cookin'."

Laughing, too, Bodie punched the youth's arm. "I knowed there was a real reason, all right, all right."

The tractor rumbled back to life. Whatever the Minnicks had done had given that ancient engine yet one more round of effort. As Mr. Minnick climbed again up into the scoop seat, Will gestured toward the road.

"Bodie, see that girl riding in? Know who she is? I don't recognize her."

"Where? Oh, ain't that there Sadie Bean's gal—Ronda, I think. After her pa, Ron Bean. Ain't seen her here for couple'a years, don't think." He turned to Greg for confirmation of his guess, but the young man was studying her with such obvious interest that Bodie grinned.

"If that is Ron Bean's gal, she never looked like that before," Greg commented low.

"Been a while since you took notice of her?" Bodie chuckled.

* * * * * * * * * * * * * * * * * * * *

In the yard, Doris stood with her bony hand at her brow, watching to see who was coming. Rose watched her grandmother for a few moments then turned to dig at her Raggedy Ann doll's eyes. Nandria had gone into the kitchen for lemonade. Wearied by her anticipation, Doris sat down again in the rocker just as Ronda rode up the lane into view.

"Ah!" cried Doris. "Tether your mare near that fence where she can feed, why don't ya, gal? You hot from the sun?"

Nandria stepped out from the enclosed back porch with a tray with three glasses and a pitcher of fresh-squeezed lemonade. "Please come," she invited, and Ronda dismounted and led the mare near the fence where the grass grew wild and tall. She dropped the reins and turned.

"I—I…" she started, then stopped, embarrassed.

Smiling, Nandria gestured for her approach. "I'll fetch us another chair while you join Mrs. Minnick."

Doris patted the chair beside her. "I knowed you when you was little, didn't I? You been out here with your mama."

"Yes'm," Ronda acknowledged without sitting down.

"Do come closer, girl, and let me look at you. No, don't tell me. It's fun guessing, but you've changed. A lot. Now let me see. Seems like I remember you sitting down with us womenfolk. But not for long, as I recall. Antsy, are you?"

"Mama's said so a few times," Ronda answered, adding "a few times a week," under her breath.

"You was mighty pretty as a kitten underfoot, as I remember."

She's not just saying that, Ronda realized. *She's not even looking at me to see my reaction, so she must remember it that way.* It did Ronda's heart good to have ever been thought of as pretty, even if it was only in the past.

"We was sewing, weren't we? We women. No, quiltin'! That's it. When the quiltin' group come here. And other homes, too, weren't it? Your mama is a quilter."

"Was," Ronda corrected.

"She dead?"

"Oh, no, ma'am! I just meant Mama has no time now. Workin' for…"

"Wait! Don't tell me. Years back. Four?"

Nodding, Ronda acknowledged. "Your memory sure is good, Mrs. Minnick. Four, or near so. The summer he come."

"Doc Ricartsen!" Doris blurted. "You're Sadie Bean's gal. Named for your pa. Ronnie."

Nandria returned with an oak chair from the kitchen; Ronda was still standing shyly beside Doris in the rocker, but both were laughing.

"Here, my dear, sit down next to Mrs. Minnick," Nandria invited, but Ronda wouldn't sit until Nandria had. As Nandria poured the lemonade, Ronda finally forced herself to speak.

"Thanks kindly. I—I'm Ronda Bean."

"And just as grown up as your mother boasts about you, Miss Bean. Welcome. I'm Nandria."

"Just the spittin' of Sadie," Doris chirped.

"Yeah, well, thanks," Ronda managed, not at all sure she wished to look just like her huge mother. Her eyes strayed to the playpen, where Rose had crept close to stare at her. "The—the baby's cute."

"Ain't he precious?" Doris agreed. "And so smart."

"Rose is a little girl," Nandria explained patiently. "She is doing quite well, thanks be to Heaven. Is the lemonade to your liking, Miss Bean?"

"Oh, yeah, it's real good," Ronda exclaimed, taking her first sip. It was good. She took another, glad for the distraction. When she lowered the glass, she found all three generations of Minnick women looking at her expectantly. "Looks like you're awful busy."

"This here is a farm," Doris sighed. "On a farm, folks are always busy. But it's a fine thing to have neighbors call and give us a break."

"How is your mother, Ronda?" Nandria asked. "Does she need anything we can help her with?"

Blushing, Ronda set down her glass to answer. "Oh, no, ma'am. It's me. What needs. I mean, mebbe you could help me, if you would."

"If I can, of course I will be happy to help you. What is it you need?"

"I'm takin' algebra," Ronda all but wailed. Her round face puckered in dismay.

"This summer?"

Ronda nodded.

"It may be that summer is a fine time to be studying the subject. In the school year, there are so many distractions. Quite a number of people struggle with algebra at first."

"Too many unknowns," Ronda mumbled, and Nandria chuckled aloud.

"Well put!"

"You—you think so?" Ronda stammered, then smiled at her own joke, though she wasn't quite sure what was so funny about it. Her shoulders relaxed, and the smile made her rather severe expression soften into sweetness.

"Quite!" Nandria laughed. "Would you happen to have brought your text with you, by chance?"

Ronnie glanced at the satchel dangling from her mare's saddle horn. "Oh, jeepers, if you could help me!"

CHAPTER SIX

In the Minnick kitchen, Nandria watched as Ronda cut the lard into the flour and salt mixture until it looked like coarse crumbs. At first she'd used too much water, and the dough had been too moist. Nandria had taken over that portion and had her start again. This time the dough was near perfect. "Go ahead and add the egg and water and vinegar," Nandria said, smiling her praise.

Ronda mixed and carefully moistened any dry bits as she tossed and lifted with her fork. At last the dough adhered into a fine, large whole.

"Are we ready to roll it out?"

"Well, not quite yet," Nandria decided. "Ordinarily we would wrap and chill this in about six sections about now, but perhaps we had best divide it into the six sections…"

Ronda hurried to help.

"…and roll each section out into a circle of approximately twenty centimeters."

Ronda frowned. A confused, "huh?" escaped her lips and then a blush overtook her neck and cheeks.

"Forgive me, Ronda," Nandria chuckled. "Your American dimension would be about eight inches. Something like this."

"Oh, yeah," Ronda agreed as she understood.

"Then we add the filling, nearly half a cup set right in the center of circle."

Ronda hurried to scoop filling into each of the remaining circles.

"Then we brush the edges of the pastry circle with just enough water to help the edges paste together as we fold the circle over on itself. And crimp or flute the edge as though it were pie crust."

"Oh, okay," Ronda laughed. Finally she was doing something familiar. She'd been helping her mother make pies since she was just a little girl. Her father loved pie and they treated him often.

"Another time, we could cut triangles so the pasty edge resembles a little dinosaur. Or twist the corners to look like devil's horns. Or the miner's wives would cut vent slices in the form of their husband's initials so there was no argument underground about whose food this was to be."

As they completed each pasty, Nandria crimped the raw edge of her creation with the flat of the fork's tines. Grinning, Ronda tried something similar with her pasties. "That makes 'em pretty," she exclaimed as they brushed each with the slurry of egg and water for a glaze and set them in the hot oven. Those Nandria had completed from the earlier dough were nearing a golden brown.

"Well done, Ronda," Nandria murmured, concerned that Ronda's pasties might not be finished baking when the men arrived from the field. But the earlier ones would be, and Ronda's could be served hot out of the oven when they were ready.

Ronda wiped her forehead with the edge of the apron Nandria had loaned her. "Pasties. I ain't—I mean, I never heard of 'em before."

"British coal miners' wives would make them for their men so they would have something filling to eat to keep them going as they worked hard deep underground." Together, Nandria and Ronda set the pasties into the oven to bake.

"Ugh, working under the ground like that. I can't imagine not seein' the sun and the blue of the sky," Ronda moaned.

Nandria lifted her eyebrows in wistful agreement.

"You thinkin' about England just now?"

"How did you know?"

"I dunno. But Mama sometimes gets a look like that sometimes when she's thinkin' about Papa. And since your Will's here on the farm now, I just guessed you miss the country you're from. What's it like in England?"

With a lilting laugh, Nandria leaned forward to take the girl's hands in her own. "You are so like your dear mother, Ronda Bean."

Ronda's eyes strayed to her own bosom and she frowned. "Want I should ring the dinner bell?" she asked to change that subject.

"Our men's stomachs are remarkably accurate. They will toddle along any minute now."

As Nandria turned to check the pasties in the oven, Ronda spoke softly to her back. "You're awful nice."

Straightening, Nandria turned to face her. "Not what you expected from a Negro?"

"No, yes. I mean…"

"Never mind, Ronda. Few folks in this area have met a woman of my skin color as a person and do not know quite what to expect." She turned again to check the green beans on the stove.

"You ain't like no other darky I know, mebbe because you're from England." Concerned by the startled expression on Nandria's face, Ronda gulped and changed the subject again. "Mama says we get nasty when we feel small and afraid."

"And we all do, one time or another. Your mother is a wise and compassionate woman. I think you will be, as well."

Ronda opened her mouth, but, unable to think of anything to say, was gladly distracted by the sound of the men entering at the back door onto the porch. Minnick, still shuffling into his slippers, entered the kitchen first, leading Doris and seating her at her place at the table nearest his own. Bodie was next, gesturing to Greg Paisler behind him to seat himself on one of the chairs against the wall so the porch end of the table would be free for Will and his wife. After a quick peck of a kiss on the back of Nandria's neck, Will sat, with Rose on his lap, at the end of the table opposite his father.

"Sit and eat, Greg Paisler," Minnick commanded. "A workman is worthy of his wages."

Doris's face brightened. "I think it was St. Paul said that, Mr. Minnick," she told him, delighted.

"Well, he got one thing right, then."

As Ronda turned with the platter of pasties, she saw what she feared and yet could feel her heart beating rapidly to see. How many times had she gazed at the back of that young man's head and shoulders as he sat with his family in the pews ahead? How many long, long sermons by Pastor Kylie had she dreamed away staring at him and dreaming that he'd take her in his muscular arms? The platter tilted; the pasties slid—and would have splattered to the floor had Nandria not twisted to right the platter again to level position in the girl's hands.

Ronda blushed a fierce red; Greg laughed aloud.

"You go to spillin' stuff as bad as I do there, young lady," he called. "Must be I'm rubbin' off on ya even from across the room." *So awkward you could be my sister. But I'm glad you ain't.*

With as much grace as she could muster, Ronda set the platter on the table in front of Mr. Minnick and backed away toward the sink. But Nandria caught her in her arms in mid-kitchen, and spoke. "Everyone, this is Ronda Bean. She is not only a great help in the kitchen, she is one very wise young woman, studying algebra this summer. She has agreed to help me brush up on my mathematics as we study together."

"Math? In the summer?" Greg asked, incredulous. "By choice?"

"Is that not a wise decision? To study with full attention," Nandria defended her. "Sit here next to Mother Minnick, Ronda."

Doris beamed as the girl sat beside her.

"Well," said Will, reaching for a piece of homemade bread to give to his hungry little girl, "I hope it doesn't interfere with your fun this summer."

"No season's strictly for fun," Minnick groused.

"Maybe not, Pa, but summer probably comes closest. Are you going to get to see the fireworks on the 4th?" He scooted to one side to give Nandria room to sit beside him.

Ronda saw that Will was looking to her for an answer. She felt the heat of yet another blush rising up her throat, but she swallowed to answer. "I—I don't know. Prob'ly. We usually go to Shute Grove."

Seeing Bodie and her husband lifting the pasties from the plates Minnick had served them, Doris chirped, "Oh, Mr. Minnick, we got so busy talking, we forgot to say grace."

"So we did, Mother," he said and lifted his hands after setting down the dough pocket of meat. All bowed in anticipation. "Bless our Lord, we beseech thee, this food to our use…"

As Minnick continued the words of blessing, Greg opened his eyes and peered under his brows. He was as startled as Ronda was to catch her peeking at him. Both flushed red and quickly looked down at their folded hands.

* * * * * * * * * * * * * * * * * * *

In town that afternoon, Pastor Kylie slid his forefinger under his turned collar to relieve the chafing of his neck. That new darky he'd hired had used far too much starch. He would need to speak to her, and then, if it happened again, to send her packing. It wouldn't do to have him go out among his flock fussing away his discomfort. It made him feel, and look, small. A pastor is supposed to lead his flock, not draw their pity. While he was fuming, a mare trotted by with a young girl riding astride the animal. Her calf-length skirt ballooned out to either side. She hurried by without acknowledgment, apparently not even seeing him. "The hussy," Kylie breathed, flushing anger onto each successive double chin.

At the post at the end of Dr. Ricartsen's walkway, Ronda pulled up on the reins, though her "Whoa" had been enough to slow her mare. The girl jumped down, dropping the reins rather than tying them, and ran up the walk toward the door. She'd reached to push it in, when it flew from her hands and Mr. House stood stiffly erect, wincing at the jarring of her working the door against his hands.

"Young lady," he admonished through gritted teeth.

"Sorry, Mr. House." She backed out onto the stoop to give him ample room to get by her through the doorway.

Mrs. Drangler, rising from her seat in the front room to see what was going on, chuckled until the pins glittered on her collar as Ronda burst inside. At the ruckus, Sadie marched from the back hall.

"What in the world? Ah, Ronnie-girl, it's you. Got your homework straightened out then?"

"Ah, Mama! They're wonderful!"

Sadie beamed her I-tried-to-tell-you-so smile, until she saw in her daughter's face that it was more than the younger Minnick couple that was "wonderful." But as she glanced around to see who was there to listen to their conversation, her question for Ronda got lost in the cry of distress from Dr. Ricartsen's office.

"Oh, Lordy! Lordy!" Doc cried. "No!"

The three women hurried to his office door. Sadie entered even as she knocked. Mrs. Drangler and Ronda pushed in behind her. Moaning into his hands, Ricartsen sat, butt deep in his pushed-back chair so he could lean close over the brown, table-top radio on his desk. He was fiddling with the ivory-colored dial, all but weeping in his frustration at trying to keep the station tuned in. As he heard the women enter, he raised tear-stained cheeks.

"Lord help us, Sadie Bean, the Krauts have reached the Channel."

Ronda stared at him. "There's sauerkraut in the creek?" Confused, she shook her head, and turned to her mother, but it was Doc Ricartsen who answered.

"Would that was all there was to it, Miss Bean," he told her kindly. But devastation again drew his narrow features until Ronda had to look away. He continued his explanation while looking deeply at the scars in the oak desk top. "The Nazis now sit at the eastern edge of the English Channel. Nothing but choppy waves between them and the brave folks of England, Ireland, and Wales."

"Oh, Mama, Nandria is from England. I best go tell her."

"Yes, Ronnie, I think she would want to know. Go, child." Sadie touched her daughter's shoulders, hugged her briefly as though she knew that if England did fall to this German terror, there was no possible way that her United States would be able to stay out of this second European war, dread that prospect though they all did.

Ronda looked up, saw the tear on her mother's cheek and cringed, but Sadie again hugged her close and sent her off. "Minnicks will want to know," she whispered. "Good girl for thinking of them. Thank you."

Without looking back, Ronda ran past Mrs. Drangler and out through the front lobby. They heard the door close behind her. It was the little seamstress who needed clarification.

"So that's bad news about their war across the Big Pond?"

"Terrible," Ricartsen acknowledged, his butt well practiced at bringing the chair up under him and close to the desk again.

"Our boys gonna get took back over there when we're only just now gettin' our farms back heavy with good food again?"

Both women gasped at the emphatic "yes" on Ricartsen's anguished face.

Float

CHAPTER SEVEN

Ronda's mare stood patiently while the girl leapt down and hurried without tethering the animal toward the Minnick's enclosed back porch. With two trips out all this way to the Minnick farm, and this second one in some hurry, the mare was quite willing to stand where she was with her reins trailing for a time before ambling across the lane to the fence where the grass, though getting dry, was tall and plentiful, especially around each upright post.

"Miz Minnick!" Ronda hollered as she ran. "Nandria!"

Will was the first to burst from the porch door with Greg Paisler close behind him. As Will caught the distraught girl in his arms, the rest of the family hurried out to the back lawn to learn what was so wrong to bring Ronda bursting in on them. Handing little Rose to Bodie, the last to exit the house, Nandria stepped closer to brush back unruly clumps of hair from the girl's face.

"Ronda, dear, you are safe here," Nandria crooned. "Will has you. What is it? What's wrong?"

White-faced, Doris clung to her husband. "Mr. Minnick? What is it? Is it Freddy?"

He patted her shoulder and drew her closer. "No more, Mother. Never again."

Greg leaned nearer. "Trouble in town, girl? Tell us."

Breathless, Ronda piped a single word: "Germans!"

"We're under attack?" Will demanded.

"Where are they, Ronda?" Nandria coaxed. "Where are the Germans?"

"Channish englel," the girl managed, but her anxious audience froze in confusion.

"Channish englel? Uh, oh, English Channel?" Nandria reasoned. "Is it the English Channel you are trying to tell us?"

Nodding vigorously, Ronda was finally catching her breath.

"Are you telling us that the Germans have made it to the English Channel?" Will insisted on clarification.

"What's she saying, Will?" Greg wanted to know.

"Oh, Lord, Will..." Nandria stared at him, her face drawn to despair.

With a great gulp of air, Ronda tried to explain. "They squeezed through them trees."

"Squeezed through what trees?" Greg demanded. "What's this all about, Will? Nothing good, I reckon."

"Nothing good," Will echoed. He calmed his breathing before explaining. "Nobody believed the Nazi tanks could thread through an incredibly thick, gorgeous forest in northern France."

"The Ardinelles," Ronda muttered.

"The Ardennes, you're right, Miss Bean," Will assured her.

"If nobody thought there'd be threat from there, they didn't defend it, did they?" Greg figured.

"No need, they assumed," Will answered, shaking his head. "But I'd bet the French—in fact, probably all the Allies are paying for that miscalculation now."

"Sounds like they was quick gettin' that far." Minnick's usual stoic expression was creased with concern as he moved closer to Will after his son had handed the girl over to Nandria for comfort.

"Their 'lightning war.' Blitzkrieg," Nandria murmured without looking over at her father-in-law. When she did look up, he was scowling, but she wasn't sure it was because she had broken into a man's conversation or perhaps because she was showing him up, knowing more than he did about a world event. Tightening her lips, she looked at Will to continue, but could not refrain from speculating. "Near Calais, do you not think, Will? On the spit the way it is, it is only a stone's throw from England."

"It would take a pretty fair arm to hit England from there," he grimaced. "But you're essentially right, Nandria. That would be about the Channel's narrowest point."

"And the Krauts is there by this Calley?" Minnick demanded of his son.

"Most likely at least one Panzer division."

When the vertical crease in Minnick's forehead deepened, Nandria could not stop herself from again interjecting what she knew. "Tanks," she stated. "Heavily armed and very fast."

51

Minnick turned on her. "How do you know?" He was so focused on the uppity Negress that he didn't catch Will stiffening at the apparent attempt to humiliate his wife yet again.

Nandria opened her mouth to explain, but Ronda must have thought the challenge was directed at herself.

"That Edward Arm Arrow guy on Doc's radio told us. Doc keeps bendin' over it, listening. Mama's worried about him, he gets so wrapped up in the war news," the girl explained.

"I think Sadie Bean is worried about all of us," Greg added. "You, especially, Miss Bean." He felt a flush rising as Ronda pinked, but quickly changed the subject to what concerned him the most at the moment. "Will, there's gonna be a lot of people pushin' to get us into this now, ain't there? You think Rousy-velt's gonna declare war?"

Ronda's face fell. "We're gonna be in a war?"

It was Doris who spoke, the others having gone silent with their own thoughts. "When've we ever not been at war with the elements, eh, Mr. Minnick?"

CHAPTER EIGHT

The next day, just after noon, Mr. Owens poked his head through the curtain from the butcher area behind Boonetown General Store. He'd heard his gentle wife's soft call. He wiped his hands with a clean towel. With a practiced flip of his blood-crusted apron over his head in the storeroom, Isaac tossed the towel into the corner and settled a more presentable bib apron over his head. Already moving forward into the public part of the store, he tied the apron's long strings, crossing them behind his back and knotting them over his beginning paunch. He stepped into the large, crowded single room of the store he and his Bernice had worked these many years to build into a thriving business. Son Eugene Isaac Owens had wanted nothing to do with the bothersome people one needed to deal with in retail. He'd left for Springfield as soon as the principal of the high school in Fox Haven handed him his diploma. So, the graying couple were left with what they'd poured sweat, blood and tears, but not soul, into. Neither spoke their boy's name and hoped no one in small town ever saw fit to name a child or grandchild Jean or Gene.

Bernice nodded her thanks for her husband's quick response and gestured toward the Minnicks entering the double-wide front door. She tucked back a knot of field mouse-brown hair that had escaped her hairnet and turned again to smile at Mrs. Freshstalk and her prissy daughter.

With a quick swipe with the bottom corner of his fresh apron at his weeping right eye, Isaac Owens plowed forward to greet Grover, Doris and Will Minnick.

"Good afternoon, Mr. Minnick." Owens extended his hand, regretting, as always, the difference between his softer palms and the thick calluses of Grover's pressing into his. As he extracted his hand and willed himself not to wince or rub it, he turned his smile to Doris. "Mrs. Minnick, welcome. You are lookin' well. Glad to see you out and about." He looked over at Will with eyebrow lifted. "Nothing botherin' the baby or the little woman, I hope, Will?"

"No, no, Mr. Owens," Will assured him, pleased that he'd noted Nandria's absence as though it mattered to him. "My wife stopped first at Doc Ricartsen's for a word with Sadie Bean."

"Beans are full of news about the Krauts. Some folks are sure them Germans are gonna override us any day now. We've had a run goin' on for folks stockin' up on supplies like we ain't seen since them tornadoes in '38. You're with the Army, Will. Any truth to the rumors the Nazis is near at our door?"

"Not our door, Mr. Owens. But the Londoners are feeling their hot breath."

When Doris stirred uncomfortably, Minnick intervened. "Didn't come to monger, Owens, but for a radio, and that's near as bad."

Will looked over at his father but tightened his lips and said nothing. Instead he turned to watch his mother wandering over to peer into the glass jewelry display like a child drawn to the candy jar.

"Oh, ain't they purdy?" Doris breathed.

Minnick followed her and came to stand close beside her, the corners of his mouth lifting as he took in the joy of her expression. "Which one do you want, Mother?"

"I can have one, Mr. Minnick? Really and true? They're so purdy." But she looked up, sure he was going to need to tell her how tight their means were.

He laid his hand gently on her shoulder. "Been a good many years since you've had somethin' new. If'n we're goin' under, mebbe this time you can wear somethin' just because you wanted it."

Will glanced at Mr. Owens' concerned frown and walked midway between his parents and the storekeeper to explain. "We aren't going under, Pa. The radio is only to be able to keep track of where we are."

"So we know just when we *are* goin' under," Minnick argued, daring his son to contradict what he'd determined to be true. Owens was openly staring between the two.

"I know it looks bad, Pa. I can't argue that, though I know it's what you want me to do."

With an audible exhalation of disgust, Minnick turned his back on Will and bent over the jewelry case with Doris. Owens stumbled a few steps toward Will, his forehead creased in deep furrows.

"They say you're with Intelligence, Will, like a spy. You know stuff."

"Not really, Mr. Owens. I did some calculating for them, but right now I don't know any more about what's going on than you do. That's why I want a radio."

"Radio, yes!" Owens again wiped at his irritated right eye and, dropping his apron front, motioned for Will to follow him to a far corner of the store. "We have a couple over here. RCA's got some handsome models. What range'll you want?"

"Worldwide, if you have it."

Shaking his head slowly side to side, Owens gaped at this young man he'd hoped would be able to assure him of their future.

CHAPTER NINE

The Minnicks had elongated their day with that extra trip into Boonetown. By that evening, even Bodie and Greg seemed extra tired. Bodie took off for his place soon after supper. Nandria glanced again and again out the kitchen window at the sky thickening with dark clouds as she finished the supper dishes. From her high chair where she was busy gnawing a heel of bread into a soggy lump, little Rose watched her grandmother grow bored seated beside Ronda at the table.

Doris tugged at the corner of Ronda's textbook to pull it across the oak kitchen table toward her. "Ah, Mama, don't…" came to the girl's lips before she remembered where she was. "Oh, Mrs. Minnick, are you interested in mathematics?" she managed instead.

"Math-me-atics?" Doris recoiled. "Is that what your book is all about? I was hoping it was a purdy story of a handsome prince winnin' his lovely princess."

"Don't I wish!" Ronda grinned conspiratorially. "You and I know what's really important, don't we?"

"Don't we, though?" Doris hunkered closer, delighted with the girl's including her in her playfulness.

"Ah, but it is only my Algebra homework. Miz Nandria is helping me. Isn't she wonderful?"

Doris stared her, her eyes blank. She raised a sparse eyebrow as though to question who this person might be calling herself "Miz Nandria."

Nandria let out the last of the dishwater and turned away from the sink. Wiping her hands on the tea towel and smiling gently, she walked over to the table. She laid a gentle hand on Doris's shoulder as the older woman fussed with the scarf at her throat and puckered up in dismay.

"All is well, Mother Minnick. I think Mr. Minnick would enjoy your cheering him on in his dominoes game with Greg Paisler, if you feel up to it?"

"The mister wants me?"

"Yes, in the living room," Nandria nodded. Ronda sat without saying anything as she watched them both until Doris rose and wandered out of the kitchen toward the sofa in the living room. Sitting in the chair beside the bewildered Ronda, Nandria leaned close to explain. "Mother Minnick does pretty well most times, but in the evenings she gets overtired and loses track of reality a little. Please just treat her gently. She cannot help herself. You have seen for yourself how well she can do, especially in the morning."

"Oh, yes," Ronda hastened to assure her. "I really didn't know what might be wrong."

"I fear neither does Dr. Ricartsen nor any of the other physicians Mr. Minnick has taken her to see." Nandria sighed and reached for one of the papers spread in the center of the table in front of Ronda. "So, how is the lesson coming?"

The girl was about to answer when they both looked up at the muffled exclamations of frustration erupting from the enclosed porch. They'd been hearing the scratchy noises intermittent with garbled, deep-throated monologue for quite a while without being fully aware or alert. Now Will's voice was half-raised in exasperation. With a quick apology to Ronda, Nandria rose to hurry to her husband.

"Just when I hear something, it turns to static," Will complained in answer to Nandria's look of inquiry. Smiling, she approached to sit beside him at the edge of their brass bed. He swore under his breath again and returned to fiddling with the radio dial.

"Well, when you are as tired as you are this evening, it should not be surprising that fine tuning is more a matter of blind luck than skill."

"Which would be a ladylike way of telling me I am clumsy."

"Why do you not consider 'turning in,' as you Americans would say?"

"Turn into what? No, don't answer that. I hear your point. I guess I was waiting to see Ronda safely home. And don't tell me that you can tie her horse to the back of the truck and drive her into town. Who would see you safely home then?"

"It may be that Greg Paisler is more unhappy with his family than he has given us to believe. He is still in the living room with your father, trying to win at dominoes."

Grinning, Will relaxed and reached for his wife. "Or stalling until Ronda is ready to go. What young women do to poor, unsuspecting young men!"

Float

Nandria returned his quick kiss before rising. "Shall I send them on to Boonetown, then?"

"Right soon, and then we should turn in." He rolled his eyes and Nandria smiled at that prospect. As she re-entered the kitchen, Ronda was gathering up her books and papers in her satchel.

"I'm sorry; I should have left for home hours ago, but I was so excited to be gettin' the hang of this algebra stuff."

"Once you have grasped the concepts, you will find that you use it far more often than you realized you would." She stopped to lean close to ask quietly. "I was about to prevail on Greg Paisler to see you home, if that is satisfactory with you?" The girl's deep blush was a clear sign of agreement. Nandria smiled as she headed then for the living room.

Evidently Minnick had already escorted Doris to her room, for only the two men were to be seen in the long living room. The low coffee table that normally stood in front of the sofa was now arrayed at hand to Minnick's easy chair. On it lay a long, intricate pattern of domino tiles spread in testimony to the competitiveness of one farmer and another farmer's son. Greg, sitting on the floor with his long legs splayed, leaned on one elbow to twist to acknowledge Nandria as she approached.

"Miz Minnick, has my thinkin' rattled my brain too loud and bothered your teachin'?" he chuckled.

"Girl, you ruined my concentration, bargin' in like that," Minnick scowled, but his voice was soft as though thanking her for ending the ordeal of hours-long strategy.

"So sorry," she murmured, hiding her smile.

"Well, I ain't!" Greg was awkward, extracting one leg from under the low table and rolling over onto hands and knees to get up. "Mr. Minnick was about to beat me into the ground again. You're sending me home with mebbe a draw I didn't deserve but like right 'nuff.'"

"You'll never come closer to a win from me, young fella."

"You're probably right, sir." Greg was up now, and grinning, though his hard work in the Minnick fields left him with pudgy gray-green half-circles under those dark chocolate brown eyes. By choice, he probably would have gone to bed much earlier.

"May I ask a favor?" Nandria began.

"She's gonna ask you to see that nurse's gal home. See if'n she don't," Minnick warned. "Not too much of a hardship, is it?" He said it all straight-faced, but there was a stray light in his eye that Nandria had only seen once before when little Rose reached from her grandmother's arms for her grandfather to take her. Nandria was about to comment something foolish when they all turned at a loud outcry from Will on the porch.

"Oh, Lord Almighty!"

Twisting on one foot, Nandria was the first to dash to her Will. Greg also turned, then went back to help Minnick scramble up, untangling himself from the legs of the low table. Nandria rushed by Ronda getting up from her chair. The girl backed away to let Mr. Minnick pass her. Blinking, she felt Greg slow and come back to her as he hurried through.

"You okay, Miss Bean?"

She looked up at him, her mouth an 'O.' She opened those gray eyes that sparkled green in the sunlight, he'd noticed. They were brimming now with tears.

"Here, come with me," he told her protectively, taking her arm to keep her close. They untied the long diaper that had been used to strap Rose safely in her high chair. Greg lifted her with an expertise that surprised Ronda, although, when she thought about it, he'd had a passel of younger brothers. Of course he knew how to handle a little one. She clung to one of his arms. They were the last to get to the porch, where Nandria glanced up at them gratefully for having taken over care of the baby. Frowning, she huddled close beside Will as he worked to keep the radio broadcaster's voice audible. Minnick plopped into the rocker, drawing it close and straining forward to listen.

"...*Dunkirk... only beach... German Panzers rac...*" The voice scratched and was taken over by incomprehensible static.

"Oh, Lord," Nandria whispered. "No."

CHAPTER TEN

Nandria leaned the long handle of the hoe against her shoulder and turned, rubbing her sore palms, to check on Rose in her playpen. Drooling into her grin, the little one greeted her mother's attention with an enthusiastic wave that toppled her to a sudden sit-down. She laughed. Doris looked up from snapping the long green beans and chuckled, setting one and then the other off into long peals of laughter. Hands still sore, but heart warmed, Nandria glanced around before returning to her garden work. It was from the corner of her eye that she caught the powdery dust cloud that meant someone was coming up the Minnick lane.

"Company, Mother Minnick."

"Company, oh, no. My hair. My dress. My apron," Doris fussed, staring down the lane hoping to see who was coming. Her drawn face took on animated anticipation. "I wonder who it could be this late in the morning."

The truck that pulled up might well have been one of the milk delivery trucks belonging to Ron Bean's firm. It was old, but evidently sturdily built. Both long doors were open, if indeed they could be closed. The driver had to stand behind the high steering wheel of the squat van. The sides had been painted over, which worked well where they had been white. But the milk company's logo showed faintly beneath the goldish-brown coat.

"G E M, Working to Make Your Life Luxurious" was emblazoned in rich yellow that gleamed iridescent in the sunlight.

Nandria shaded her eyes to peer in at the youthful driver. A slight man with thatch of straw-brown-yellow hair that went well with his topaz GEM jumpsuit. His eyes, though, when he stepped from the van carrying a tray of glittering and mundane items for the household—his eyes were green and somehow belied the grin of a born salesman that opened below them. As he turned, from the side Nandria caught what seemed a golden gleam from those green eyes. Eerie, and, at the same time, oddly attractive.

Nandria swallowed before she lifted her hand in welcome. "Come in, come in," she echoed her mother-in-law.

"Hello, Ladies," the young man called, smiling widely. "I'm Ben Struan, with Kleinwares' GEM traveling stores. We bring the shopping to you."

"Welcome, Mr. Struan," Nandria said, standing her hoe and coming to approach the playpen. She gestured to her mother-in-law. "We are the Minnicks; Mrs. Grover Minnick."

He bowed; Doris giggled.

"And I am Mrs. Will Minnick," she added as she picked up her wide-eyed little one. "And this is Rose." She waved the baby's pudgy right hand. Rose, feeling safe in her mother's arms, nearly smiled. "Would you like something cold to drink?"

"That's right kindly of you, miz," he nodded toward Nandria, then turned to bow again toward Doris.

"Whatcha got there, young man?" Doris asked, her excitement showing on her face. "They's for sale, ain't they?"

"Caught me dead to rights, ma'am. I am here to afford you fine opportunities for some high-quality merchandise for you to choose from in the comfort of your very own home."

With an impish grin, Doris chirped, "Sounds expensive."

"It isn't," Struan leaned in conspiratorially. "But no one needs to know that."

"Oh, then we must see everything in that case." Doris's face glowed with anticipation.

Rose, watching her, grinned widely, drooling. Nandria set the child back into the playpen where she could watch her grandmother. She turned toward the house saying, "I shall fetch us those cold drinks then."

"Anything I can help carry, miz?"

Hesitating, Nandria turned back to look at the young man, strangely fearful. But the three were already gleefully engaged, and Nandria shook her head again, scolding herself. *Nandria Brown Minnick, do not allow yourself the distorting influence of paranoia. You do not know the ways of these people well enough to superimpose your own feelings onto them or their motives.*

Nandria frowned as she looked back once more from the doorway to the porch. When she emerged a few minutes later with the Minnicks' tray of glasses and pitcher of lemonade, she'd slipped her slender wallet into the pocket of her apron. Young Struan had already spread a shiny blanket on the grass at Doris's feet. He was bent, setting housewares out for display, but rose quickly to come to take the tray from Nandria.

"How very kind you are," he repeated quietly so only Nandria could hear as he set the tray on the small table beside Doris.

Nandria shook her head once more, uncomfortable with his degree of praise and gratitude. But she poured freshly squeezed, pale yellow liquid into each of the three glasses, handing one first to Doris and then Struan. Doris waved hers away; she was too interested in the display of goods, especially the trinket glass-jewels Struan had set sparkling at the corner of the blanket. He watched her interest, and, sipping his lemonade, strode back to the van. Emerging a moment later with a small tray spread with a purple-black velvet cloth that showed wear at the back edge. On it were pins, lockets, gaudy rings of impossible gems surrounded by glass diamonds. Two pearl necklaces; one ivory cameo with an intricate lock already showing green at the margins.

This is used jewelry. Why would a merchant company be selling used jewelry? Nandria wondered, but, saying nothing, she went to sit beside the playpen to be near Rose.

"Would you have a radio for sale, Mr. Struan?" Nandria asked quietly. They already had the only one they were likely to buy, but she was curious as to whether he would carry one and how much he would charge for it. She nodded with understanding as he ruefully shook his head and set his glass of lemonade aside to concentrate on the elder mistress of the house.

"Anything of interest there, Mrs. Grover Minnick?" Struan asked, wiping his mouth with the back of his hand.

Doris barely looked up, and when she did it was with the delight of a child taking her time choosing from a tall jar of candy. She shook her head impatiently at his interruption.

"Well, I see a cheese grater," Nandria interjected. "Ours is, frankly, elderly to the point of creating a mass rather than singular, grated strands."

The young man eyed her curiously. He'd never heard such formal speech from a country housewife. But then he'd seldom been asked to serve a lady with a Brit accent or a Negro wife of a white farmer, either. *Wherever this one comes from, she'd be foreign to these parts even if she'd been lily white.* Struan lifted the cheese grater from the back corner and handed it to Nandria for inspection.

"Two bits, ma'am," he shrugged. "Or less, if'n you're buyin' something else as well." He turned to the older housewife. "Are you finding something to your likin', ma'am?"

Doris was obviously tiring, but she bent forward one last time to set several of the bracelets and a round pin back on the blanket. She sat back in her chair, sighing, clutching a brooch of impossibly red and purple stones. She looked over at Nandria with pleading in her eyes.

"Would you like that stunning piece, Mrs. Minnick? I can wrap it in tissue for you. Or if you'd like a cushioned box for it, it would only cost a nickel extra." He turned to Nandria. "And the grater? It'll only be a quarter for the utensil and the box, if you want them both."

"How much you gonna stick my mister for for this here pin, young fella?" Doris asked, sounding like a seasoned negotiator.

Struan hesitated, but only for a moment. "How about $2.95? That'd be three dollars with the cushioned box."

"And the grater another quarter?" Doris sighed as though incredulous he could ask so much of a farming family barely scraping by, but her eyes were on Nandria who was shaking her head slightly.

Struan rose, lifting out a small, rounded-topped snap box of soft lavender. He opened it to show Mrs. Grover Minnick the lilac colored, mounded satin inside. When she nodded, he closed it was a sharp snap that startled little Rose. The little one whimpered, then puckered up as though she would cry until her mother stroked her arm and murmured to settle her.

Ben Struan held out the lavender box to Doris and stepped back to address Nandria. "Sorry, ma'am, I forgot how little ones startle to sounds." He shook his head as though to apologize and then quickly gathered within the good feelings engendered by Nandria's acceptance of his apology. "For such a gracious family, I couldn't charge you more'n, let's say two dollars for the whole kit and caboodle. How about a dollar and ninety-eight cents? Then you'd have your jewel, your grater that'll grate rather than mash and your own two cents worth, too."

Doris chuckled aloud, Rose chortled, and Nandria smiled as she fumbled in her apron pocket to hand him two worn one dollar bills. He handed her the grater and took the bills without expression, but she caught the glint of superiority in his eyes. He frowned as he realized she was again more than he had allowed himself to believe. But he recaptured his flair in presenting the elder Mrs. Minnick with two shiny pennies and then, with yet another bow, offering her the new-to-her brooch.

"Madam," he intoned as though the brooch was set with rubies and amethysts.

Doris opened the box slowly, gazing at the glimmer from the glass facets from all angles.

Both Nandria and Struan gazed at her, smiling, this time with good will. The young man turned to ask quietly of Nandria, "Were those pebbles in there, too?" His gaze fell on her apron pockets before looking at her face. In her own turn, she recognized (and he saw that she did) that he was more observant, sharper than she had given him credit for.

"Yes, they keep me grounded."

"You're a deep one, aren't you? Not from around here."

"London."

"Illinois?"

"England."

"That country's at war, isn't it?"

"Yes, Mr. Struan, it is."

"Losing," he commiserated, shaking his head.

"No. You do not know the British if you believe they could lose this war."

"But obviously you think they will," he countered. "You're here."

He caught her reaction; labeled it guilt. And then he saw something in her eyes that told him it was time for him to leave.

"I am sorry, ladies," he managed, gathering up his wares. "It has been a delight to get to know you, all three. But I really must be getting on to my next farm. Thank you so much for the delicious refreshments."

They watched him pack and leave. He waved, standing at the steering wheel of the van and Doris waved back. Rose moved her arm. Nandria stood fingering the pebbles in her apron pockets, considering.

As his dust settled on the lane, Doris once more gazed fondly at the brooch as though conjuring up memories from long ago.

"It sparkles," Nandria commented. She picked up Rose to check her diaper before going back to the hoeing.

"Ugly as sin," Doris told her, "but Gerald Teagarden got it for me when we was only two sillies in grade school. Such a crush he had on me. Saved up his egg money to buy it. You should have seen his face when he gave it to me. I thought he'd burst, he was so red. Didn't know anyone could get that red. And then he got redder when I wouldn't take it. I had no idea he'd kept it all these years."

"Teagardens? Do they reside near here?"

"Gerald married Elisa Ramford not so long after I found my Grover. Two boys and three gals, they had. All grown up and married. Only the one—the second gal—stayed on their farm with her husband, but Gerald has grandchildren runnin' around at his feet." Doris stopped, again peering at the brooch. What she added Nandria almost did not hear, she said it so low. "Heard the

Teagardens got robbed a month ago—mebbe more. I'll need to check with Mr. Minnick this night. Mebbe I'm wrong."

Float

CHAPTER ELEVEN

"Nazis are coming!"

"How in heaven's name could them Allied leaders let that happen?"

"They're on our East coast, ya say?"

"I heard they was at the tip of Cape Cod. Ain't that so?"

Boonetown's folk clumped in worried, fast-talking knots. Buzzing, heads together in worry and resulting anger, their clusters shifted and regrouped again and again as they gathered near the railroad shack where the tracks crossed town and on the boardwalk.

Women who had done their weekly shopping only the day before carried their baskets hanging from their arms and congregated near the entrance to Owens' store, eager for news. Their near-hysterical whispers among their shifting clumps slowed and then stopped actual would-be customers as they came in, until even Mrs. Owens' patient smile sagged to a frown. Again and again Bernice persuaded one or another small group to move on outside, but each victory was only momentary. She was gently herding her ninth or tenth cluster of frightened women past the printed "cheap" sign at the base of the next-door window toward Ludwig's when Mrs. Zorn gasped so loudly that all the women—and the men who watched and listened from the road—turned as one to look where she pointed.

"Mrs. Drangler, ain't that?" Mrs. Zorn cried. "Who's she pushing?"

"Looks like she's throwing whoever it is out of her shop."

"Looks young, don't she? Who...?"

"No, look, she's bustling the gal across the road."

"Yeah, looks like she's steerin' her toward Doc Ricartsen's."

After all her efforts to dislodge the crowd, Mrs. Owens felt suddenly bereft as people melted away to get a closer look at Mrs. Drangler, collar pins glistening in the sun, step-marching slender Ida Freshstalk from her small house catty-corner across the partly paved street. Ida was red-faced, distressed and half-pinned into a peach-colored waistcoat of pieces basted together with heavy, dark thread. The girl was gasping for breath.

A neighbor reached the doctor's door and hollered inside. Sadie came to loom at the front windowsill and then disappeared. By the time Ida and Mrs. Drangler reached the doctor's front stoop, Sadie had returned with a paper bag in her hand and, with an imperious sweep of her arm, all but lifted the fashionable young lady inside. Mrs. Drangler entered behind them and closed the door, sure that someone would surely have gone to alert Ida's mother by now.

In front of the nearest chair, Sadie held Ida's back upright with one hand and the bag to the girl's mouth and nose with the other.

"Breathe!" Sadie commanded, brooking no alternative. Ida inhaled, shuddering at first, and then more smoothly and deeply. Her body relaxed and she took more of her own weight on steadier legs. Her cheeks faded from red to a becoming pink.

Sadie helped her to sink into the chair, but continued to force the bag against her nose and mouth. "Here, you hold it," Sadie told her. "And keep breathing. Slower now. Easy. That's it."

"Feelin' better now, Ida Jane?" Mrs. Drangler tittered from the other side.

"Here, what's goin' on?"

Mrs. Drangler jumped at Dr. Ricartsen's sharp question behind her. She scurried out of his way so he could see the recovering Miss Freshstalk in Sadie's capable hands.

"Oh," the doctor muttered. "Freshstalk." It was obvious to both Mr. House, seated uncomfortably in the far corner, and to Mrs. Drangler —much to her delight—that the doctor had dealt with this high-strung young lady before. He turned on his heel as though to stalk back to his office, but he stayed, twisted like that, to watch Sadie Bean deal with her. He'd caught sight of townspeople under his front windows, peering in.

"There, Ida Jane, feel better now, do you? That's a gal. Sit up and tell us what triggered all this," Sadie coaxed, if not gently, at least without malice. The nurse dug in her pocket for a large man's handkerchief, which she held out in front of the young lady. Ida took it, blew her nose loudly into it and handed it back to Sadie. Sadie sighed, dropping it inside the now crumpled paper bag. "Ah, yes."

"She might have took it home herself, laundered it and give it back," Mrs. Drangler murmured. Sadie nodded, but Ida Jane gave no indication of having heard.

"Let's get her to an exam room," Ricartsen said, nodding toward the front window to let Sadie know they had an audience. "I'd like to examine her and that should be done in private."

Ida Jane's eyes widened, but she didn't resist Sadie's hand at her elbow insisting that she move to the second small room along the hall. Mr. House averted his eyes as the parade passed him, but he did manage a woeful glance at the doctor who was taking this young woman next although House had been there first and had been waiting.

"In just a minute, Mr. House," Ricartsen told him as he hurried by. "Emergency."

Even Ida Jane heard the man's disgruntled "humph" behind them, but no one turned. Mrs. Drangler patted his arm as she trundled past him. His second "humph" was even louder.

Ida was sitting up with ladylike poise on the edge of the exam table when Dr. Ricartsen entered the small exam room. He loosened the stethoscope hanging around the back of his neck and bent to listen through the partially basted upper garment to the girl's heart and lungs. His hindquarters were foremost when Mrs. Freshstalk and two of her dearest, gossipy friends crowded into the doorway.

"Oh!" and "Oh, dear me!" behind him brought the doctor starkly upright.

"Mrs. Freshstalk," Sadie greeted them. "Ladies, why don't you have a seat in the front room for a moment until the doctor has finished his examination? Please?"

Tittering, the pair of friends withdrew, but Claudia Freshstalk held her ground, looking down her nose. "I will stay with my daughter, if you please," she stated, implying strongly that she would remain whether or not it pleased anyone else. "Ida Jane? Are you all right?"

"Oh, Mama," the girl whined, reaching for her. Brushing by Ricartsen, the crenelated woman settled against the far edge of the exam table beside Ida and peered deep into her eyes, frowning at her daughter's disheveled appearance in the basted waistcoat.

"You went through town in this…this…garment?"

"She pushed me," Ida wailed, turning to Mrs. Drangler squeezed now against the far wall.

"She weren't breathing," the seamstress explained reasonably.

"Why?" Dr. Ricartsen demanded of Ida Jane before Mrs. Freshstalk could raise objections. "What is going on, young lady, that had you so flustered?"

"Well, you should know, Doctor. You was the first to tell the town. Ain't you scared now that we're about to be bombed?"

"Not 'ain't,' Ida Jane," her mother admonished. "'Aren't' you scared…?"

"Bombed?" the doctor questioned over the grammar lesson. "Here in Boonetown?" He looked up gratefully as Sadie re-entered the room with a glass of water. He hadn't realized she'd left. Shifting his hips, he made room for his nurse to approach Ida and watched while the huge nurse coaxed the slip of a girl into drinking from the far rim of the glass.

Float

"Now, then, Ida Jane Freshstalk, you drink this just like I'm showing you. Prove you're back in control of yourself and this situation."

Ida drank. Ricartsen nodded to himself; he was swallowing along with her and knew he would have drunk at Sadie's command. Swallowing again, he turned to face mother and daughter and regain control of this examination now that Sadie had them cowered.

"Now, then, miss. What set this off? What's this you say about bombing?"

"Well," Ida smoothed her ample skirt with nervous hands. Without looking up at her mother, she explained. "Mrs. Drangler, she's sewing my dress for my engagement reception— you knew that Mr. Paisler and I are announcing, didn't you, Mrs. Bean?"

"I was glad for you both when I heard," Sadie began. As Ricartsen rolled his eyes, she continued, "But his proposal was weeks ago, wasn't it? Why all the hiss-terics now?"

"Wasn't hiss-terics, neither! Mrs. Drangler made me stand still and stand still for ever so long while she pinned my hem, and I got to thinkin' about Boonetown gettin' bombed and how unfair it was for Mr. Paisler and me gettin' bombed before we could get hitched. And then she started on this here top and I had to stand still and all and I got to thinkin' how unfair it was for us to get bombed when all we were doin' was what every young couple's gotten to do before us, and why was it happenin' to us when we had so much to look forward to and it was all gonna be taken away, and then I started shakin' and that old hag pushed me out her door and shoved me here." She was breathless again.

Sadie patted the paper bag sticking up out of her pocket.

"Boonetown is to be bombed?" Ricartsen questioned to forestall the comments already spilling from the tip of Mrs. Freshstalk's tongue.

"Everybody knows it's true. You told us, from your radio. We're gonna be trapped," she ended in a wail.

"Not us, it's the Brits what's gonna be trapped," Sadie managed to keep her tone civil, but it was an evident struggle. Mrs. Freshstalk glared.

"Brits? Not us? You sure, Sadie Bean?"

"Doc here's been listening on the radio to word about what's goin' on in Europe."

Ricartsen's shoulders lowered in obvious relaxation. He re-set the stethoscope around the back of his neck and explained patiently. "Allied Forces entered Scandinavia months ago to defend when the Nazis moved troops west. Later they had to give up Norway, but they were still helping France to the west of the Maginot Line for fear of German invasion into France when the Panzers got behind them through the forests of the Ardennes…"

His audience stared at him blankly. Rolling his eyes, he turned on his heel and stalked out of the exam room toward his office.

"What?" Ida expressed their collective confusion.

"All that's happening in Europe," Sadie took over trying to explain. "The Brits are part of the Allied Forces— most of 'em, I guess, but not the only ones. Anyway, they were up in the corner north and mostly west of France, and German tanks cut them off and now they're gettin' pushed against the English Channel. So many soldiers on that stretch of beach, but they're gonna be bare targets when the Nazi tanks and planes get to 'em. How do they get so many men out to the big boats, even when they get there? Miles from home, and nowhere to go with the sea water right there and the Panzers comin' up? But they're miles from here. Miles and miles from America. Miles and ocean and miles again from here. You're safe, girl."

The huddled women heard sharp static, then a booming, sonorous voice. "…French Resis… thousands…" The radio voice broke off abruptly. Scratchiness, a few low cusses, and then a click that had to be from the radio dial. Silence.

Confused, Ida Jane turned to her mother and saw a thoughtful expression she'd seldom see on Claudia Freshstalk's severe face. Frightened, Ida Jane turned to Sadie.

"In Europe? Then we ain't gonna be bombed here in Boonetown?"

"Not now; mebbe never, if we can keep out of that war."

"Oh, thank the Lord. Mr. Paisler and me can…" Ida Jane blushed.

"Yeah, you can, most likely," Sadie nodded. "If'n that new Brit head man…"

"Prime minister."

"Prime minister the Brits got—what's his name? Churchkill?— if'n he's anything like he seems he'll be."

"Good for the Brits, and good for you two, too, when you can," Mrs. Drangler added, her pin-covered collar twinkling in happy agreement.

Ida looked down at the floor, her blush deepening.

CHAPTER TWELVE

That evening in their living room, Ron Bean tilted back in his chair, the better to grin and chuckle at the story Sadie was telling him from her day at the clinic.

"Imagine! Three different families paid down on their bills. I've never seen Doc so happy," Sadie beamed. "He kept muttering, 'I can just about catch up on my mortgage payments on this place.' I don't think he'd've been gladder if'n he and Sally Rand'd gotten hitched."

"For the night, at least," Ron suggested, and they both burst into raucous laughter, which muffled as they heard Ronda's footfalls clatter down the stairwell. The girl rushed in to join them.

"Who's gettin' hitched?" she wanted to know as she entered. Throwing herself down at her father's feet, she looked up expectantly. "Doc?"

Ron stifled his red-faced laugh and lowered his tilted chair carefully. "That'll be the day."

"But I heard you," she insisted.

"Eavesdropping is no virtue, Missy," her mother observed as she rose and shuffled off to the kitchen, leaving her spouse to deal with the consequences his raunchy quip had caused.

Ronda peered after her mother, then looked back at Ron, expecting to be let in on the fun. "Pa? What were you laughing so hard about? Who's getting married?"

"Nobody I know," Ron shook his head, then remembered. "Oh, except that Paisler boy somebody was talking about at Owens' store when I delivered this morning." He lifted his paper, as much to hide the redness of his cheeks as to end the conversation.

"P-Paisler?" Ronda faltered. But Ron, behind the news sheet, did not see her face.

"Yeah, I think so. To that prissy gal of Phil Freshstalk's. Ina, is it?"

"Not Ida Jane!"

Ron lowered the newspaper a bit to turn the page. "Yeah, that's the one, if I remember right." He lifted the ink and paper barrier again, unaware of his daughter's devastation.

"Oh," Ronda muttered, biting into her balled fist. "Wh—which one, do you know, Pa?"

"Not sure. One of the older ones, of course, but not Eli. The one with the yellow-brown hair?"

"Greg?" she whispered.

"Uh, yeah, mebbe. Sounds about right."

* * * * * * * * * * * * * * * * * * * *

The next morning, dawn struggled through a low bank of compressed clouds to take over the sky and the attitude of the day.

"Lovely," Nandria whispered as she emerged from the enclosed back porch lugging a basket of damp laundry. She stood a moment at the doorsill drinking in the sky. Goaded back into today's demands by her daughter's squeal from the high chair in the kitchen, she stepped out onto the lawn to set the basket under the clothesline and returned to being a temporary (she hoped) farmwife running any number of chores at the same time. Throwing the bib of the men's overalls over the line and securing them with a wooden clothespin, Nandria was quickly finished setting the first load of laundry out to dry. She hurried back to the kitchen where Rose was still engrossed in picking up each small square of waffle and stuffing it into her mouth. She grinned a syrupy smile at her mother.

"Hello, precious. Thanks for being such a good, patient little girl," Nandria praised and went to the stove. She lifted the fry pan of simmering turnips and red onions for today's pasties away from the heat to allow them to cool before dicing them evenly and consigning them to the ice box. Strange that having the vegetable and meat cubes the same size made the pasties taste better, but she knew from long experience that it was true.

Checking the rising bread dough, Nandria realized it was ready. She pummeled and kneaded it, and set it again to rise. Rose watched intently, squealing in delight when her mom punched and worked the dough.

"Oh, you like that, do you, little miss?" Nandria washed and wiped her hands again after handling the dough. Checking once more at the progress of everything on the stove, she turned to lift her daughter into her arms. "Hi, precious. Ready to go out to see a very lovely morning and help me hang the second batch of clothes?"

Rose was ready for anything—and dry, for once. Nandria carried her out to sit with her stuffed toys on Minnicks' Great War Army blanket. Nandria was lifting the second wet-heavy-despite-two-times-through-the-wringer set of men's bibbed overalls toward the line when both she and her baby looked over at the sound of the tractor starting up in the barn.

"That must be your daddy," Nandria called to Rose. "Even the jouncing of riding that tractor keeps opening up his side," she complained, mostly to herself. *But Lord knows my pointing that out to him only causes friction between us, so I must grit my teeth and let him do what he will without my nagging.* Working to lift her frown into a smile, Nandria turned to wave.

Rose sat upright, staring until the tractor emerged. She was distracted only when her mother hurried by her toward the barn to kiss that man who made her smile.

Leaving the tractor motor running, Will bent low for the kiss. Fanning off the engine fumes with a laugh, they talked over its rough noise.

"I did not see Greg Paisler this morning." Nandria raised her eyebrows in question.

"I flat out told him we couldn't pay."

"He was not working for pay."

"I know, it was just his way of protesting to his brothers, but it put us under obligation."

"Oh, no, Will."

"Especially Pa." His forehead contracted into vertical creases.

"Oh, I see, I suppose," she nodded. "Any word on Dunkirk?" She had heard Will fiddling with the radio as she prepared breakfast, but Grover Minnick, after Doris's emotional upheaval over the last news of the Germans approaching the Channel, had expressed his displeasure at news of "thet blamed war" being brought up at the table.

"Tough, tough going." Will shook his head. "They're dead ducks getting slaughtered. No cover. Nowhere to go except that sliver of beach the French still control."

"Hopefully someone will figure a way to help them. What enormous courage people have."

"Not everyone."

"Of course not, but those do not negate the ones who do."

Will dismounted to take her in his arms. "You are beautiful inside as well as out, do you know that?"

✶ ✶ ✶ ✶ ✶ ✶ ✶ ✶ ✶ ✶ ✶ ✶ ✶ ✶ ✶ ✶ ✶ ✶

Sadie Bean slid the cloth handles of the bag of condiments onto her left wrist to free her right hand to pull open the back screen door of the home she loved. Entering by backing in, she was all the more startled to find Ronda slouched at the kitchen table.

"Ronnie, you're home. Did you have half day today?" she cried as she set the bags of groceries sprawling on the counter to the right of the sink.

"I—I didn't go."

"Didn't go to class with the professor? Why? Are you feelin' sickly? You know he made a special effort to hold these summer sessions at the lodge so he'd be in between Fox Haven and here, just for us." Turning quickly for such a large woman, Sadie bent over her daughter's shoulder to peer into her face and touch the smooth forehead with the back of her hand. "No fever."

Annoyed, Ronda leaned far to the other side to get out from under her mother's hand.

"Well, I don't see nothing obvious. I'd take you over for Doc to see, but he stuffed his mouth with bread and took off to check old Mrs. Pilford north of town. You been feverish? Puking?"

"Oh, Mama, no, I ain't been upchucking, but if you keep talkin' about it like that, I might."

"Well, then, what is it?"

Shrugging, Ronda frowned and looked down at her forefinger tracing the swirling grain of the edge of a knot in the maple table top. "Oh, nothin' like that. I just…I just don't feel…"

"Well, Missy, shrugging sickness ain't enough to keep no girl of mine from what she needs to do. You sit there and I'll fix you lunch and then off you go to afternoon class. That professor comes halfway from Fox Haven for you five kids and you gotta be there for him. You hear me?"

Ronda nodded, but looked down, again tracing the patterns in the wood. Frowning, Sadie busied herself with the groceries. Whatever it was, her usual scolding command had not touched the core of the problem and they both knew it. The girl seemed heartbroken, but Sadie had no idea why—nor how to get her daughter to tell her.

* * * * * * * * * * * * * * * * * * * *

"Thank you, Pastor Kylie, for coming so far," the widow woman murmured.

She is so demure, so refined. Such a pleasant change from the roughened women—and men—of Boonetown. The Bishop knew where he was sending me. I had no idea how much he resented my superior education until he assigned me to that culture-forsaken backwater.

Kylie might have continued with his bitter musings, had not Mrs. Struan delicately coughed to draw his attention to the fact that she held the silver coffee pot poised over his dainty porcelain cup. She was asking mutely whether he would like more of the Turkish blend. He roused himself to nod graciously. "Yes, if you don't mind. It is delicious." And that, too, is a welcome change. Graciousness. *Ah, even the town of Fox Haven is at least reminiscent of a cosmopolitan city where men are gentlemen and ladies...*

With suddenly warm cheeks, Kylie watched the slender wrist and long, tapered fingers gracefully bared from the lace at the cuff of her long-sleeved, satin blouse. Mrs. Constance Struan poured as though for royalty. Even this setting, as superior as it was to what Kylie had known these last years, was not enough for such a lady. He longed to give her what he knew she deserved. It startled him to think such thoughts.

"More sugar, of course," she murmured. "Three lumps, wasn't it, Pastor Kylie?"

He nodded, a trace of smile coming to his lips. *She pays attention; she remembers.*

She set the silvered pot on its salver and sighed. He looked over sharply.

"I fear you have made a long journey on my behalf for nothing, sir. Forgive me."

"Dear woman," he cried, feeling at that moment that there was nothing his manhood could not tackle and conquer for such a woman. "How you slight me to think that there is anything I would not gladly attempt on your behalf."

She blushed; a chill, and then a decided warmth flushed through him.

"Name it," he commanded. And then, more softly, "Please, Madam, do let me know how I can be of service to you."

She sighed, head down, lace-edged hankie dabbing at downcast eyes. "My son," she whispered finally.

Kylie startled. He had thought she was alone in the world.

CHAPTER THIRTEEN

After a filling noon picnic, the men had hopes of finishing the entire field that afternoon, even though it meant working in the heat of an unusual day in May. But—naturally, as far as Minnick was concerned—the tractor had turned recalcitrant. That was a word he had not known prior to his tractor's nearing old age. Doc Ricartsen had mentioned it, and it fit the ancient implement with such formal exactitude that he'd tried it on the thresher as well. But that decrepit monster was beyond even "recalcitrant" and so he had labeled it with Freshstalk the banker's word, "vindictive." Maybe there was something to all this fancy education, after all, if it gave you the undeniable labels to condemn the inanimate tools that were contributing to your defeat.

Will was up in the seat, having just finished one single row. As the stubborn vehicle swung to start the next row, it sputtered, coughed as though it would expel a hardy bolus of phlegm, and staggered to a stop—silent. Resentful, from the look on its grill. Definitely defiant of any attempt to make it work longer or farther.

Greg Paisler walked up just at that time; Grover Minnick scowled.

"Don't blame me, Mr. Minnick." Chuckling, Greg lifted his palms in mock surrender. "I just come to give you a hand. No payment needed or expected from a neighbor."

There it was, out in the open. Will and Bodie looked away, but covertly sidled a glance at the farmer to see how he would react to Greg's defying his dismissal. Without looking at Mr. Minnick at all, Greg went to the tractor and lifted its awkward cowl to peer at the dead motor. Frowning, Minnick peered over his shoulder, then shrugged in disgust.

"Just once on this farm," Minnick complained, "I'd like to be able to do a job clear through to the end without somethin' sloughin' off."

"Ain't that the truth?" Bodie agreed. "Ya never gets to pick up a tool and just do a job through. Somethin' always breaks or needs somethin' else to be done afore ya kin finish what's at hand." He wiped his brows and forehead with the back of his hand, revealing pallor beneath the splotches of dirt. Again, Will wished that the old man had gone back down to the house with the women and their picnic basket. The old man needed to fully heal from the sneak attack by Horace Bratton and his idiot brothers. It wasn't enough for the drunken bully to beat his young wife, who was Bodie's kin. He had to try to kill Nandria for not taking the blame, and Bodie would die for Nandria and little Rose. He'd proved that, if there was ever any doubt.

Will pressed his side, and, with a wry smile, allowed that he had little right to say anything to Bodie about that. *My own wounds are barely closer to health than they had been when I got back to Pa's farm. There's just so much that needs done. How could a man simply sit back when the work demanded much more than Pa could do on his own? Why—why won't he simply admit this was beyond him and my mother and sell out?* Will wiped his own forehead, twisted his back to stretch and hopefully settle his side into a more comfortable position. Frowning, he stepped up to peer over Greg's shoulder at the tractor's innards.

"Or it's manglin' 'stead'a cuttin'," Greg was contributing to the general funk as he poked at the motor, "and ya gotta stop and sharpen the blade."

Minnick began his contribution so low, Will wasn't sure he was saying something rather than merely adding a low groan. But the words came, startling Will. "Or one of your boys is caught in the balin' wire and ya gotta slice up your hands cuttin' the mutt loose."

Will stared up at him; Minnick nodded, yes, that happened.

"Twas yer brother. You, I always knew'd be at the back steps with a book in yer hands. But Winfred…"

At the mention of Freddy's name, each man looked away from Grover Minnick while he pulled a huge blue and red handkerchief from his pocket and blew his nose. Each coped with his own sense of guilt at the death of the wild son. Greg was the first to break the awkward silence.

"I think she's past her prime, Mr. Minnick," he suggested as quietly as though to break gently the news of the tractor's loss of function. Only then did Will realize that his father must have been thinking of selling the farm if he let the implements go to rack and ruin without replacing them. He'd have had this tractor worked on if he were going to try to keep farming this land. But if they were to be leaving soon, what was the use of spending that kind of money?

Will glanced up at his father with more understanding, but Minnick was busy stuffing the used blue and red cloth back into his pocket and not looking at any of them, especially Will.

"Bodie," Will said as he straightened up, "would you mind hiking back down to the house and checking on our women folk?"

"Good idea, don't you think, Mr. Minnick?" Greg chimed in. "Will and me'll have this bugger working in no time."

Will's inhalation sounded very like a gasp. He rolled his eyes at Paisler, but added his vote to the two older men retiring to the house. There wasn't much to be done here without the power of the tractor to help.

"Ma looked pretty tired, Pa. Might be good to be sure she made it back all right and is lying down. Oh, and if you think of it, would you check if the mail's come?"

Minnick peered at him, but it was Bodie who put their thoughts into words. "Spectin' somethin', Will? Like new orders?"

"One way the army is like a woman—if it does change its mind," Will recited, "it'll insist it had it that new way all along."

Rising to the family joke, Minnick snapped "Women!" with the expected gusto and turned away from the tractor in disgust. But he turned back a moment at Greg's rather pensive. "Women…" The corners of his mouth turned up, only for a second, but Will caught it, and smiled.

"Onliest time I kin catch 'em is afore they kin crawl fast," Bodie shared wistfully.

Minnick chuckled aloud but bestowed a rare compliment. "You do good with the littlest ones."

"Sorry you never had one of your own, Bode?" Greg asked before he thought. He really didn't know for a fact that Bodie had been childless throughout his past. At Bodie's expression, he hurried on. "Little Rose must be outcrawlin' you by a long way now."

Chuckling and exchanging barbs over their individual abilities, Minnick and Bodie started their hobbling path back toward the farmhouse.

"'Fixed in no time,' eh? What've you got us into, Paisler?" Will griped as Greg lifted his large hand, shading his eyes to survey the hills and fields of the farm before bending again to peer at the tractor motor.

"Bodie's evidently got a story I didn't know of."

Will nodded and crouched beside him.

"It's his'n to tell or not tell, that I understand. Sorry I brought it up without thinkin'."

"He may say somethin' to you about it later, if he wants."

Shaking his head that that would not be necessary, Greg poked at a piston and shook his head in dismay. He stood. "So, Will Minnick, how else can we do this field?"

"You mean without the tractor?"

"You're good at fixin' things, Will, but you're no miracle worker. It needs a complete overhaul by a trained mechanic, or at least one with lots of experience with tractors."

His hand pressing his side, Will rose to amble over toward the shade of a lone tree at the edge of the field. Greg followed him and sat down with his back against the base of the trunk to think and talk. He watched Will shade his own eyes and look out with a play of different emotions as he surveyed the acreage.

"It's time for Pa to sell the place, if only he would."

Greg's nod was vigorous enough that Will looked down at him, realizing something he'd only barely thought of before. "You thinking of settling down one of these days, Greg? Is that why you came back even after Pa's pretty broad hint that we couldn't pay?"

"Don't want to see the place get any more run down than it already is, maybe? Well, it's fine land and good water. That's a real plus out here," Greg admitted. "Think he'd consider sellin'? I been savin'. Don't have a whole lot, but I could do a bit at a time. Enough, probably to keep them in good straights in town."

"Have you talked it over with Ronda?"

"What makes you think...?" Greg started up, then relaxed, laughing. "That obvious, is it? Hell, I ain't even kissed her yet."

"You'll get around to it."

CHAPTER FOURTEEN

Rose lunged from Nandria's arms toward the metal mailbox at the end of their farm lane.

"Will you look at him?" Doris chuckled. "Nosy already, and such a little one! You're gonna be one fine gossip, little man. And glad I will be to have you searching out the news in the neighborhood for me when I'm too old and gray to sniff it out for myself." Laughing, she pulled open the mailbox door and stepped to the side so Nandria could let the child reach in for mail.

But Rose was intrigued by the red metal flag.

"Don't need that this day, little one," Doris explained as she reached deep in the box for the mail herself. "Don't have no letters for Josiah to pick up from us today. We get to town often enough now that the weather's good. We can drop it at Owens' and not bother Josiah with it. He's gettin' feeble enough, he don't need more'n we have to give him to do. Been at this route for thirty, no, closer to forty years now. And he was no spring chicken when he give up his farm and started haulin' the mail."

"Caught up in the Great War, was he?"

Doris looked back over her shoulder as she dug her arm deep in the metal box. "Josiah, a soldier? Why he's the most placid man I ever seen. I'm afraid my boys used to laugh at him," she confessed as she drew out a small envelope, a days-old newspaper refolded not quite pristinely from someone's sneak read-through, and a long official envelope plus four of what had to be bills.

"We got us a passel this day. Most days there ain't nothing at all." Doris pulled out the small missive, squinting to make out the cramped handwriting on the front. Her face brightened. "A letter for me! Really and true!" she squealed. She squinted again to be sure. "Yep, a letter for me!"

"Are you not going to open it?"

Doris hugged it to her chest and shook her head. "Oh, no. Mr. Minnick and I always open letters together."

"From what I have read of United States history, it sounds almost pioneering to be that thrilled and excited to receive a letter in the mail." With her British accent, Nandria's statement sounded stilted even to herself, but Nandria needed to keep her own style, her own being or be swallowed up in this morass of ill-education. If Nandria had sounded strange to Mother Minnick, she gave no indication but charged right on with her own thoughts.

"It was a thrill, girl. It was. Oh, and here is something for Will. I wonder what the U.S. Army…"

Nandria's hand went out to take the official envelope from her, but she pulled it back when she saw her mother-in-law's expression. The woman had straightened her shoulders and taken on an air of important purpose.

"Willard will be grateful to you for delivering that to him, Mother Minnick," Nandria managed, though she longed to hold it in her own hands. It held the future of her small family. She reacted quickly to Rose's lunge for the long envelope.

"Oh, no, you don't, little man," Doris scolded playfully. Instead of Will's letter, she handed the child one of the bills to maul and chew on.

* * * * * * * * * * * * * * * * * * *

All the rest of that afternoon, Nandria glanced again and again at the stack of mail at Minnick's place at the head of the oak table. By evening when Bodie and the family gathered at the table, Nandria had worked herself into a state of anxiety. She met Will's eyes as he entered from the porch and sat down to settle Rose in the high chair beside him.

"What?" he mouthed, but just then his father entered, bent to touch Doris's shoulder and sank into his seat at the head of the table. Minnick waited for Bodie to squeeze behind him before pushing back and tilting his chair against the narrow wall behind him.

Nandria took a deep breath and disciplined herself to concentrate on setting the serving platters and bowls in front of her father-in-law. She sat quietly beside Will and bowed her head with the others as Doris led them in grace. "Bless our Lord, we beseech Thee, this food to our use and thus to thine service…"

Minnick served. Nandria and Will could only exchange glances, but Will's concern for her showed in his frown.

When everyone's plate had been filled and passed, Minnick set to eating. No table talk this evening. Not with the apparent mood Minnick was in tonight. Everyone except Doris sat, tense, as they finished the meal. Before Nandria could rise to clear the supper dishes and serve dessert, Doris, grinning like a child on Christmas morning, reached to straighten the stack of mail between them that her husband had been ignoring. She slipped the U.S. Army letter from the pile and waved it.

"Here, Will. This come for you today."

"Well, thank you, Ma," he said, taking the long envelope, glancing at it and stuffing it into his pocket.

"Ain't you goin' to open it?"

"It looks official and boring," he answered, smiling at the disappointment on his mother's face.

"How can a letter in the mail be dull and boring?" she wanted to know.

"If'n it comes from the government, you'd be lucky if it weren't bad news," Minnick told her.

"Or a big bill," Bodie chimed in.

"Amen to that," Minnick growled, and Will nodded, grateful for their siding with him.

"Later. This evening," Will promised. "What else was there?"

Minnick reached for the stack, but Doris beat him to the small envelope at the bottom of the pile. "Well, this one for me ain't from the government, but maybe it's dull and boring, too," she sniffed and tucked it into the pocket of her apron.

"What you got there, Mother?" Minnick questioned.

"Nothin' very interestin'."

Rose had been watching with her head cocked to one side. But patience was not yet her best virtue. She picked up her tiny silver spoon and banged it on the wooden tray of her high chair.

"Another country heard from," Bodie commented. "Must be she knows there's somethin' comin' for dessert."

The family peered at her, and then at each other, smiling. Minnick chuckled aloud. "You said just what I was about to, little one."

Taking her cue, Nandria rose to bring the apple and berry pies to the table. She set the five small plates and a bowl beside Minnick and took away the dinner plates Bodie and Will had gathered and stacked for her at the bottom corner of the table. She glanced at Will's pocket and raised her eyebrows, but Will shrugged. He did not know what the Army's message was. They would read it together as soon as they could get a moment of privacy.

"He'll need a bath," Doris chuckled, seeing the berry mess Rose was making of her bowl of pie. She'd laughed aloud when the child insisted on berry rather than apple. Mothers know when a disaster is coming.

Minnick belched low and satisfied before again tilting back his chair. Nandria knew it was his way of praising her baking efforts, but she could not bring herself to respond. Will glanced over, understanding what she was feeling but unable to help her by correcting his father's manners. Instead she gathered the dishes and set them on the sink board. Behind her she heard Minnick scrape his chair and rise. He must have leaned over Doris, because she heard his bantering growl. "I'll settle with you later, woman."

At Doris's giggle, the men laughed. Sighing, Nandria could not contain a smile.

"Well, good night, all," Bodie told them. He brought to the sink two large bowls and the remains of the apple pie. "Good supper, Miz Minnick. I didn't dare touch what was left of that berry pie of your'n. Not the way the little princess was lookin' at it."

Nandria chuckled. "We should let her daddy dare that one, I suppose, Bodie."

"G'night, ma'am," he smiled, and Nandria nodded in recognition of his thanks.

Will came over with the last of the dishes from the table—excepting the berry pie. "Why don't we wash the wee gal in the sink here before we start the dishes?"

It was a joy for the three of them. Rose loved splashing. Will pulled a bath towel from the hamper to wipe up the floor when Nandria lifted the baby from the sudsy water and wrapped her gently in her own fluffy yellow towel to hand to Will.

"Here, my love," Nandria told him, setting the floor towel back down on the speckled linoleum. "You enjoy some moments with your daughter. I suspect there will not be that many for you soon." She glanced at his pocket that held the dreaded letter.

"Come," he whispered. Quickly drying her hands, she followed them to the porch where she took the baby to diaper and dress her for the night while Will drew the letter from his pocket and opened it slowly.

"Orders?" she asked.

Grim-faced, Will nodded and handed her the letter as she sat to nurse Rose.

"Oh, Will. '...further training before duty in Europe.' When?"

"Monday, July 1st."

"But I thought you were to be stationed in Washington, D.C."

"Things have changed a lot across the Pond. Gabriel Heatter says the Italians will undoubtedly declare war on France."

She handed back the letter and concentrated on her suckling child. "We could not expect Norway to go it alone. We knew that when we had to abandon her."

"Abandon..." Will murmured, green eyes gray with guilt. Biting his lip, Will bent over his wife as she rocked forward. He was nearly broken by the thought of leaving her here. But what else could he do?

They hugged around the sleeping Rose.

Float

CHAPTER FIFTEEN

Doris strayed to the narrow window at the far end of the living room as Minnick sank heavily into his overstuffed chair. She looked out toward her favorite hillock, watching its bare side take on the glow of reflected sunset mauves. She sighed.

"You all right, Mother?"

"Just thinking. Remember our boys out roamin' these little hills of ours? How they'd escape the house as soon as they'd done a lick and promise to the supper dishes and run and hide from each other or just lie on the ground and look up at the sky, watchin' for the stars to come out?"

Minnick lowered his newspaper, nodding. "They're gone, them boys," he murmured, mostly to steel himself.

"And sometimes," Doris continued without turning to see him bracing himself against the memories she was luxuriating in. "Sometimes Will, especially, would fall asleep there in the tall grass, and we'd have the devil of a time finding him until he started snoring." She chuckled, then again sighed. "We didn't know how quick them days would be done and gone, did we, Mr. Minnick?" she asked. Quietly, she came to sit close beside her man.

His hands clutched the edges of his newspaper but he met her with a stiff expression of the peace he knew she wanted, though he did not feel.

"It's been good, our life here, Grover," she said so low he had strain to catch her words. It was only later that he realized she had called him by his first name. Minnick folded the newspaper and set it on the crowded table beside his chair. Smiling in anticipation, she drew the small envelope from her pocket and handed it to him. "We haven't opened what come in the mail."

"Addressed to you, Mother. From Ohio—Massillon, looks like from the stamp cancellation. No return address. Why don't you open this one?"

Pleased, she slid her index finger under the edge of the flap and carefully lifted it so as not to tear the envelope any more than she needed to. "Oh, I know from that tiny, squarish handwriting it's got to be from Cousin Mildred."

"They got some prime soil there in Ohio, but them Amish livin' so close by…"

"Good farmers, they are," Doris reminded him.

He shook his head and lowered his chin. "Still, havin' 'em so close would give me the willies. Strange."

She'd extracted the blue note paper and held it up between them so he could read with her.

"Never mind, just read it to me. I ain't got my glasses, it seems. No wonder I wasn't gettin' much out of the news, though Lord knows there ain't that much to concern a farmer in there, anyhow."

"Oh, Mr. Minnick, they're havin' a reunion. Says she sent us an invitation weeks ago, but she ain't heard from us on whether or not we're comin'."

Minnick shook his head. "Don't recall hearing 'bout no reunion."

"We never did get no invite, did we? Haven't have a card from Mildred since Christmas."

"You know Millie. Once she writes it, she's sure it's done. It's probably lying in a stack on her desk right now, still without a stamp."

"She says the get-together's comin' up on Sunday, May 27. At Boris's place in St. Louey. That's not far, Mr. Minnick. Can we go?"

Minnick scowled.

"Oh, my, what day is this?"

Minnick checked the date at the top of his newspaper sheet. "Says here it's from Sunday, May 20. What's today, Monday? Tuesday?"

"Then it must be—oh, my, the gatherin' must be comin' up this weekend, ain't it?"

Minnick took the note from her to peer at it close up. He shook his head, scowling, but when he looked over at her, she was in tears.

* * * * * * * * * * * * * * * * * * * *

There was enough light from the lantern hanging at the wide door of the Paisler barn that a strip of the lane and the yard was bright. Will pulled up in the Minnick truck to park near the back door.

"I'll wait here," Nandria told him quietly. She settled the small, light blanket around sleeping Rose and nodded to him to go ahead into the house.

"Call if you need anything. I won't be a minute," he said, getting out of the truck and heading toward the neighbors' back door.

He knocked; it opened almost immediately. Eli Paisler stepped back, surprised. "Just on my way out to the barn to help Sam." He turned, hollering over his shoulder. "Greg! Company! How are you, Will? How's that hip and side? Healing finally? Come on in. Ma'll be mighty pleased to see you."

Will followed the eldest Paisler brother into the warm, ample kitchen. Mr. and Mrs. Paisler were seated at the huge round oak table. A slender baby, probably not much more than a year old, with a thatch of straw-blond hair, sat on Mrs. Paisler ample lap, reaching for any left-over scraps within his lunging reach. Their electric refrigerator hummed. Greg stood at the multi-burner gas stove behind a small boy working at scraping a heavy pot back and forth across the burner. The smell and rapid-fire, nicking sounds of popping corn explained why he was laboring to keep the pot moving so the kernels wouldn't burn.

"Will! Welcome! Ma, it's Will Minnick," Greg said as he half-turned, but he kept close watch over his little brother. "Just keep going, Todd. Almost ready and then we'll have a hot treat for our guest. Say, why don't you get the butter from the fridge so it'll be ready? I'll do these last couple minutes for you."

The skinny blond seven-year-old looked up, ready to protest that he'd wanted to do it all by himself, but he saw only kindness in his brother's face and turned the wooden pot handle for Greg to grasp. He jumped down from the chair he'd been on and scurried to open the refrigerator door. Will watched him lift a large tub of freshly-churned butter past the doorless, well-stocked pantry and set it, with difficulty, onto the sink board near the stove.

"Yes, Ida, yes," Frank was saying into the telephone on the wall, growing redder and redder with each effort to hang up. "Yes, dear, but I need to go now. We got company. Will. Will Minnick…" He looked up and rolled his eyes as he was met by a fresh torrent of questions from the other end of the line.

"Party line," Eli told Will, though both knew that was not what was keeping Frank with his ear glued to the receiver. "Our ring is four of the gall-darndest buzzy-sharp noises you ever did hear."

Mr. Paisler spoke up, grinning. "Ma here says that if we had a passels of girls 'stead of boys, that phone'd never get no rest."

"Pa hates that you gotta pay for it every month. Figures once you buy something, it ought'a stay bought," Greg said, carrying the pot to the sink board where Twig was ready with two huge bowls and slabs of butter.

"Welcome, Will Minnick," Mr. Paisler said, patting the seat of the chair next to him at the table to invite him to sit. "Been a while since we seen ya."

"Maybe that's true for the rest of us, Greg. Not for you," young Sam laughed, entering from the barn. He moved as far from Todd and Greg and the popcorn as he could before washing his hands at the sink.

"You done good with that popcorn, young Todd. Welcome, Will Minnick," Cyndy Paisler smiled and gestured around the baby on her lap to have him sit at their table.

"Thank you kindly, Miz Paisler," Will told her, "but my Nandria is waiting in the truck."

"Well, have her come in," Eli invited.

"She's holding little Rose—asleep."

Leaving his small brother to officiate the popcorn, Greg stepped up to Will, wiping his palms on his trouser legs. He offered his right hand to Will. "Anything wrong?" he asked low.

"No, no," Will assured him. "I just come to ask a favor."

"Name it!" Eli, Frank (finally settling the receiver in its cradle), Greg and Sam chorused in unison.

Will stepped back in surprise and gratitude at the overwhelming response, though he shouldn't have been surprised, he realized immediately. Not at the Paislers. So many of the boys were rugged as their father but also held the steely optimism of their mother.

"Just you name it, Will," Greg prompted.

"It's—it's just that our family may be going to some reunion or something this weekend. No firm plans yet, but I wondered…"

"You want me to look in on the stock and generally keep an eye on the place? Sure. You go. Have a great time. It'll be good for the womenfolk," Greg assured him heartily and the others nodded.

"Nandria said she'd leave word tomorrow for Miss Bean not to come out to the house—that we won't be home."

Will caught the swift change in Greg's expression. "Well, I'll be," Will chuckled. "All this time I thought it was us Minnicks you were coming out to help. I should have known it would have to be something a lot cuter than my father that would make it worthwhile to you."

At the rising interest and inevitable teasing from his brothers as they realized what was being said, Greg protested. "I was out there in your fields awhile before anybody started coming for lessons, if you'll remember, Will Minnick."

"That you were," Will laughed, resting his hand on Greg's shoulder. "That you were. And I'm sure I never thanked you proper for bein' such a good neighbor."

"I reckon if you had to thank me, I wouldn't be no 'good neighbor.'"

Float

CHAPTER SIXTEEN

Though she was hurrying not to be late to Doc Ricartsen's, Sadie stopped to look at her pale daughter. She drew the girl to her for a gentle hug. "The Fourth is coming up, Ronnie girl," she whispered. "And your dad has plans for us this summer. We'll have fun then. You just wait and see."

Ronda shuddered. How she'd wished and hoped when Greg Paisler had said what he did that first night at Minnicks' about a good time on the 4th of July. *But he's engaged—to Ida Jane Freshstalk, of all people. Ida Jane, so slender and pretty. Ida Jane only wears the latest fashions from the magazines from St. Louis, thanks to her mother's hiring Mrs. Drangler. Ida Jane doesn't get a dress when she needed one; she gets a new dress whenever there's a new fashion wrinkle for Mrs. Drangler to sew for her. It ain't fair!*

A quiet knock at the front door startled mother and daughter. Releasing Ronda, Sadie leaned to open the door to find Greg Paisler standing there.

Ronda drew excited breath and then again remembered his playing with her emotions and turned away as he removed his cap and stood hat in hand. He smiled shyly at her. He looked so innocent.

"Why, Greg, you're out and about early this day," Sadie joked, but Ronda hugged her books and started away back into the house. Sadie caught and held her there at the door. "Good morning. What brings you from your farm so early in this fine day?"

Greg answered Sadie while looking directly at Ronda. "It is a beauteous day, isn't it? Ma needed a few things from Mr. Owens when he opens his store. So I thought I come ahead and let you know that the Minnicks is plannin' to be away this weekend, maybe."

Ronda turned to stare at him. "Miz Minnick ain't gonna be there to help me? I got a big test comin' up next Tuesday." She ended in a panicked whine.

"I—I could mebbe…"

"You're going to be there alone, Greg Paisler?" Sadie demanded. "Bodie going with them?"

"I'm not sure, ma'am, about Bodie. I keep thinkin' he's just part of them. I was just gonna go up early to tend to the stock, and then again late in the afternoon. Will said somethin' about a family gathering or reunion or such, in St. Louey."

"They never said nothing," Ronda complained.

Greg shrugged. "Evidently arrangements was made by their Aunt Mildred."

"Well," Sadie sighed. "That explains it. They were lucky to hear about it at all then, until it was over and done. Mildred Nease was the most scattered lady I ever saw when she came to visit once years ago. That was when she was younger. Don't reckon old age has brought her more together in herself."

Greg had been listening politely, but in reality had been watching Ronda and her avoidance of him. Puzzled, he caught her eye, but when he tried to speak she deliberately turned from him to pull at her mother's arm.

"I'm gonna be late for class. Mama."

Hurt, he stepped back. "Sorry, ma'am. I didn't mean to keep you back. I'll go now, unless I can carry something for you?"

"No, thank you, Greg Paisler," Sadie declined his offer, shaking her head and gathering what she'd need for the day at the Doc's. "We're just fine. We're runnin' a little late, that's all. Tell your mama we sent our best."

Nodding, Greg reset his cap. He backed away still glancing at Ronda, but she kept her face turned away from him. Sadie waved as he turned and strode toward the center of town.

"Well, now, Missy, what was that rudeness all about?" Sadie began, but when Ronda looked up, the mother saw such misery in her child's face that she let the girl hurry away without explanation.

* * * * * * * * * * * * * * * * * *

Later that morning, Mr. House paused at the bottom of Dr. Ricartsen's walkway, angry and pained. Grimacing, he waddled to the stoop, reached to knock and pushed the door open without waiting. In the lobby he muttered impatiently for Sadie, who came around the corner from the back hallways with a basin in her hands and a filthy red and brown towel over her forearm. Mr. House looked at the towel but refused to look into the basin. He stiffened, rheumy eyes glowering.

"Ah, Mr. House," Sadie greeted him. "Another?"

Mr. House's only answer was an angrier sharpness to his glower, but Sadie shrugged off his seeming attempt to make his continuing problem her fault.

"Have a seat," she said without irony. "I'll be back for you in just two shakes of a lamb's tail." She disappeared back into the hallway.

House muttered blue-black cuss words under his breath.

It wasn't that she didn't hear them, or couldn't imagine them, but she and the doctor had explained carefully again and again the elements of ass hygiene, and to her knowledge the House privy seat was still unplaned and unhosed and his undergarments washed only when he fell into a creek. With his wife's death—how many years ago now?—Mr. House had sewn himself into long johns and would probably change them only when they rotted away.

But try to tell him that? No, it was easier on everybody to simply let him rave under his breath about the doctor's and his nurse's incompetence. Everyone else in town could smell whose side to take.

Realizing she was being unusually critical—if not actually bitchy—this morning, Sadie emptied the basin and tossed the towel into bleach water to soak. Scrubbing her hands and arms she felt a little more like a human being as she hurried back to escort House to the dirty procedures area.

"Sadie, got that scalpel in the steamer?" Ricartsen called.

"Just nearly, Doctor," she answered on the run.

Ricartsen had stopped in his office and evidently turned on his radio as he washed up in there. A rich, but scratchy baritone voice told them that Panzers had been seen northwest of Dunkirk. And Italian forces…but the voice had faded before completing that bit of information.

"You oughtn't to let him listen to that there radio," Mr. House chided.

"I oughtn't to let them Nazis run all over Europe, but not much I can do about that, neither. Or about you gettin' infected again. Say, where you been settin' lately to be back here again so soon?"

House not merely glowered; he glared. But Sadie had turned to look out the window, glad for the moment that whoever had just turned away was too small to be any of them Bratton brothers again. How weird that had been, glancing up and seeing one of those faces staring in when Doc was doing what he could for Horace's severely beaten wife. Not that they'd ever come in to sit with Emmy. Shuddering, Sadie hurried on to fetch the doctor and get this session with Mr. House over and done with.

✷ ✷ ✷ ✷ ✷ ✷ ✷ ✷ ✷ ✷ ✷ ✷ ✷ ✷ ✷ ✷ ✷ ✷ ✷

The young person Sadie had missed seeing at the window was her daughter. Tears streaming, Ronda turned from the doctor's and ambled disconsolately toward home. She coughed into her father's handkerchief. The professor had sent her home again, afraid, he'd said, for the health of the other students. But Ronda knew it was his own health he was worried about. How many times had he expounded about the scientific basis for germ theory? All the time holding a white handkerchief of his own near his flaring nostrils.

But Ronda didn't care. She hadn't been getting anything from the man's explanations in class anyway. Only Miz Minnick—Nandria—made any sense of this math stuff for her, and the Minnicks were going away, just when she needed them most.

Why did that Greg smile at me like he done? And joked like he really cared? Making me feel stuff I never knew about…and him all the time gonna be married! To Ida Freshstalk, of all people! And even this morning, to come without warning and look at me with those huge, chocolate eyes innocent, like it was my fault. No fair! No fair! She hurried toward home at a run.

* * * * * * * * * * * * * * * * * * *

"You off your feed, Greg?" Will asked low as he slowed to let Bodie leave the Minnick barn in front of them.

"I been slackin'?"

"You? Not likely. But you haven't hummed that infernal 'Back in the Saddle Again' all day like you usually do. Just wondered if somethin' was wrong."

"I hum?"

Will rolled his eyes and laughed aloud. "Hour after hour. The tune gets into a variety of keys, so there's some variation or I'd have buried you in one of our fields long ago."

"Huh. Eli tells me the same thing, but I didn't believe him."

"Believe," Will started toward the house and Greg followed a step behind. "Seriously," Will said over his shoulder. "Anything I can give you a hand with?"

Greg hesitated at the porch steps, then shook his head and followed Will into the house, walking past him when Will stopped to turn on his radio.

"...Panzers..." Will leaned in close to listen while Greg went on into the kitchen.

"Miz, er, Nandria," Greg greeted her as she hurried on out to porch to listen with Will.

Nandria crouched beside her husband to listen, taking his arm in both her hands as she understood what was being broadcast. "Oh, Will."

"Blitz," Will spat the word, shaking his head, but patting her hands on his arm to comfort her.

"Unbelievable how quickly he moves his troops around," Nandria commented. "I suppose if you are not concerned at all about their welfare, you can make humans perform nearly to inhuman criteria."

"He gives them pills."

"Pills? To his troops? What kind of pills?"

"Something that revs them up that also makes them careless about themselves. Immediate and long-term." Will grimaced; he wasn't supposed to have told anyone about that.

"Oh," Nandria responded, peering at his face. She nodded, understanding. "I guess I did not hear you correctly," she whispered, assuring him she would say nothing. Both knew without saying that if one side in a war had come across a chemical weapon, the opponent, no matter how high-mindedly he spoke, would soon be working to match or outdo. Nandria looked down in dismay.

"Ah, love," Will whispered, setting his hand on her shoulder to thank and comfort her. Giving vent to further frustration, he spat, "But Europe is giving itself away; no one was prepared to conceive of anything but stodgy trench warfare. Nothing but a replay of the Great War. But Hitler isn't playing by those same rules, and they refuse to see." He glanced over his shoulder to see Greg Paisler stepping into the porch doorframe.

"Sorry," Greg mumbled, embarrassed to have intruded. "I heard your voice and was afraid something was wrong. War news?"

Will nodded. "The stupidity…"

"Peace in our time!" Nandria exploded. "What about in our children's time?"

Greg set his hands deep into his pockets, shrugging and shaking his head.

Will closed his eyes.

CHAPTER SEVENTEEN

The Minnick truck brake lights picked up the bristly red tail of a fox crossing the road so fast, everyone in the truck bed blinked, unsure they had seen it. Aware of Bodie's sudden tenseness, Nandria chuckled low.

"In England, seeing a fox like that first thing in the morning would be considered a good omen," she related, understanding his superstitious fear.

"For the hunters, if not for the fox," Will laughed. Rose lifted her head from his shoulder and stared around sleepily until she saw her mother smiling. She plopped her head back into its snuggle place against her daddy and was promptly safely back within her dreams.

Bodie looked at Will's dark wife, warmed by her thoughtfulness and tact, although at that moment he would have thought of neither word. He knew she'd seen him start, reacting in a fear taught to him since he was no bigger than her creamed coffee-colored little girl.

What's gonna become of that youngster? And the one comin'? Boonetown ain't no place for them two. Not even with Will here to plow a way fer 'em. People's gonna get to 'em alone and that's more'n any child should haf'ta deal with. Mean. Them Brattons weren't the only ones could be mean. Hope Will can find a way to take 'em with him when he goes. Soon, now, prob'ly, though he ain't gived hisself much time fer healin'. Still winces. Like now. Bodie frowned as the truck clamored over washboard at the far end of the Minnick lane.

Doris snuggled into the passenger seat after shifting away again from the cardboard box of tools her man had pushed over at her with his hip. She stared at it, surprised to be aware of that flap-eared collection that had ridden between them unnoticed for how many years. Smiling at its familiarity intensifying her sense of security, she continued with her own thoughts.

We are getting a good start, leavin' before sunrise like this. Praise be the Mister saw fit to have us go. St. Louey. Quite a drive. Wish it could'a been Kansas City, but then most of the family is from way east, so I guess we ain't even the ones drivin' the farthest to get together. So glad the Mister is lettin' us go. How long's it been since I seen family? Doris patted her hair, her flower-patterned, cotton housedress, smoothing its full skirt over her knees.

"You'll be the belle of the whole gathered clan," Minnick assured his wife as he recognized her familiar gestures of taking stock of her appearance.

"You think so, Mr. Minnick?" she whispered.

"Always have been the prettiest of the entire collection—still are." He reached over the tools to pat her thigh and rested his hand there until, shyly, she laid her calloused hand atop his huge, hard one.

"Well, we got the gal with us now."

"The gal? You mean Will's…?"

"She's pretty. Prettier than I ever was, but I guess the clan won't see her as one of us, being a darky like she is."

Minnick glanced over and then quickly swept his eyes to the paved road through Boonetown.

"It's a shame, really," Doris sighed as he lifted his hand from her lap and clutched the steering wheel. "She's one fine cook and she certainly takes care of that pickaninny of hers. Just as good as white folks ever did. It's a shame nobody will like her. She is worth more'n they'll ever see in her."

Minnick swallowed. *That pickaninny is your grandbaby. And mine. Now how the devil are we gonna live with that with that clan of gossips and loud talkers of yours, Doris Rose? And here I was, telling Will he had to face up to what he's done. The reality. Not that your folks are big on reality. How long it took 'em to work through Freddy's fool losing his head. Blamed Will fer the longest time... And how are they gonna react to his marryin' a darky?* Minnick jerked the wheel as though his arm had a spasm. He straightened at Doris's gasp.

"You well, Mr. Minnick? You want Will to do the drivin'? I can sit in the back with Bodie, if you need."

"I want you by my side, Doris Rose," he told her firmly and warmed to her grin. But he went silent. This was a trip he wished to his boot tops that he'd never agreed to.

* * * * * * * * * * * * * * * * * * *

They reached Jeff City with a nearly empty gas tank and emptier tummies. They filled the gas tank first, with Will doing the pumping and Bodie trying to reach to wipe the bugs from the windshield. Nandria and Doris spread their picnic lunch on the table in the grove behind the station. Doris invited the station man, who did come for chicken and stayed to share dessert. He sat all but drooling as Doris spooned the berries into the meringue crust shell she had brought separately. His eyes bugged as she sprinkled sugar over the multi-colored berries. Clearing his throat, he got up and stalked back to the cooler beside his front door to bring ice for their lemonade and said he hadn't had such a satisfying meal since his Lulabelle had passed two years and seven months before.

Doris was smiling widely with pride at their generosity—until the part about Lulabelle. "I'm so sorry, you dear man," she consoled, tears in her eyes for him.

His own eyes glistened then. He reached to hold her outstretched hands. "It's all right, Missus. You get almost used to the quiet day—and night." He waved heartily as they packed up and drove on. "You remember, pull up at the Bide-a-Wee just as yer gettin' twenty some miles east of Columbia. I'll call my cousin right now and tell him to keep the big cabin open for ya!" he called after them.

He must have done just that. As they pulled into the pot-holed lot of the Bide-a-Wee, a figure hustled out of the garish lobby toward them. The dark-haired man had tanned cheeks and neck, but white skin just under the vee opening of his shirt and white forehead when he doffed his floppy gray trilby hat. He greeted them with the same stoop-shouldered, arms opened wide pose their gas station owner and picnic partaker had used to wave them on from Jefferson City. Their cabin was nearly twice as wide as the other seven, with two double beds and a trundle bed with wrought iron grillwork at the head of each. Each mattress sagged in the middle, but the sheets had been newly tucked and still smelled of that afternoon's sunshine hanging on the line. The Minnicks and Bodie slept well. In the morning, a cousin carried a fresh bucket of well water for their wash basins and had various, assorted mugs for coffee for them as they came out to pack up the truck. Evidently that family felt that a favor done for one was an obligation to be treated as neighbors by all the rest of their clan. He hadn't said a word about Nandria being housed with them in the cabin, and that surprised Minnick. It gave him hope for his wife's clan. Hope that would be dashed before the sun was far into its downward path to the west.

"This is my wife, Nandria, and our daughter, Rose," Will told his mother's people who had gathered, open-mouthed but silent. Nandria stood tall but not commanding; smiling but not assuming. She and Will had talked so long, quietly, in the bed of the pickup. One problem was that Will did not know his relatives individually or well, either. They were who they were, and it was what it was. Not a new situation for Nandria, but one over which she had little control. She was at the mercy of others' experiences, and both she and Will knew that. She felt him reach now to cup her right elbow, both to reassure her and to let them see he claimed her as his own.

"We come such a long way to see you all," Doris told them when no one had spoken for an uncomfortably long time. The pleading in her voice made Minnick cringe.

Finally, Millie spoke. Quietly. "You might have told us…"

Float

CHAPTER EIGHTEEN

The headlights of the Minnick truck settling to level after rising up out of the dip in their lane caught the shiny back of a badger lumbering across the rutted road. The animal turned to glare at them with red, angry eyes and then disappeared into the brush. Minnick gripped the steering wheel tighter as though the animal's stare had been a bad omen, but Doris stirred beside him in the passenger's seat as Rose clapped and squealed on her lap.

"D -d- d...!"

"Do you hear that, Mr. Minnick? He's trying to say 'doggy.'"

"So she is, Mother," Minnick agreed though he didn't believe a word of it. Will had been bright, but this one...well, he didn't believe she was trying to name an animal she'd never seen before. Not that little. But he couldn't argue with his Doris. *I win more arguments by just saying "Yes, Dear."* Chuckling to himself, he was impressed, however, that the child had been delighted rather than afraid. It did take a lot to scare her. That much of her was Minnick, at any rate.

As they came almost within sight of their home, Minnick was still amused despite the aching turnout of the reunion, despite the decision to leave early that afternoon and drive straight back. Still bleary-eyed despite allowing Will to do most of the driving, Minnick blinked, unsure of what he was seeing when a brownish van seemed to ease ahead of the range of his lights. He sat up, widening his eyes. The van appeared to melt into his own back yard, but when he stepped on the gas to hurry to pull up beside the house and park catty-corner so his headlight swept the yard, there was, of course, nothing there.

All he knew for sure was that he had been damned cold and uncomfortable in the bed of the truck. And not a lot more comfortable when he took back the driving chores more than half way past Jeff City. He was just glad as hell they were home again. He left the truck parked catty-wampus.

"So we can see to cross to the porch," he told Doris when she questioned his parking angle as he took the baby from her and helped her out of the truck.

"Dear Mr. Minnick, I know my own back yard. Ain't I hung clothes here for a million years?" she laughed. He didn't tell her about what he wasn't sure he'd seen.

Will helped Nandria and Bodie down from the truck, then waited while Bodie took off across the west field and Nandria made it onto the porch before leaning in to flip off the headlights. He followed, wondering at the impression of tire tracks he thought he'd seen in the grass. They seemed to cross the lawn, skirt the elm and turn to go around the far corner of the house. He was thinking about following them to see, but Nandria called then. He hurried inside, to find her, Rose in her arms, peering and frowning at the contents of the small dresser they'd brought down from Will's room to have drawers for the baby's clothes.

"They are all rumpled," Nandria said so quietly it was almost a whimper. That was a tone he'd heard but seldom from his warrior princess wife.

He shrugged and took the baby from her so she could straighten the little garments and select what she needed to dress Rose for what was left of the night.

They turned at Doris's distant cry of dismay. "Oh, Mr. Minnick, what a mess you've made."

"Not me, Mother," he answered in a voice that protested innocence.

"Well, never mind, I guess. I'll work on this after I've had some real sleep. Come now," she said, but the rest trailed off.

They did hear, "Yes, dear," and a fond chuckle. Will and Nandria smiled at each other and hugged around their daughter, glad to be home for whatever comfort and safety it could afford.

* * * * * * * * * * * * * * * * * *

When dawn came too soon, Will groaned, turning over in their brass bed. Seeing light in the barn, he slid into his trousers and stumbled out to catch Greg Paisler just as he finished milking the last cow, Clementine. The two carried the buckets to the separator.

"Thought you weren't due back until tonight, late," Greg commented as he set the equipment into the sink to scrub and rinse. He looked over at Will. "Trouble, huh? Family didn't take well to the heavy tan?"

"Something like that."

"Beats me why so many lie out in the sun to look like Nandria—though they don't make it, by far—and then object to what comes natural to her. She all right?"

"You know her."

"She'd never tell you if'n she wasn't. Sorry, though, she had to go through that."

Will leaned heavily against the sink. "Well, I guess I should have known better. What can you expect from people who didn't know what was happening in Dunkirk? And didn't care when I tried to tell them." Grasping the filter in both hands, he swished it violently in the sudsy water. Greg went on with his cleaning without comment until Will could master his feelings. "Sorry you had to come to do extra for us, but I really appreciate it, Greg."

"Hey, no problem. You been good to and for us whenever there was need. Your whole family…" He went quiet. No sense bringing up Freddy again when, thank the Lord, that heart-pain was finally settling to a dull ache for the Minnicks. So glad that Mr. Minnick finally recognized his younger son's death for what it was: a tragic, stupid-beyond-words accident of Fred's own doing.

"Say, was there somebody out here while we were gone?" Will questioned. "Did you see any sign?"

Greg's full brows lifted; he shrugged. "Nope. Why? Something wrong? Sorry if I missed somethin'." He looked around.

"Don't think so. Just a couple of messes where we don't think we left them in the house. But you know how particular women can be about their things."

Greg shrugged again. "Ain't got a lot of womenfolk in my life to know that. Sorry."

* * * * * * * * * * * * * * * * * * *

Breakfast was later than Nandria had ever known the family to sleep in. Even Rose slept until nearly nine that morning, but by then she was ready to be up and changed and fed—immediately. Nandria laughed and obeyed. Will and his father fueled up on light pancakes and crisp bacon and over-easy eggs and then left reluctantly for the north field.

"What time will you want lunch?" Nandria asked as they were pulling on their boots.

"A picnic?" both suggested.

"Of course. About one?"

"Sounds good, love," Will whispered into her ear as his father nodded.

Nandria started the extra laundry from their trip and came in to check on Doris in her rocker in the living room. She was leaning forward to encourage Rose playing with her Raggedy Andy. Doris looked up.

"Girl, did you go through my drawers for somethin'?"

"No," Nandria answered, more surprised than offended. "Why? Are you missing something?"

"A few trinkets from my jewelry box. Nothin' I care about. I don't keep my treasures in there anyhow. But the mister says he had some cash money and wondered if'n I'd taken it for some reason."

"Oh, dear. The baby's dresser drawers were tumbled as well, and neither Will nor I remember having left them that way. How strange." Nandria looked at her mother-in-law and saw confusion settling over her. "There is bound to be an explanation."

"We been robbed, I'd say. Or burgled. Which is it? I do like the funny sound of that word. Burgled, burgled, burgled," Doris repeated, using only an exaggerated movement of her lips but keeping her jaw still. She giggled, then sobered. "Nothin' I care about missin', I guess, 'ceptin' that brooch."

"Brooch? The red and purple one your young boyfriend tried to bestow on you?"

"He weren't never my beau, but he did try hard, didn't he?" Doris giggled. "Now why would anyone want such a plug-ugly thing as that?"

Nandria wiped her hands in her apron, then fingered the pebbles in its pocket. *Why would someone have such a piece to sell in the first place? Perhaps I need to find out more about this young Mr. Struan.*

✳ ✳ ✳ ✳ ✳ ✳ ✳ ✳ ✳ ✳ ✳ ✳ ✳ ✳ ✳ ✳ ✳ ✳

Finding himself again in Fox Haven, Kylie parked in the morning shade of a mulberry tree. Frowning, he searched among its leaves as though they could give him a rational reason that he had come all this way once more. It wasn't as though Mrs. Struan was the first or only parishioner to call in tears. Nearly always before he had been able to find a reasonable way of saying, "No, not now." But again this day, here he was leaning back into his car to lift his oversized Bible from the front seat.

"Oh, Reverend Kylie, I am so glad you've come. I am beside myself," the woman sobbed, though every hair was place and there wasn't a wrinkle in her purple cotton dress with its ample, mid-shin skirt. Kylie caught his breath at the sight of those trim ankles.

"Now, now, dear lady, do not fret yourself so. I said I would come, and here I am, grateful if I can be of service to you." He squeezed past Connie Struan into her living room as she held the door wide with a long, slender, white arm.

"There is something so wrong, Pastor. My son, Benedict, is acting so strangely. I know there is something very wrong."

At the catch in her voice, a pang whipped through Dean Kylie's chest. It was like nothing he'd ever felt before. He sat down on the sofa before being invited to. His right hand pressed against the thumping of his heart.

"Reverend Kylie," Connie cried, "Aren't you well? You're so pale, I—I don't know what to do."

"It is nothing, dear lady," he choked. "It will pass in a moment, please the Lord." He hoped. And then, seeing her concern for himself, he felt his breath hitching toward ease of flow. He hadn't realized he was holding his breath until he found himself exhaling with a slight, if undignified whistle. He inhaled, feeling the air fill his lungs and lifting his ribcage so the terrible constriction gave with the expansion. He breathed again, marveling at the freedom, the flow, the ease of health when for that moment he had thought he was dying.

And all because of her. The way she had looked. The way she looked at him now.

He shook his head. "Constance, Connie…" but he had no words. *I am a preacher. I always have words. But that is what they are, isn't it? Just words. People have tried to tell me there is more—so much more. But until this moment. Until the woman looked at me this way...*

Struggling to sit up, to regain his dignity, he addressed her formally, almost roughly. "Mrs. Struan, forgive my momentary lapse. I fear I must leave now. This moment."

"But my son...what about my son?"

"I will return at my earliest opportunity."

"But, Dean, I need you now."

Kylie sat peering up at her, mouth slack. "I—I'm here," he managed, finally, fearing he could lose consciousness at any moment. "What has he done?"

Constance Struan stiffened.

Kylie felt breath seep into his chest. He was right; her reaction proved that, but for once it wasn't enough to be right. He had to find a way to tell her he not only wanted to help, but would be able to help, no matter what kind of trouble her son was in.

She seemed to see it in his eyes, but obviously could not allow herself to believe.

He struggled to sit up, though the ache threatened to re-grip his chest. He sat, peering up at her, knowing he could not leave her. "You—you must tell me," he managed. "What has he done?"

Shaking her head, she swayed in her misery. "Why must everyone simply assume Benedict is guilty? They don't even give him a chance to explain."

Explain what? And who was accusing him? Why? But Kylie remained uncharacteristically still. He inhaled deeply; he would need all his faculties to help her.

Clutching one hand in the other and then shifting to pull on each in turn as though straining into and out of unseen gloves, Constance Struan paced up and down her living room, kicking at the corner of a rug that had had the audacity to curl up at one corner when she needed the way smooth under her feet. On her fourth lap, she leaned over him, mouth twisted in anger but eyes pleading.

"Your...," she stammered, unable to find the perfect derogatory word, then finally skipping over the adjective altogether. "Your sheriff—Yates, is it?"

"Yakes."

"Yakes, then. He had the gall to call my son into his dusty office to all but accuse him of being part of..."

"Part of...?" he asked gently, telling her he truly wanted to know. Needed to know if he were going to be able to help. He was so quiet that she stood a moment, shuddering and then sat beside him. He hitched to give her room.

"Haven't you heard of the burglaries that have been going on around here in the last several months?"

He nodded. "But what...? Does Yakes think Ben may have a part in those?"

The anger shifted totally into pleading on Connie's face. Her hand fluttered to cover her eyes; she wept.

Float

With new strength in his chest he lifted his arms to do something he had done only once before in his life. Kylie drew the sobbing lady into his arms. He held her.

CHAPTER NINETEEN

That Sunday evening, knowing the Minnicks were exhausted, Greg Paisler returned to help with the evening chores, just as he'd planned to do alone. The resurrecting evening breeze haunted the door at the porch and wafted the yellow and green seed-sack curtains at the window above the kitchen sink. Nandria, hands still in sudsy dish water, lifted her chin to catch a bit of its stirring to cool the sweat stinging her eyes.

"Ahhh," she murmured, and Rose behind her in her highchair looked over from gnawing on the heel of baked potato from supper.

"Mmmm mmm," Rose commented, and Nandria turned to look and smile at her growing little one.

"Yes, darling," Nandria whispered, "Mum loves you, too."

Greg wiped his lips and chin of the last of the berry filling from his third wedge of pie. He rose, gathering his plate and the empty pie pan to carry them over to the sink.

"Mmmm, indeed, Miz Minnick. That was so good." He stopped to grin and grimace at the baby to make her laugh, then brought the remaining dishes and utensils to the sink board. "Can I help you with them dishes? I sure dirtied up a bunch of them."

"No, thank you, Mr. Paisler. I am nearly finished now. You go along. But I would ask a favor, if you please."

"Of course. Anything."

"You were so thoughtful to come here this evening, I want to be able to do more for you to express our gratitude. I would appreciate it if you would knock me up in the morning."

Greg's eyebrows lifted. He stood, mouth partly open, and then quickly snapped his jaw, closing his mouth as he swallowed.

Seeing his distress, Nandria knew she'd embarrassed herself—and him. She hurried to try to explain. "I—I mean, you arrive so early each morning. Please just knock at the porch door and I shall let you in to serve you a cup of coffee."

"Oh," he exhaled. "Uh, no, that's all right. I don't mind waiting. Gives me a chance to look over the farm."

"To dream of how you would arrange things on your own?"

"Somethin' like that, ma'am. Dreamin' don't getcha far, but thinkin', and plannin', now…"

"Yes, quite. A distinct difference," she agreed, lifting her shoulder to brush back a strand of hair that had fallen into her face. "Well, thank you for your offer to help with dishes. Good night, now."

"Yes, ma'am. Good night to you and the little miss." He grinned and made faces at Rose until she giggled as he passed by to the porch. Subdued bursts of laughter met him. Nandria had been hearing those every now and again for the past several minutes. She was curious, but first she needed to check on Mother Minnick, who had been quiet too long.

Scrubbing the last of the baked berry ooze from the pie pan, Nandria set it to drain and tipped the basin to empty it. As it sloshed and gurgled, she wrung out the dishcloth to wipe the table and stove top. She left the cloth on the hopelessly soggycrumbed tray of Rose's highchair and wiped her daughter's face with the hem of her apron.

"Ah, precious," she exclaimed. There were no words. Lifting the baby into her arms, she carried her to the doorway to the living room.

Doris, frail in her pallor, snored softly on the sofa. Her regular breathing lifted and then sucked in the section of newsprint over her face. Nandria watched and listened a moment, then carried the baby to the sink to do a better job of washing that little, round face. She tipped the basin again to dry, gave the high chair tray a lick and a promise and, hearing again the bursts of laughter, carried her baby to the porch.

She stood a moment watching Will huddled close to his burly father on the edge of the brass bed listening intently to the radio. Bodie had pulled the one straight-backed chair up so close he knocked Will's knees from the side. Greg stood just beyond Bodie, leaning forward, snorting with them at hilarious moments of the broadcast. But when one man's laughter burst loud, the others hushed him so they would not miss the next exchange of the two voices on the radio.

Smiling at their obvious enjoyment, Nandria leaned in close to listen. Minnick hushed her but made room.

"Amos 'n' Andy," Minnick explained.

"Ain't they a kick in the keister?" Bodie cried, then looked up, evidently just registering that Nandria was near. "Oh, sorry, Miz Minnick. No of-fense, if'n you please."

Without answering, Nandria asked quietly, "Are these men Negroid?"

Nodding as he chuckled, Will looked up at her only for a moment, barely recognizing her question and missing its implications. Minnick, thinking she was questioning that darkies were permitted to broadcast, explained, "Been a few niggers on the radio afore them. Remember, Bode, that Nigger Improvement malarkey a while back? Who the blamed…?"

"Somebody Garvey. Marcus Garvey, I think, Mr. Minnick. But that was before I ever heard of him bein' on the radio. He wanted all Negroes to get money to go back to Africa."

"He got that part right, at least," Minnick stated. "But he ended up in jail, didn't he? Somethin' about mail fraud? But these guys," he added, gesturing with a calloused hand toward the radio. "Amos and Andy, well, they're somethin', all right."

"I laugh 'til my belly hurts," Bodie snickered.

"Almost worth the cost of that there radio just to get to hear 'em," Minnick decided.

Nandria straightened. After one deep breath, she handed the baby to Will. "Perhaps humor will etch at the racial barrier," she said, and turned to go outside.

Hugging Rose to his chest, Will peered after her. He opened his mouth to call, then thought better of it. Handing the baby to Bodie, Will extended his left hand as he tried to extract himself from the press of men at the bedside. But Nandria turned at the doorway and motioned for him to stay where he was.

The back yard was dark, with masses of greater darkness where the barn loomed, and blotches of black for the chicken coop and doghouse. The mulberry tree had twittered—as nearly every evening—while the last of the roosting birds, finally nearly satisfied with the territory they had claimed for the night, began to quiet. It was still now. The elm hovered, a mosaic of darkness and reflected bits of light from the porch.

Nandria wandered in the grass, from Fred's and Emmy Lu's grave-sites to the edge of the Minnick lane and far side of the barn. Shuddering, she returned slowly to grasp the rope swing hanging from the elm's broad horizontal branch. With her back to him, Nandria felt as much as heard Will approaching. She did not turn, but neither did she flinch when he rested a hand gently on her shoulder.

"Sorry, love."

"You need not have come out, Will. I am fine."

"I know," he agreed, moving around to come to her side so he could peer at her face. "You have a strength inside you that lets you deal with hurt. You've probably already forgiven me for being such a blind, white fool."

"No, darling, no."

"You haven't forgiven me?"

"Nothing to forgive," she sighed and sat on the swing seat. "It is merely that at times I stumble over the differences in our cultures. Did Greg Paisler tell you about our misunderstanding?"

Seating himself on the grass beside her, Will shook his head.

"I—I asked him to please knock me up in the morning."

Will guffawed. "Oh, I can picture his face when he heard that one. What did he say?"

"I could see that he was shocked, so I tried to explain that I had meant for him to knock at our door and awaken me if he arrived as early as he sometimes does. Did you know that he merely waits outside until there is stirring in the house?"

Nodding, and still chuckling, Will stretched up to explain. "My precious Brit, Americans use the expression 'knocked up'..."

"Never mind. I have gathered that Americans have made it something with innuendo."

"Let's just say, it has been my privilege, twice now."

"Oh."

"Unless you'd like to..."

"Nourish the new little one coming?" Nandria smiled at Will's grin.

"Will those people on the porch never quit listening to that infernal radio?"

CHAPTER TWENTY

In Dr. Ricartsen's front room lobby, Ida Jane and Mrs. Freshstalk sat primly, waiting. Claudia sat taller in her straight-backed chair and exhaled slowly in a sigh that spoke tellingly of her displeasure. It was a posture and a sound that Ida Jane knew well.

"I suppose we must be grateful that a doctor is willing to stay here in our little town..." the mother of the bride-to-be huffed. "... but we do wish we could have procured the services of someone more efficient and respectful of our time," Ida finished with her. The girl's words were barely audible, but when she looked up, she realized that her mother had caught her mouthing them. She flushed, wishing she'd kept her rebelliousness to herself.

"Well, really, Ida Jane," Claudia snapped, and twisted in her chair to stare at the doctor's office door.

They waited awkwardly a long while before the girl gathered courage to try to speak. "Really, Mama, Dah will be all right. We're not really telling tales on him—just letting the doctor know why we're concerned. You mustn't worry so." She raised a small, white hand to the outer corner of her left eye as though to remind her mother of wrinkles. But even that gesture, although understood, only served to make the air between them more tense. "Dah is so strong. He owns the bank!" Ida stated as though that fortified him against all threats.

"But we had plans for this day, you and I," Claudia donned her martyrdom pose, and Ida Jane wriggled just a little before catching herself. She'd have to think fast to find something to distract her mother or there would be sighing and flopping onto beds and couches all day and her needing to stay close and listen to complaints and nothing much else accomplished.

"Yellow and purple," Ida blurted.

"What?"

"I think I've decided on my wedding colors."

"Purple and yellow. Purple, for a wedding?"

"Oh, yes, Mother. Purple is so rich and then the yellow will soften and brighten everything. I can just see it. It'll be beautiful."

Claudia's expression said clearly what she thought about such an outlandish color for a celebration on which the Freshstalks would be judged. But she cleared her throat delicately and asked as though innocently, "Just what flowers were you imagining?"

"Irises, mostly. They are so stately and elegant with just the right amount of fluff and curve." Her slender face lit in pink rapture, but her mother's smile was not warm.

"You are planning a spring wedding, then?"

"Oh. Irises. Spring. That's right. Must I, Mother? Must I wait that long?"

"I would imagine you would wait at least a year so as not to appear to be in too great haste."

Ida Jane twisted on her chair, staring at Claudia, comprehending her mother's meaning and gasping in response.

"Mother!"

Ida was still open-mouthed as Sadie came to the head of the hallway to summon them to the exam room. But Ricartsen groaned in his office and Sadie strode—with the Freshstalks behind her—the few steps to open his office door and peer in. The three women looked at him, bleak-faced, huddled over his radio.

"Really, Dr. Ricartsen, your obsession with matters going on in Europe would seem to be interfering with your devotion to your practice," Claudia huffed.

Sadie turned on her; Ida Jane shrank back. Ricartsen snapped off the radio and stood up to full lanky height. He galumphed by her and into his front room but paused just beyond his accuser.

"No, Mrs. Freshstalk. Never. Medicine is my life," he intoned and brushed on by them and out of sight down the back hallway.

As they followed Sadie and were ushered into the small exam room, Ida Jane turned on her mother. "Really, Mama. Dah is the one he's gonna examine tomorrow. What if he's mad when he does it?"

"If that man so much as looks mean, let alone hurts my husband, we shall not only find another doctor, but we shall be sure no one else is harmed by his distracted state either."

Sadie looked back into the room and then down the hall as Ricartsen—who had obviously heard the woman's threat as well—approached. He stopped, looking at his nurse and shaking his head. It was all Sadie could do to keep from saying, "I told you so."

Ricartsen stomped on by and into his office. He slammed his door and slammed himself into his chair to fiddle once again with the dial on his radio.

The Freshstalks waited a long time, growing more unsettled minute by minute. And then they heard sharp static penetrated finally by a booming, sonorous voice, "...fishing boats, ferries, anything that floats...pulling off hundreds, no, rescuing thousands..."

"They're gettin' them fightin' boys out!" Sadie whooped as she ran back up the hallway and into the Freshstalks' exam room. "Praise the heavens," she added softly leaning into the doorsill and closing her eyes.

"What?" Claudia rose, her right hand over her throat.

"Dunkirk," Sadie explained.

The radio voice broke through again, "French resist..." it started, then broke off abruptly. Scratchiness, a few low curses, a click of the dial and Dr. Ricartsen bounded back to the doorway to the exam room. He peered in, beaming. "They're getting them!"

Blinking, Ida Jane turned first to her stunned mother and then to the nurse. "Why's he so happy?"

"They're taking small boats across the Channel to Dunkirk and slipping the Brits off the beaches to take 'em home!" Ricartsen boomed.

"Huh?"

"Those young British soldiers were bare on the beach—no cover, just open targets for strafing, for artillery, for firing practice for tanks," Ricartsen roared.

"They was gettin' slaughtered," Sadie explained. "And now, thank the Lord, they are escaping. People with any kind of little boat are coming from England to pick them up. To get 'em out of there!"

Claudia Freshstalk's face softened. "Oh, my word. It's a miracle," she whispered. "I lost a brother in the Great War..." Her eyes brimmed with tears.

Ida Jane stared at the expression on Claudia's face that she did not remember seeing before. Instinctively she reached out to grasp and hold her mother's hands.

Float

CHAPTER TWENTY-ONE

Sadie and Ron clung to each other as they walked home from the bewildered but joyous Dunkirk celebration in town; Ronda stumbled behind them up the back stairs and into the kitchen.

The winds had picked up a little that evening, lightly starched to tell you they had power, but still "gusties," as Ronda had called them as a delighted child. Ron Bean leaned back in his chair at the kitchen table to open the back door wider to give them welcome.

"I love this time of near night," he said, smiling.

"You love night, period," Sadie remarked and the glance between them was one that Ronda might normally have picked up on and blushed, but she sat hunched over her plate, pushing her food around with her fork. Both parents watched her. Ron looked up, questioning Sadie with a look while she was at the refrigerator tucking away left-overs, but the large woman could only shrug. "Of course, you get up so unearthly early for your milk route," Sadie murmured as though to explain her comment.

With a worried frown, Sadie came over to sit at the table, assessing Ronda as she came, but the girl did not look up. "You know, Ron, I hoped when you first got off the people route and were scheduled to deliver to stores that it would mean you could sleep in just a little, but if anything, I think you need to go even earlier."

"Folks want the milk in the store early if'n they've forgot to pick it up the night before." He laughed, as he always did when faced with unpleasant realities.

Sadie sat wearily at the table and their hands met under the table where the parents could console each other as they studied their daughter's face. It was Ron who pulled out from under the black cloud that was settling over the three of them. He reopened the discussion from the night before, asking, "July 4th, then? Is that when you want me to get somebody to cover my route? Take a couple days off together, maybe get a cabin at the Lake of the Ozarks?"

Sadie sat up straighter, fixing a smile of anticipation on her face and turning to Ronda. "So Fourth of July, don't you agree, Missy?"

The girl looked up, surprised that her parents were both looking at her to answer whatever the question was that had been posed. "May I please be excused, Pa? I got homework to do."

"Surely, child," he told her after a glance at Sadie. "Go on now. But don't work too late. Get yourself to bed early tonight, you hear?"

"Yes, Pa," the girl assured him and rose heavily.

Her parents listened to her trudging footfalls up to the second floor. Her door closed without its usual defiant click. Ron and Sadie looked at each other and then away, seeing no consolation, only mirrors of their own anxiety.

"What's eatin' her, Sadie? It seems like weeks she's been nothing but a damp dishrag moping around here. You sure Doc Ricartsen checked her good?"

Sadie nodded, assuring him Ricartsen had given their daughter a thorough going-over.

Ron's expression grew even more pensive. "Worried me some when it first started; more now."

Sadie nodded sadly. "It's like her heart is broke, but I don't know what did it. Think I should go up and talk with her?"

"What'll you say? I wouldn't even know what to ask."

"Neither do I, but maybe just sittin' with her will let her know she's loved." Sadie rose, her whole being taking on a task she had no hope for.

In her room, Ronda sat at her desk with her books and papers spread out before her, staring out her window. She looked up as Sadie approached from behind and leaned to envelop her precious daughter in her arms.

Ronda wept, but said nothing.

* * * * * * * * * * * * * * * * * * *

As the dawn crept and then flushed in at the porch windows, Nandria stretched and turned on her side to smile at the look of pure contentment on her sleeping beloved's face. Some moments are worth all the struggles of the day. But even that moment did not erase the feeling of dread coursing through her limbs. She was turning over to snuggle against Will's back when the flannel sheet slipped from her shoulder, pulling her nightie's strap with it. Not-yet-warmed air caressed her upper arm, sending a chill into her chest and throat.

Will is not home, except to heal. The United States Army will be taking him away. Oh, Lord, please keep him safe. Please.

Will awoke to her silent, shuddering sobs. It took several minutes for him to discover what was hurting her so.

"But, angel love, I am less torn apart by the thought of being killed than you are. I guess it was when I was lying in that field and then again in the hospital outside London, I realized that in this war, my body no longer belongs to me. All the training. Makes us soldier-things, I suppose. React as we've been taught and drilled to react. No, I don't like the idea of pain again…"

"Or still."

He chuckled. "You're right. Or still. But it's only the price I pay. I guess the way a woman accepts childbirth. I don't know, it's as though I know it is a possibility, but that can't keep me from…"

"…from doing your duty," she finished bitterly.

He lifted her chin so he could study her face. "You have little to say protesting duty. You stay here, working yourself far past what I could wish for you."

She would not acknowledge, but he could read in her eyes that she understood what he was trying to tell her.

"Stiff upper lip," he whispered as an accusation, and she had to giggle.

"I always thought that must be decidedly easier to manage with a flourishing moustache," she muttered.

"Probably," he laughed and drew her to him.

* * * * * * * * * * * * * * * * * *

Pastor Kylie lay awake, his body splayed across his double bed, miserable with thoughts of frustration and fear of failure. *Is the boy a thief? Could the son of such a fine woman truly steal from his neighbors? He must have been coerced in some ungodly way. Surely. I need to find a way to speak to him—but how? He does not know me. Not truly. Constance, Mrs. Struan…*He paused, chest tight, picturing her gazing at him with those eyes that flashed golden. He needed to breathe deliberately for a while before he could go on with any semblance of planning.

Perhaps it would be prudent to find out for myself what the sheriff thinks of the situation. Sheriff Yakes. A slovenly man, but experienced. Yes, perhaps I need first to sound him out. After all, it behooves a man to keep himself from becoming entangled in a woman's hysterical assumptions. Yes. I will talk with Sheriff Yakes in the morning.

Turning onto his side, Kylie slept more deeply than he had throughout the night. He snored, although he would have denied the fact.

* * * * * * * * * * * * * * * * * *

A late start for this day, but even Grover Minnick dawdled at the breakfast table sipping his third mug of coffee.

Will tipped back his chair and quietly watched his parents and then Bodie, who had drawn the little princess's high chair to him around the corner of the table. The old man was feeding her heaping spoonfuls of oatmeal that guaranteed oodles would ooze onto her cheeks and plop in gobs from her chin. Watching her, Will was filled with a suffusing warmth.

These moments of nothing, of ordinary. These are what life is. Funny, I've never stopped to think of it just that way before. He knew his murmured conversation with Nandria this morning had spurred that realization.

He looked over to his wife at the kitchen sink and the inner warmth deepened. Rising, he gathered the soiled dishes at his end of the table and carried them to her, setting them in the sudsy water in the basin. He touched the hem of hair that 'curdled'— she always rolled her dark eyes when he called it that—at the wide, rounded strap that held up the bib apron at the nape of her neck. She went still, and then lowered her chin. He saw that she was fighting morning sickness nausea again this day, so he caressed her shoulder and went back to the table to collect the last of the dirty dishes for her to get them quickly under the soap foam. The less she had to deal with the remnants and odors of what she'd cooked for the family, the easier it would be for her. He was going back for the last when a knock at the porch door startled them all.

Greg entered without waiting for an answer.

"Good morning, Mrs. Minnick. G'morning, all." He greeted the family as Bodie pulled the high chair closer to let him sit at his place against the wall. Nandria gestured to the stove, offering to cook him breakfast, but he shook his head and rubbed his mid-section to tell her he'd already eaten. "It's gonna be a scorcher right early this day."

"Best we get started then," Minnick groused. "Hate that heat beatin' down on us. If that sun wasn't so good for the crops, I'd hang a tent over the whole place and give us shade to work in."

Muttering, the men swallowed the last of their coffee as they stood up. Almost in unison, the mugs slapped against the oak table, startling Rose, who glared at Bodie as though it were all his fault that her eating had been disturbed. Greg did snatch up two of the last three of Nandria's biscuits from the table before following Bodie toward the porch. Minnick raised his hand palm up.

"Won't need ya this mornin', Bode."

"You sure, Mr. Minnick?"

"Till we get that tractor doin' what it's supposed to, don't hardly need the three of us out there breakin' our backs."

As Bodie backed to his chair and settled again to feeding the little princess, Minnick plopped onto the bench to haul on his boots. Greg stopped Will beside the brass bad, lowering his chin to speak quietly.

"That schoolgirl..."

"Ronda, you mean?" Will frowned. *You know her name as well as any of us here. Why the mystery?*

"Well, yeah, Ronda. She ain't comin' out here no more for help with her math?"

"I guess she hasn't been feeling well for a while. Staying close to home, as I understand it. You haven't called? Or gone into town to see her?"

Biting his lower lip. Greg shook his head. "She don't seem to want me around." He peered up, but Will shook his head and lifted his hands palm out. Gnawing at his lower lip again, Greg went on by him and out the door to the yard.

Will returned to the kitchen; he bussed the nape of Nandria's neck, whispering, "Ronda say anything to you about not wanting Greg around?"

Frowning, she shook her head. "Not to me. Is he missing her as much as we are?"

Shrugging, Will kissed her again, but noticed from the corner of his eye how intensely Bodie was concentrating on the baby rather than looking anywhere near them at the sink. "Not half as frantically as I would be if you were missing."

"Rather like my feelings when you are away, I suppose. I am so grateful that this time when you are called we will all be together." She twisted to look up at him, but his eyes told her of his uncertainty.

"Oh," she said so quietly, he probably did not hear her as he left. He did not turn back. Nauseated, Nandria stared a long time at the dishes poking up from the vanishing soap suds.

Bodie spoke up from the table. "Never you mind, Miz Minnick. You come here and finish feedin' this here little one. I can gather up them dishes and clean this kitchen slick as a whistle. And, hey, ain't you and the missus goin' to some party at lunch time?"

Lifting her hands from the basin and drying them elaborately on the tea towel, Nandria faced him wearily. "We are to help Mrs. Paisler prepare the picnic for tonight."

Chapter Twenty-One

"Picnic?"

"To celebrate Dr. Ricartsen's anniversary or birthday, whichever it supposedly is."

Bodie's expression of disbelief was so bewildered that Nandria chuckled despite herself.

"The doctor has evidently served this town for four years now, I believe."

"Four years already? Fer a while I wasn't sure the boy was gonna make it. Sure was one awkward colt when he first come."

"The celebration is to be a surprise."

"Oh, it'll knock his socks off, fer him to find people care fer him 'nuff to give him a party."

"Dr. Ricartsen is a fairly self-effacing gentleman, from my observation," Nandria offered as she came to sit down beside her oatmeal-coated offspring.

Bodie grinned and rolled his eyes at her, obviously not understanding.

"Rather like you, Mr. Bodie," she told him.

"And that's good?"

"Quite."

Float

CHAPTER TWENTY-TWO

Rather than getting around to return to talk with Doc Ricartsen, Yakes sat, chair tilted and hands on belly, with his legs resting just above the ankles on the edge of his desk. His feet were crossed, but that was putting a strain on his belly. He had about determined to shift position when Pastor Kylie startled him by entering the sheriff's office. Yakes groaned as he drew his feet from the desk. He clutched and rubbed his protruding belly as he half-stood to gesture toward the vacant chair.

"Sit, why don'tcha?"

"Yes," Kylie replied, looking down his nose for a second before pasting on his smile. "Thank you, Sheriff. I will, if you have a moment." He sat, although it took steeling himself to do so without first taking out his handkerchief to wipe at the chair's seat. Lord knew who had occupied the chair last.

"Coffee, Pastor?"

"No, no, thank you. Don't trouble yourself. I have just finished breakfast. I was merely curious about the rumors I had been hearing from many of my flock."

"What kinda rumors, Pastor?" Hiking up his belly in his left hand, Yakes settled more comfortably in his chair although he wished he'd had warning so he could have gone in back and relieved some of the gas that had been building. He concentrated on listening and not squirming. He'd have to get up in a minute and excuse himself if the pastor turned long-winded.

"Well, I suppose they aren't mere rumors. Several of my parishioners have told me that they have been the victims of robbery. Or is it burglary when items are taken from the home?"

Ignoring the question, Yakes sat up straighter. "Who's told you that?" He reached to draw a sheet of paper from the top drawer of his desk. "I got a list here of the people's told me. You know anybody that ain't said nothing to me yet?"

"Well, I did jot down a few of the names of people who've spoken to me…" Fumbling in the large pocket of his black cotton jacket Kylie laid a wrinkled paper on the edge of the desk to straighten and smooth it with his hand. "I copied this at breakfast this morning for you, Sheriff, so you may keep it and consult it at your leisure." He swallowed to hide a sly smile at the man's reaction to his words. And then Kylie was a bit ashamed of himself. *The sheriff is not a bad man; he is merely uneducated. Probably his family could not afford to send him for any work beyond high school, if he had that. But he is bright in his own way. He seems to be trying to see people around him as human beings with failings and foibles. What if they are as unsettled in their worlds as I find myself, thanks to the Struan woman? She looks at me and my foundation crumbles. What if other men are experiencing such bewilderment and finding no one to whom to communicate? Unsettling, indeed.*

* * * * * * * * * * * * * * * * * * *

The sheriff meticulously checked off each name on Kylie's list and handed it back to him. "Just Mrs. Zorn. I got all the others, I reckon. Thank you, Pastor. I'll ride on out to the Zorn place this day or the next and talk with her. Mebbe she'll have some ideas."

"No thank you needed, Sheriff," Kylie said and found that he meant it. His eyebrows raised of themselves to realize that was true.

"Appreciate your help, Pastor. Anything I can do for you?"

"Well, as a matter of fact, I am puzzled…or rather, so many have asked me if there is any progress being made in finding out who might be behind these series of small thefts. I was wondering if there was anything I could tell my people—without interfering with your investigation, of course."

Yakes lifted his hands, palms up. "Don't know. Ideas, mind you. But to be honest, in all my years, I ain't never seen the like."

"I understand," Kylie said quietly while looking down at the paper he'd given to the sheriff, "I have heard that you are bringing in people to question them. Suspects, Sheriff?"

"Nah," Yakes expelled. He rose, tightening his sphincter and wishing the pastor would leave about soon, if not right now.

Suddenly realizing the poor man's dilemma, Kylie stood. "Well, I would like to stay and talk a spell, but you, of course, understand how busy a professional man's days can become…"

Relief showed on the sheriff's anxious face, until Kylie turned at the doorway, speaking back across the turned collar. "The Struan boy? Did you speak with him?"

"The kid from Fox Haven that's working a route for GEM? Yeah, I thought I'd ask if he'd seen anything suspicious. He offered to keep his eyes open on his travels."

"Well, Sheriff," Kylie ended as he reached to turn the doorknob, "I won't keep you. But you will let me know if you gain any leads, won't you?"

Nearly cross-eyed, Yakes nodded vigorously and was deeply grateful when the pastor opened the door and closed it firmly behind himself.

Kylie hurried away from the office, glad he'd put the question to Yakes. He could let Constance Struan know that her son was not being accused of anything. He would be the bearer of good tidings. Kylie pictured her face as she looked up at him as he consoled her.

Dr. Ricartsen sat frowning at his desk. He twisted the knob to turn off the radio with such a decided click and grunt that Sadie leaned in to check on him

"More bad news? Ain't they still getting them boys out of Dumbchurch?

"Dunkirk," Ricartsen correctly automatically. "Yeah, I think that is still in progress. Unbelievable what people will do to help. What a people the British are."

"So?" she asked, one hand cradling clean linen while the other settled on her hip, elbow out, demanding an answer.

"Belgium surrendered."

"Belgium? I thought you told me that a day or so ago, didn't you?"

"I said they'd have to. Didn't know till just now that it was official." He shook his head sadly. "Sometimes I miss the official announcements with this blamed radio."

Chapter Twenty-Two

"And with seeing patients, but that you gotta do. So you knew it was comin'."

"Yeah," he agreed, tightening his lips to a thin smear.

"Well then? Anyhow, the sheriff's here. Says you wanted to see him again this morning."

"Yeah, I did. Early. Like before we got started with patients. Schedule another time with him, will you, Mrs. Bean? A long one. I want a long stretch to really examine the man."

"Worried, are you?""

"No, not yet. But enough to want to be sure we got nothing to be worried about."

Sadie resettled the clean linen on her arm and went about setting the pieces ready-to-hand in each room. What her doc had just said made perfect sense to her.

Float

CHAPTER TWENTY-THREE

Clouds, wispy rather than promising any relief from this early dry spell, lazed in the southwest, teasing the hilltops. On their back stoop, Cynthia Paisler looked up from wiping the jam faces of her twins just in time to get a peek at Todd—or Twig, as he made his brothers call him—leaving stealthily, fishing pole and empty tin can in hand. He was just rounding the corner of the barn. If Cynthia had not the experience of seven younger brothers and sisters and eight sons of her own, she would never have looked up in time to know where the bit of a lad was headed.

She raised her chin, ready to call him back to keep an eye on Ned and Travis, but she smiled instead, willing to give a seven-year-old a cherished moment of his own. Shifting baby Levitt on her hip, she admonished the nearly five-year-old twins to play within sight of the house. They nodded solemnly.

I know both them boys—Travis, especially—fully intend to heed my command. But they'll get engrossed, likely in something gross. Like as not, they'll follow a mother field mouse out into the tall grass to find her nest. Probably bring home a squirming mass of tiny, squeaking rodents.

Cyn smiled again. *People think I run this here busy household well, but they ain't got one idea how often what happens is nothing I either chose or wanted. A momma's gotta accept with a smile because it's part of her sons' growing, part of the ordinary little things that make up a fine, loving man in the end, the good Lord willing. And that was what me and Zeb wanted for our boys to be: hard-working, good neighbors, upright farmers, husbands and fathers. There's no higher calling for a man. If that means overlooking the dry worms forgotten in overall pockets that I need to pick out before laundry, then that's the price.*

Oh, I just got a picture flashin' across my mind tryin' to picture fussy little Ida Jane discovering crawling or dead fascinating critters in her own sons' pockets. Will she have come down to earth by the time her own boys need her to swallow and carry on without carrying on? Ah, well, Frank has made his choice, and if anyone can bring out the best in a city girl and bring her to love country life, it would be Frank—or Greg. Ah, now there was a heartache both Zeb and me has decided to stay out of. It was the boys themselves that had brought on that tension when they wouldn't listen to Greg at all about the cotton, and they'll learn most by finding a way to settle it themselves.

Dear Zeb. Dear self-giving man. This rips at you even more'n me, my love. But you'll prod and poke quiet-like, like always. You'll teach our boys, pointing out insights so easy they'll think they thought 'em up on their own.

"Levitt, child, you are one lucky little guy to have the father you do," she teased the baby gurgling at her hip. "Do you know that?" They laughed together. They did that a lot.

Cynthia re-entered the enormous Paisler farm kitchen to find her oldest sons and their father still at table. "Scoot, you Paislers! You got enough lunch in you to last two days. If'n you want a decent meal for that party tonight for Doc, you gotta let me get to work on it now. Scoot, the gaggle of you!"

She set Levitt on the floor in the middle of the good-natured traffic as Zeb, Eli and Frank clamored up, grousing happily as they left for outside. Zeb stooped to snuggle his youngest son, then set him down again right in the path of young Sam who had stopped to gather half the dishes to carry to the sink for his mother. Sam side-stepped with an elaborate lifting of his left knee. Cynthia wasn't quite so agile. She rocked to a halt, bent low over the empty sausage platter, and spoke with comically screwed up face to the baby. "Levitt, you gotta learn to stay out of my way this day, littlest man. I've got work and enough without trippin' over the likes of you. "Travis!" she raised up to call. "Ned! Come in here and watch after your little brother!"

In the lower field, Twig halted when he heard her voice, listening hard for his name. But when she called only the twins, he crouched and hurried along, as near as he could come to being out of sight and out of ear range, too, he hoped, before she thought of him. He didn't see the low-slung, purple-magenta Studebaker until he heard it and looked up. His instinct was to duck, but he realized almost instantly that the seamstress with the murderously fascinating collar of pins and needles surely must have seen him already. To be rude to a visitor was something no son of Zeb or Cynthia Paisler was at liberty to do.

The tiny woman, her eyes and nose just visible above the driver's window sill, slowed and called to him. "Goin' fishin', are you, young man? Well, good. Catch a bunch. I love fish for lunch." She waved and struggled to put the car into gear again. The Studie coughed and lugged, and finally lunged forward up the grade toward the farmhouse.

Twig waited to see that the woman would be able to stop and park safely. He saw his mother come to the door to greet her. Her expression was unexpectedly clouded. "Ned Paisler!"

The twin popped up from beside the barn and reluctantly shuffled toward her. He raised his shoulder to try to surreptitiously wipe grime from his chin.

Even from where Twig stood, he could hear his mother's voice scolding. "Ned Paisler, I called you, young man."

Twig supplied the compulsory, 'Yes'm' that his little brother must have murmured.

"I called you, but I am not going to ask whether you heard me because I don't want you to even consider lying. I needed you to help with the baby. But Mrs. Drangler is here now. She will do a much finer job."

Oh, that was anger—something the boys seldom heard from their mom.

"Ya gotta answer if'n she calls your name, Nedder," Twig told him under his breath. "What if'n she wanted you for something needful? You gotta answer, ain't I told ya that a hundert times?" But the scolding had sunk in, Twig could tell by the slump in his little brother's shoulders. And then he remembered that he had heard his mother call and had kept on going when he wasn't specially named. "Oh," he whispered. He stood a moment, considering. Then, reluctantly, but knowing it had to be done, he turned to march back up the grade to stow his pole and can in the shed and go to the house to see how he could help.

When Twig entered the kitchen, Ned was draped with a half apron around his shoulders like a cape put on frontwards instead of back. He was drying dishes and climbing on a wooden chair to set the clean cups and plates into the cupboard. He glanced up at Twig sorrowfully.

Twig nodded. His was just punishment, and the little boy knew it. All his next older brother could do was assure him as he washed his hands at the sink, that sooner, probably, rather than later, he'd be accepted back into the good graces of the family.

Travis played with the baby on the floor near their mother's feet as she sat forward on a chair leaning over the wooden step stool that Mama kept specially to serve as base for the metal food grinder. The thick wooden plank of the uppermost step was just the right thickness for the grinder's screw grip.

Mrs. Drangler, at the table, was chopping long sections from the ham for Mama to feed into the oval top and grind with the long gray handle. Twig had always loved to be the one to turn that handle. The wooden sheath that covered the perpendicular hand piece also turned loosely, even spun on itself, though Mama didn't particularly like him doing that. "Waste of time and energy, Todd," she'd say. On a farm, you gotta be aware of time and energy. There's always more needs to be done."

"Ham salad sandwiches?" Twig asked. "Want me to get a jar of pickles from the fruit cellar, Mama?"

"Ah, Todd, if you would, that would help a mighty some," Cynthia cried, surprised that he'd returned. "No fish biting this afternoon?"

So she did know where I was going. Couldn't'a been the twins telling on me. They didn't know. But Mama always knows. She knows just about everything.

He glanced at Mrs. Drangler, but she shook her head. She hadn't told on him.

When he came back up from the cellar, Todd carried the large jar to the sink board and wiped the lid and wire mechanism clean before working to open the pickles. He carried the jar to the table for Mrs. Drangler to pick out the misshapen ones for the grinder.

"Might as well leave the prettiest for the table," the seamstress giggled. She was always laughing, making those pins and needles gleam and glitter wickedly on her collar. Twig sidestepped, almost backing into his brothers Travis and baby Levitt asleep on a blanket on the floor under the table. Sidestepping again, Twig hurried to the far end of the table to sit with Ned, who was paring potatoes.

Cynthia had risen to check the loaves of bread baking in the oven. "Within an instant," she declared, looking up, her face flushed.

The boys were quiet. Mrs. Drangler must have forgotten they were there, because she brought up a topic Twig never remembered grown-ups discussing in front of children before.

"When do you expect Doris and that colored gal gonna get here?"

Cynthia glanced at her two sons but answered, "Any minute now. I told them not to eat so we gals could enjoy a women's meal together." Rather than slice the loaves, she wrapped them in clean flannel and laid them at the back of the table. Frowning rather like a bewildered child, she stood a moment assessing before confiding, "You know, Ella Mae, it's funny, but I don't even think of her as colored anymore."

"Will's gal? Really?"

"She's just Nandria. Skin's dark, I'll grant you that. But then so are my boys' by the time summer's half over."

Mrs. Drangler unconsciously screwed the food grinder down tighter. She turned the handle twice more, concentrating on the slender fingers of pink meat oozing from its dial of holes. "I hope," she said low, long after Cynthia had turned to other tasks, "I do hope that happens for me sometime. Soon."

Wiping her hands, Cyn came to sit at the table. Her boys scooched to one side out of her way, quietly grateful to be allowed to remain for the adult conversation.

Mrs. Drangler eyed them, then set her small mouth in resolution. They were fine boys. Perhaps it would help their own growing up to hear discussion of her difficulty. She cleared her throat and continued. "I mean, I still hafta steel myself to drink from a cup she's handed me. I know it's clean—prob'ly more so than ninety percent of the cups I take from neighbors without blinkin' an eye. But still, inside, I know she might'a drunk from it in time past and it gives me the shivers to put it to my lips."

Cyn was shaking her head gently. "Should be the other way 'round. Her being unsure of what we've touched."

The boys' eyes grew round. They stared into each other's face but said nothing.

"She's one strong woman," Mrs. Drangler commented.

"She is that. And educated. One of the finest I've ever known. Wish we could talk her into teaching our kids."

"School mistress? Oh, Lord, wouldn't that cause some kind of volcano right here in Boonetown?" Mrs. Drangler giggled, and Cyn's serious expression dissolved for a moment as she, too, pictured the area's reaction.

"But Nandria doesn't deserve that. I won't bring it up as a suggestion, and don't you, neither, Ella Mae Drangler."

The seamstress raised her sticky hands in joyful surrender. "Not at the moment, anyhow," she promised. "She's the daughter of a British diplomat. Been all over the world, did you know that?" Drangler said, returning to her destruction of the ham.

Carrying over the salt cellar to fill the shaker on the table, Cyn replied wistfully, "All the more experience to share with our school kids, if only she'd be allowed. Is that why she can always be so…"

"Contained? Beats me how she can keep from screamin' her head off at times. I couldn't."

"Prob'ly raised for self-discipline."

"Shame to have to do that." Drangler studied the little boys asleep at her feet. "Kids! They do what they need to do when they need to do it. We should learn from them."

"Ain't that the truth?" Cynthia laughed.

CHAPTER TWENTY-FOUR

The Minnick men had seen the truck's dust, and their midsections told them Nandria was coming up into the field with lunch. Will and Greg strolled down to meet them at the edge of the lane while Minnick sat down heavily against the base of a scrawny, half-grown oak, glad for what little shade it offered.

Rose had been fascinated to look out at the movement of the farm from her grandmother's lap in the passenger seat of the truck. But her mother slowed the truck and Rose heard her father's voice. Gurgling, she clambered across to her mother's lap to get to him. Will raised his eyebrows, questioning whether he was too sweaty and dusty to take his little princess, dressed as she was in frilly pinafore.

Nandria smiled. "I have extra clothes with us," she assured him, handing the baby up into his arms.

"I'll fetch the basket," Greg offered, determined not to lose sight of the true object of this meeting. He rolled his eyes as he lifted the basket from the truck bed in appreciation of the weight of the lunch Nandria had made for them. There would be plenty of food, thank you very much. "Did you womenfolk get to eat?"

"Mrs. Paisler distinctly instructed us not to; that she would have a spread, as you call it, ready for all us women helping make the meal for Dr. Ricartsen's. But I did feed Rose."

Grinning, Will rubbed the baby's rounded tummy, making her giggle. "Good idea. My girl doesn't wait all that well."

"And we fed Bodie and sent him on home," Nandria added. "I hope that was the right course of action?"

"Oh, yeah. I think Pa saw this morning how peak-ed he looked and that's why he told him not to come out with us. He tries to do too much."

"Is it possible he does not understand how close he came to dying when the Brattons shot him?"

"Oh, he understands all right, but he isn't about to admit it to the rest of us. He's a Missouri farmer, after all."

"Stubborn," Greg agreed as he lifted the cloth to peek into the basket. "But if this here shindig tonight is to thank the doc, you might as well plan another surprise celebration for that pastor," Greg added without looking up from where he was fishing out chunks from the potato salad with grubby fingers.

Will frowned at him.

"What? Not gonna want any of this delicious food now? Okay by me. My dirt; your dirt. We're both workin' in the same field." He shrugged. "My brother Frank used to lick something of mine he wanted so I'd give it to him. But that only worked twice. After that I'd deck him and eat it anyhow."

"Well…" Will was undecided but chose to change the subject. "That's not a bad idea. Planning for Kylie, as well. You know he's not going to take kindly to be snubbed when honors are being passed out."

"A mite sour on the gentleman, are we?" Nandria asked.

"Are we? Never knew anyone more self-righteous, myself."

"Ah, but when he finds someone he loves, he will humanize," Nandria speculated.

Will looked at her thoughtfully around the small, dimpled hands that were squeezing his nose. "Especially if that love is threatened in any way. Well, I hope you're right; you usually are," he added nasally.

Nandria cocked her head at her husband and reached to take Rose from him.

"Have fun, Mother," Will said in closer to his normal voice. Doris waved across to him and took the baby back onto her lap. She handed her the large, green yarn angel Nandria had made for her. Rose settled at once to pick at the embroidered eyes.

Will pressed his hand to Nandria's cheek and she held his fingers a moment before re-starting the truck engine that had died as they spoke. She worked the gas and the clutch until the truck eased forward.

"Give yourselves time for a bath before we go to town tonight!" she called back, although she was not sure the men heard her over the rattling of the ancient truck. *Missouri farmers are not only stubborn, they also seem to believe that any smidgen of luxuriating is unmanly. And woe be to the man who dares be unmanly. Thank the Lord that Will's military experience has been enough to keep him out of that myth goal. But, oh Lord, he is not immune, is he? Else he would be allowing his hip and side to heal properly, would he not?*

* * * * * * * * * * * * * * * * * * *

Rose slept most of the way in Doris's arms. The woman who may or may not have realized she was the child's grandmother was delighted to hold her and croon soft, lilting lullabies until Nandria pulled up beside the maroon Studebaker near the Paisler farmhouse.

"Ella Mae Drangler must be here," Doris speculated. "Yes, there she is."

Drangler and Cyn came to the door, with Ned and Todd close behind them and to one side. Todd hurried out to help Mrs. Minnick from the truck while his mother took the baby and Nandria gathered some of the bags of garden produce from its bed.

"Help Miz Nandria with the rest of them bags, Ned," his mother instructed. He jumped quickly to help.

They carried their various treasures into the Paisler kitchen.

"My goodness, you ladies have been working hard," Doris exclaimed. "Look at all this food. It looks good enough to eat!"

"That's the general idea."

"Is there any sign that Dr. Ricartsen is suspicious?" Nandria asked.

"Talk about suspicious," Doris vented as she gathered up a plate from the stack at the corner of the table and sat where she could reach nearly all the choices of food.

"Suspicious?" Cynthia cocked her head to peer at her neighbor. "Did something happen?"

"Well, that's just it," Doris sighed, "we aren't completely sure. But when we came back from that sad trip to St. Louey—oh, I never expected a greeting quite like that…"

"What happened when you got back?" Mrs. Drangler prompted, with a glance at Nandria's discomfort with where the story was heading.

"Nothing much. Who can be sure you didn't leave a mess, but it didn't seem likely." Doris shook her head. "And the gal here says she didn't get into my things."

"What things?"

"That's just it. Nothing worth much of anything, but the strangest thing was I'd just bought a brooch—ugliest thing you ever seen, but it reminded me of a would-be boyfriend from early elementary school days. And now it's gone. Who would want such a glass monstrosity? But I can't find it nowhere."

"You had a boyfriend in grade school?" Mrs. Drangler smacked her lips at Doris with an impish grin, but Doris turned to Nandria, her frown conveying mounting confusion.

"Teagarten, did you tell me, Mother Minnick? Nandria reminded her. "Was that your young friend's name? A neighbor, recently robbed…or burgled," Nandria laughed, remembering her mother-in-law's delight with saying that word.

Cyn and Ella Mae, watched as Doris mouthed "burgle, burgle, burgle" and joined in the merriment.

"You missing anything, Miz Minnick?" Cyn finally asked, wiping the corner of her eyes with the edge of her apron.

"Not that I can tell," Nandria answered. "But I was surprised to find everything in the night stand and drawers had been ruffled up. I know I did not leave the baby's clothes in that condition."

"How odd," Cyn Paisler shook her head as she invited Nandria to take a plate.

"You said you'd just bought the brooch?" Mrs. Drangler queried. "Where did you buy it, Doris? From Owens?"

"No, not at the general store. From a polite young man come in one of them old milk delivery vans painted over brown. Nice young man, weren't he, gal?"

"Very pleasant," Nandria agreed. But from her frown, the other ladies guessed she was as suspicious of that transaction as was her mother-in-law herself. She set a slice of the golden-crusted homemade bread at the edge of her plate and smiled at Cyn Paisler. "Again, referring to 'suspicious,' what is our status with the good doctor?"

"We're to call Sadie Bean later this afternoon to see how his day is going," Cyn explained.

"Unless he's called out on a house call, we're to gather about six or so at his clinic." Drangler shook off the offers of lunch to take Rose in her arms. "Ah, little one, how you are growing." Rose gazed up at the shiny pins on the woman's collar, closed her eyes as she lay across the seamstress's lap, and promptly, as though in self-defense, fell asleep where she was.

"That was fast," Doris remarked as she reached for freshly sliced homemade bread.

Cynthia's eyebrows arched. "They call you the miracle worker, but I wasn't inclined to believe it until I saw that."

"I do enjoy the little imps," Drangler sighed.

Cyn pushed the sliced pickles closer to the Minnick side of the table. "I'm telling you, Nandria, enjoy the quiet now while Rose is still mostly in your arms. It won't last long, especially with another one on the way. Sorry I don't have no ice cream for you to go with them pickles."

"Really?" Drangler reacted so sharply she nearly awakened Rose.

"Hopefully," Nandria admitted, smiling. "I certainly have the morning sickness."

"As though it comes just in the morning!" all four women chimed, almost in unison, laughing.

Float

CHAPTER TWENTY-FIVE

The sun was still bright, but from a slant, being as it was in its elder hours for this day. Dr. Ricartsen's lawn had not been mowed, but then it had not grown much except yellower in the long days of unusual heat. The few scraggly Queen Anne's lace that thrust themselves green and tough-delicate at the edges near the walk were soon trampled by dozens and then hundreds of feet as the town's people gathered.

In the church yard, Grover Minnick drove their faded truck up near the elongating shadows of the far stand of trees, but Sheriff Yakes beckoned impatiently. "Put 'er here, Minnick!"

"Why? There'll be shade in a bit, and…"

"That shade is for the horses," Yakes bellowed as though he'd explained it a thousand times before, which he had, but not to Minnick. "Put 'er here, I tell ya!"

Grumbling, Grover hauled on the steering wheel to pull up beside Nicklebergs' feather-coated sedan with its back half sawed-off. With their kids grown and gone, they'd customized their car to fit their hen-and-egg livelihood. Scowling, Grover grumbled under his breath about needing to wash them feathers off his truck, but Doris patted his knee, knowing that many worse things had stayed plastered to this truck for weeks until the next rain. Undoubtedly those feathers would, too.

The family needed to get out and unload quickly as Yakes was sending newly arrived country folk in fast succession now. The whole region seemed to know about this party, and they were coming in droves. The Paislers' truck was two rows in so they must have gotten there earlier. It was so like Cynthia Paisler to be early to help set things up.

But, then, Paisler has all them boys to help with the evening chores, so of course he can come early and show off how efficient he is. You're gettin' so you sound like a bitter old maid, Grover Minnick! Stand up and take what comes like a man, will you? Straightening his shoulders, Grover took the Minnick picnic basket on his arm and settled his wife's hand on his other forearm to walk toward Doc's house-turned-clinic.

Ricartsen's lawn was already crowded with people from town and surrounding farms in all directions. Even a few folk from Fox Haven, although how they had heard about this wingding was beyond Minnick, and many others. A number of women had set up portable tables in a long line to one side. Some tables had cloths; others had no draping material and so must have been bare under all the food platters and bowls, but who would know?

Small, grimy hands reached—disembodied—over the edge of the table to snatch bits of goodies, but nearly all were promptly slapped down without treasure.

Cynthia Paisler slipped from knot to knot of women quietly settling disputes about whose prize contribution was to be placed on which section of table. Cyn welcomed Doris and Minnick and miraculously found room for their additions.

Will, carrying Rose, and Nandria stayed to one side of the milling but quiet crowd and eventually found themselves to one side of Ricartsen's front door with Ron Bean standing protectively near his daughter.

"We are so glad to see you, Ronda," Nandria told the pale girl, frowning as she noted the purple-gray bags under both of Ronda's eyes.

Thank you, Miz Minnick," Ronda answered, but her voice was as timid as it had been when she'd first showed up at the Minnick farm.

"Been draggin' a bit, Miz Nandria," Ron muttered. "She's gonna be fine, Doc says, but we don't know how soon before she can get back to you for her studies. We surely do thank you for your help so far."

"Our pleasure. Your daughter is a fine young woman."

Over Ron's shoulder, Will spied Greg Paisler working his way toward them through the shifting, chatting crowd. "Hello, there. Come to check on our favorite pupil, Greg?" Will greeted him quietly.

Nandria watched, surprised at the instant delight and then sudden sadness and a trace of anger that transformed Ronda's face.

"Oh," the girl moaned, and turned away from young Paisler.

Surprised at Ronda's unexpected rudeness, Ron drew his girl to him and addressed Greg. "Ev'nin', Greg, good to see ya. We're keepin' everyone out here to hang onto the surprise. Can you believe Doc still don't know what's goin' on?"

"You're kidding," Will exclaimed.

Ron shook his head as though bewildered. "Sadie swears he don't."

"And she should know," Greg laughed. He sobered and then frowned as Ronda glanced up quickly at his face at the sound. Her eyes held such longing and then such dismissal, that Greg rocked back a step before she looked away again.

"Perhaps he is occupied listening to his radio," Nandria suggested.

"Yeah, he sure is het up about that war over there." He'd seen the quick interaction between his daughter and young Paisler and his frown told Greg he had no idea what was going on in the girl's mind.

"That rescue effort out of Dunnerd…?"

"Dunkirk," Will supplied.

"Yeah, Dunkirk. That's tearing him apart," Greg managed.

"Terrible mess," Bean agreed. "Evidently planes was flying right over them guys exposed on the beach with no cover. Strafin' 'em. Mowin' 'em down and nothin' they could do to protect themselves."

"Bombs droppin' right over crowds of soldiers and sailors bottled up and nothin' they could do but take it," Greg shuddered. "No shelter. Nowhere to hide or take cover. Praise the Lord all them little craft was goin' over to pick them boys up and ferry 'em home."

"It's a miracle, I guess, that Dunkirk has been as successful as it has," Will added. "Though they're having to leave a lot of equipment that they'll sorely need later on."

"And ships," Nandria said low. "Landing craft, even some of the larger ships that would have ferried the men back to England across the Channel." She looked devastated but was controlling her grief.

"A lot of brave men dyin'," Ron Bean agreed.

"It makes you think serious about goin' over to see if'n you can help," Greg said low. At Ronda's sudden glance of horror, Greg blinked, and then tried to smile. Her pale face softened; he was sure she was about to smile—until Ida Jane Freshstalk sauntered near, giggling with several of her close friends.

"Why, Mr. Bean," Ida tittered, "good evening. And Ronda," she added with a hint of disdain. She nodded to the Minnicks, then turned to Greg with a broad grin of possession.

"Hello, Mr. Paisler," the tallest of the giggling girls simpered. "It won't be long until Ida Jane shares that last name, will it?"

"Evenin', Ida Jane. Girls," Greg nodded to include her companions. "No, not long now. Bye," he added as, giggling, they began to move away.

Ron Bean lifted his hand in farewell. Greg swung around to Ronda, but she twisted away with a low moan, and scurried into Doc's house. Startled, Greg looked to Ron, but Bean could only lift his other hand, now in surrender. He shook his head, bewildered.

"What was that all about?" Ron asked of Greg.

"Wish I knew," Greg sighed. He looked so sad, Will stepped toward him, but then stopped as he spied Pastor Kylie working his way through the crowd toward them.

"Uh oh," Will said under his breath, and the others peered out where he was looking. Each took a moment to conquer his feelings.

Bean was the first to recover his attitude of hand-me-down host. "Good evening, Reverend. Glad you got here."

"I had no foreknowledge of this gathering," Kylie huffed, and Bean donned a suitable expression of regret.

"It was more or less a spontaneous thing. Word of mouth rather than specific invites," Ron explained. "Mostly the women talking among themselves. My Sadie said she'd tried a couple times to reach you."

"Since you ain't got a woman..." Greg started, but realized immediately the pastor did not find that amusing. He went still.

"I have been away a good deal of the time, ministering to a troubled parishioner in Fox Haven. All this is to honor the good doctor, I presume?" Kylie's eyebrows went up as though demanding explanations, but Ron Bean seemed torn about how much to say.

"Yeah," Greg ventured, "been four or five years now Doc's been doin' for folks around here."

They were gratefully interrupted by the front door of Doc's house opening. Sadie, wiping her hands on a small towel, leaned out to signal to her husband. Ron grinned and lifted his fingers to his lips to whistle shrilly.

"Folks!" Ron cried, and the crowd hushed and stared. Sadie disappeared inside, and a moment later pushed Ricartsen into the door frame like a newborn colt shaky on his stick-like legs.

Chapter Twenty-Five

"SURPRISE!"

Doc swayed, open-mouthed. He looked lost in the in-pouring of congratulations and greetings.

Sadie peered at Ron, who shrugged and laughed. "This town sure likes to party," he mouthed to her, and watched as her heavy shoulders relaxed. She stepped out to stand beside her husband.

"Good folk," Sadie observed when they were close enough for him to be able to hear her.

"Not sure whether they're happier to give their best to Doc or just to get the waitin' over so's they can eat."

"Either is good," Sadie grinned.

"Bean!" Doc was stammering. "What in this world…?"

"Four years you been with us. We're grateful, Doc."

"Besides," someone called, "ain't it your birthday, or somethin'?"

Ricartsen blinked, but he didn't deny it, and, as far as the gathered friends were concerned, that settled the matter. Doc was joyously dragged onto his lawn and over to the tables groaning with food. Not that he would get to eat for quite some time, with everyone coming up to shake his hand.

Around about the pickles and condiments, Doc was accosted over his towering plate of food by a bearded farmer he scarcely recognized. Ordinarily he would have glanced at Sadie, who would clue him in to the name, but she was nowhere in sight among the crowd of people. "H-hello," Doc stammered.

"Never did get 'round to payin' ya fer comin' out to dose the kiddies when they was so sick last winter," the man was telling him. His wife peered from around his shoulder to add, "We done butchered our yearling boar fer ya. Kept a little fer ourselves, a'course, but brung ya the extra. Hope that settles us up, Doc?"

"Uh, yes, of course," Doc told them, not having a clue which account to credit. But from the small size of the bag carrying the payment meat, it didn't seem to matter much. Most accounts dragged out months or years. Doc had long since already thrown his hands into the air, knowing his chances for payment on those were slim to none.

Grinning, the farm couple wandered off to pile more onto their plates—and probably squirrel away with the plates, as well, Ricartsen thought. He did hear the wife exclaim to her man, "I told ya slaughterin' thet crippled boar would prob'ly do it..."

Ricartsen would have sighed, if there had been a moment, before two large town ladies approached him with small plates of individual desserts. Each was determined hers would be the one their doctor would choose. He ended up taking both and trying to balance them up his arm.

Watching him from beside the door to the clinic, Greg chuckled at his predicament, but knew better than to try to intervene. Instead he stared at Doc's clinic door, gathering courage. With a deep breath, he turned the knob and pushed against the door. It had only moved a few inches before it hung up, and indeed, started to swing back toward him.

"Go away," a small, choked voice told him.

"Ronda?"

"You leave me alone, Greg Paisler!"

He rocked back, astonished.

CHAPTER TWENTY-SIX

Out on Doc's lawn, the noise level of the people enjoying food and each other rose. Folks milled about talking, discussing, and, when they were thoroughly enjoying themselves, arguing. As the western horizon gathered a spent-violet undertone, several older ladies drew their shawls closer around their shoulders. Men refilled their cups of coffee and settled in for loud, un-listened-to positions of discussion that had been tread over many times. Grover and Doris Minnick sat with several other older couples discussing farming practices and the weather, specifically what to do about the long dry spell. They were wagging chins into argument over the benefits of spreading dry hay when Yakes, holding his belly, came up to stand near Doris.

"Miz Minnick, if I may?"

"Why, Sheriff Yakes, of course," Doris said, patting the seat of a near-by chair. "Come sit down with us, won't you?"

"No, no, thanks just the same but I was gonna ask, ma'am. Mrs. D was tellin' me you might'a lost a valuable pin or somethin'. You think you folks was robbed?"

"B-burgled," Doris exaggerated her lip movement and looked up at Nandria, laughing. "Oh, I don't think it amounted to much. Just a glass gem brooch is missin', that's all."

"You bought it from Owens?"

"Oh, no, from that nice young man on his GEM truck. It reminded me of my grade school days, is all I wanted it for. Made me think of the Teagarten boy."

"Jerry Teagarten?"

"You know him, Sheriff?" Nandria asked quietly. She frowned as Yakes nodded. "But, Mother Minnick, you were raised near the Canadian border, were you not? How old were you when you came to Missouri? Nearly a young lady then, is that not so? How could it have been Jerry Teagarten who tried to give you that brooch?"

The wrinkles on Doris's forehead and around her eyes deepened as she sank into confusion. Sensing his wife's discomfort, Minnick turned from his farmer talk and grimaced at Nandria and Yakes, who went immediately quiet. Grover drew his chair closer to his wife's and turned his back on the two offenders who had made his Doris uncomfortable.

"So you don't think it could'a been the Struan boy had anything to do with these here robberies?" the sheriff questioned Nandria low. "Think it was just the missus confused-like in her rememberin'?"

"I hardly know, sheriff," Nandria began.

"Thought so," Yakes nodded and walked over to stand and talk with the Paisler youth. Nandria joined them.

A few minutes later, Ricartsen finally broke away from the general greetings and, flustered, came to stand with Nandria and Will, Yakes, and Greg's two older brothers and next younger, Sam. Frank proudly held the hand of his fiancé Ida Jane as she gossiped prettily with her brothers-in-law-to-be. The Minnicks stood stiffly, worn by the girl's apparent shallowness. At last Ricartsen interrupted the girl's prattling.

"They're getting 'em out, Will. Did you hear?"

"Dunkirk? The rescue is still going on? No, we didn't take time to listen. Came straight from the fields to wash up and on to here."

"That bloody beach across the Channel?" Sheriff Yakes questioned as he joined them. "Got 'em all, did they?"

"Not by a long way, but the rate they're bringin' in every shape and size and kind of boat to get 'em, they're gonna," Eli exclaimed.

"Except for the dead," Nandria murmured, knowing that must be true.

The men gaped at her, then quickly lowered their eyes, and she realized she'd said aloud what they had been thinking but 'manhood' had not allowed them to bring up. "But the brave French stayed to cover their escape. That will cost them dearly, I fear."

Eli and Will nodded as the sheriff voiced his agreement. "Praise the good Lord that they're still workin' it. But all them tanks and artillery and Jeeps and stuff. Had to leave it right there, did they? How the devil are they gonna replace all that equipment?"

"And what are they going to fight with now?" Eli asked.

"Oh, I hate to talk about that war. It makes me shiver so, Frankie-pooh," Ida pulled at her fiancé's arm. "Make 'em stop, will you?"

"I know, dear. We'll talk about something else."

Ricartsen stiffened, his hand on his belly after consuming an unaccustomed amount of food. "Your shivering don't exactly balance out the terror and pain of those thousands of troops trying to keep the Nazis from taking over all of Europe."

Frank stiffened as well. "A little harsh on the lady, aren't you, Doc?"

"Yeah," Eli said, "she's just a girl…" he began in Ida Jane's defense, but she lifted her delicate, pointed chin.

"I am not 'just a girl,' Eli Paisler," she corrected him sharply. "I'm soon to be a married woman."

From a nearby clump of young women, Ida's girlfriends heard her irritation and hurried over to comfort or defend her.

"Anyway," Frank placated, "suppose we talk about what the women will enjoy?" He cast about for some topic to suggest. His eyes lighted on his beloved's golden curls. "Like, how about that Shirley Temple?"

His brothers gaped at him openly.

"Ida tells me that little lady earned over three hundred thousand dollars one year." He jerked his chin at his brothers, telling them to listen up. They could learn something important from his girl.

"From her movies?" Will asked to steer the conversation away from sibling derision.

"And dolls and stuff," Ida chimed in, lifting her hand to fluff her own hair. "People seem to just eat up them curls." She was about to say more, but saw Greg approaching from the doctor's house, and she knew she did not want to have to explain again whatever her next remarks would have been to yet another Paisler brother.

Eli picked up the conversation for her. "I bet that was even more'n that Orson Wells fellow got for scaring half this country to death on the radio with his broadcasting about aliens landing on Earth last Halloween."

"That was the Halloween more'n a year ago," Greg stated as he joined them.

"Okay, so it was the Halloween year before last. How much do I know about movies and such-like? I got a farm to make pay," Eli griped. He stared at his second-younger brother's long face, but Greg shook his head, asking not to be questioned.

"So how's the cotton growing?" Greg asked, as neutrally as he could manage. He really did want to know.

Ida frowned and left Frank with a pretty little kiss on her fingertips, which she waved. She flounced away to more entertaining conversations with her knot of tittering friends.

Frank let out his breath, seeming relieved. Greg looked to one side so his next-closest brother would not read his expression. *Your choice, Frankie. I'll support you whatever you decide. She wouldn't be my choice, but maybe you won't take to my brave gal with folks so decent I'd like to live up to their expectations. But you're gettin' yourself one pretty fluff, all right.* He glanced over and, knowing Will and his missus as well as he did, knew they had reached much the same conclusion. But they, too, were keeping their judgments to themselves.

Everybody relaxed when Frank glared around, squared his shoulders and changed the subject. "I still think they shouldn't'a fired Coach Choppy. The Gunners were goin' great..."

Eli jumped him. "Great? They were 5 - 6 - and 0!"

Ricartsen hawked and spit into the overgrown lilac bush. "Poland, Belgium, Denmark," he grumbled as he peered at Nandria, embarrassed by having spit in her presence. Flustered, he hurried on with his indignant speech. "Holland, Luxembourg— all of them crumpling under Hitler. Norway and France've gotta give up any day now, and all you can argue about is curls and baseball?"

With a sardonic grin, Greg made a comment that cut the tension. "At least it ain't about hemlines." He met Frank's glare with a grin, knowing his brother couldn't hold his anger against that smile. He tried to hold his laugh to a chuckle, but they all saw that Frank's pique had given way.

Ricartsen nodded to apologize but was still punished by being swallowed up in well-wishers who carted him away.

Will looked after the doctor with sympathy, but he wanted to continue talking with these friends about the war. "With the French troops desecrated as they are and the number of men they still haven't moved out from the Maginot Line, France is going to be on her knees."

"That's over there, Will," Eli tried to get them to drop the discussion. "We can moan all we want, and I don't blame anybody for doin' just that. But it's not our fight. At least baseball is something I can do something about. Even if it's only to go to the game or stay away."

"Is that not also our choice for the people in Europe?" Nandria murmured. "Going, or staying away?"

"Well," Frank said, "we can grow cotton for uniforms. That we can do. And we are."

"Food might be good, too," Greg commented. "Troops need to eat, as well as us drudge farmers."

"I do not understand why Americans are—how do you say it?—'dead set' against joining this war sooner rather than later when the fight will be ever so much more difficult to win."

"I hate to contradict no lady, Miz Minnick," Frank said, looking pained to be doing just that. "But it's your war. We should'a never gotten pulled into the last one."

Eli agreed. "Cost us a bundle and we didn't get much out of it, that I can see. We don't want to be drug into another one."

Nandria lifted her chin to ask quietly, "Is Mr. Hitler giving you that choice?"

Float

CHAPTER TWENTY-SEVEN

The party ground on in good-natured boisterousness until Dr. Ricartsen couldn't stand it any longer. He escaped to his office. Sinking with a sigh into his desk chair, he leaned forward to turn on his radio for war news.

"Who the blue blazes has been fiddling with this dial?" he exploded. Fortunately for whoever it had been and for Doc's blood pressure, he was quickly able to tune in a rich bass voice to tell him: "...ordinary fishermen, weekend yachters... to the gunwales... so many dead..."

"Uh!" Ricartsen worked the dial, not looking up as Greg Paisler entered even while he was knocking at the door frame to the office.

"We could use that radio," Greg announced. When Doc merely glared at him, Greg shrugged and sat down uninvited.

"You get your hands on this dial, did you?"

Realizing it must have been Ronda who had fiddled with the doc's radio, Greg merely tightened his lips and met Ricartsen's angry eyes, willing to take the blame. "We intruded. I know that, and I'm sorry, Doc. But we meant well. Somebody mentioned it was about this time of year some four or five years ago you come to us. It just kinda got away from us for the town to throw a thanks for all you do. And then I think somebody else said it was near your birthday. Is it?"

Doc glared, admitting nothing.

"Well, anyway, the town took off and surprised themselves as well as you." He lifted his hands, palms up.

"All the damn fuss…"

"And you ain't any happier about fuss than I am, are you? But the way it turned out, people got a kick out of telling you how much they appreciate you coming. And staying. They wanted to honor that."

"They could pay their bills," Ricartsen grumbled, but it was only half-hearted, Greg could tell.

"With what, Doc? But that ain't what's buggin' you, is it? Look, I know that war over there is goin' bad."

Ricartsen reared back in his chair. "Even if they do get most everybody off that Dunkirk beach, the Frenchies are gonna find that their whole Maginot Line—less than useless. And stupidly they'd counted on it. A huge chunk of the income for the whole nation, and now it's less than nothing. It's gonna end up a trap…"

"That's there, and we're here, for tonight, at least. Look, can't we just put aside the tough bull droppings of the last dozen years for one night and have a good time? Together. You placate your annoyance and remember laughter's supposed to be good for your soul or your health or something? Think of this as medicine for our neighbors."

"Medicine for a little gal who shivers and wants to be sheltered from even talk of war?"

Greg sighed. "Yeah. Ida Jane's flu-flu enough to keep me grinding my teeth so much at times that I gotta get out of the house to get away from her. But she's not a bad sort. And those people out on your lawn ain't a bad sort, neither. Look how they've tolerated a darky just because she's a decent person and married to Will. Come on out, Doc. Bring the radio and find some dance music. Let's have some fun."

"Dancing while Europe falls to the Nazis," Ricartsen moaned, but he rose and bent to unplug the radio from the wall socket.

"We'll be dealing with that soon enough. We gotta celebrate sometimes, and tonight I guess it's you. Sorry."

"Not as sorry as I am." Pulling the length of the cord through his hands, Ricartsen shook his head. "The nearest socket to the front door is under the front window. This cord won't be near long enough."

"Sadie can probably scare up a couple extensions. If not, Mr. Owens can no doubt sell me some from his store."

They looked first before going to Sadie. Found two—one with frayed places that threatened to set up a fireworks of sparks; that reminded Greg of something else the crowd could use. "Got any lights, Doc? It's comin' up dusk out there."

"Yea, Doc!" the crowd cheered as Ricartsen, Will and Greg hooked up the radio and lights from the clinic lobby on long, taped-over cords. Close neighbors carried chairs and small tables from their homes, and even a few tall torches to light for flickering illumination for darker corners. This party was getting to be a major event for the annals of the countryside.

Greg was left in charge of positioning the radio for maximum pick-up. He worked the dial for a popular program out of Kansas

City that played modern music that the young people were happy to dance to. The volume, when he found that station, was turned up to full. The young people danced and swayed. Their elders sat and watched, some cheering, some harrumphing in distaste, nearly all remembering the rhythms of the music of their own young days.

Frank joined the Freshstalks' table but left a chair empty on the other side of Ida Jane. Ronda, eyes red from crying, slipped onto Doc's front stoop and looked around. Spying the empty seat beside the engaged Miss Freshstalk, Ronda looked immediately for Greg. There he was, busy with the radio. Lifting her chin and murmuring blue words she'd only heard occasionally in her growing up, she ducked away from the clinic-house and hurried along the edge of the crowd.

From the large circle of Minnicks and Paislers, Sadie spotted her and lifted her hand to call her to her worried parents, but Ronda merely waved. She gestured that she did not feel well and wanted to go home. Ron caught only the last part of the message, but Sadie nodded and gave permission for Ronda to go on home, that they would be joining her soon.

"What?" Ron wanted to know as he watched his girl slip away from the party.

"I thought she must've been in Doc's house. I couldn't find her nowhere else. Feeling poorly, I guess, Ron. I think I'll go on home and make sure she gets whatever it is she needs."

"Let's go."

"No, there's no sense both of us missing out on the festivities. You stay so you can tell me later everything that went on. Stay, please?" Her huge hand covered his shoulder; he stayed seated.

"I'll come home in a bit and we can trade places. You're better at catching what's really goin' on. Besides, my early-to-rise time comes mighty early. Best I get to the early-to-bed part right soon."

She wanted to kiss him, but he'd have died of embarrassment if she had where everyone in town could see them. Instead she smiled and hurried away.

A slow, romantic piece began. The younger set melted away, the boys, especially, too embarrassed to want to be seen moving the way that rhythm and those words would suggest. People broke off conversations, looking at their neighbors covertly or their spouses or loved ones with memories imprinted on their faces. Doris's smile as she beamed at Grover made her look like a young maiden.

At last, Frank rose to bend to ask his Ida Jane to dance with him. Murmurs of joy and appreciation seeped into the evening to see the engaged couple moving closer together as they lost themselves to the music and each other.

Gnarled men slipped a flask or bottle from their overall pockets or their wives' carry-alls. Near the lilac bushes beside the road Will led Nandria in closed-eyes response to the slow, swelling strains of the music that gave voice to their tender feelings.

A second slow piece started. A few older couples joined Frank and Ida swaying on the lawn. They, too, lost themselves in a romantic atmosphere that descends seldom on farm folk or small, rural towns.

"Everybody's watching them," Todd muttered, with a seven-year-old's incomprehension that they weren't dying of embarrassment.

"Better them than me for a while," Doc groused as he hauled in a chair to sit beside Eli.

"Everybody remembers the pure good feeling of bein' in love," Cynthia looked over at her Zeb with a gentle smile that made him blush, though it was hard for the others to see in that dark of the evening, thank the Lord.

"I for one can't wait to get this blamed wedding over and done," Sam complained. At the far end of the table, Todd nodded vigorously, nearly awakening his twin younger brothers as they sprawled beside him with their heads on his lap. Cyn rolled her eyes at her middle son over the head of Levitt, content and nearly asleep in her arms.

The music selection changed pace. Hand in hand, Will and Nandria walked over to join the Paislers and Ron Bean. Greg gave up on toning down the volume of the boisterous music and came to sit heavily just outside his extended family's circle.

Moving now with more animation, Frank and Ida Jane danced near them. As Ida swirled close, Cyn beamed.

"I declare, Miss Freshstalk, you are about the prettiest thing," her future mother-in-law told the pink-cheeked girl. "But then I may be prejudiced."

"Aw, Mama, not again!" Todd complained loudly. "There's plenty and enough of us now!"

The families gaped at him, then burst into laughter.

"Not pregnant, boy," Todd's father admonished, "prejudiced. Though at times it seems like the same thing."

Mr. Owens walked near, embarrassment flickering on his face in the dwindling light of the torch just on the house side of the lilacs. He joined in the laughter as the joke was explained to him, much to Todd's chagrin. Nandria could tell the boy would have gotten up and run away from them had he not been caring for his little brothers. The Paisler family's teasing was rough, but, as it was never allowed to become mean-spirited, it gave good stead to the boys as they grew up learning to take it and move on.

"Doc," Owens said quietly when the focus of conversation had moved on. He lifted an envelope from the inside pocket of his jacket. "This here is for you. It come late today. I would've sent it over, but I knew we'd be here tonight. But then once the festivities started I plumb forgot to give it to you. Sorry, Doc."

"A telegram?" Minnick asked.

"From the War Department," Ricartsen declared, turning the envelope over in his hands. The families looked over.

"At least we know it ain't news you got killed, Will," Sam quipped. His mother glared at him, furious. The others stared, but Greg, seeing his next younger brother stiffen in humiliation at the collapse of something he thought would be funny, soothed his mother.

"Now, Ma, he didn't mean nothing by it."

"Sorry," Sam managed, head down.

"Do not be sorry, Samuel," Nandria told him. "You just said aloud what I was thinking as well."

"Thank you, Miz Minnick," Greg said for him. "Our Sammy has a big mouth but an even bigger heart when you get to know him."

Meanwhile, Ricartsen had opened the envelope. He handed the telegram to Will to read. Nandria eased closer to be able to read over his shoulder.

"Oh, Will," she cried, "'Immediate,' it says. Shall we go home and pack now?"

"I think tomorrow afternoon's train will satisfy them, love. That is, assuming you are going to release me to return to active duty, Doc?" Will leaned closer to the frowning doctor. "This makes it sounds almost criminal that you haven't made the judgement before now." He caught a bitter glint in the man's drawn face.

"Don't much like 'Mr. Anonymous,' 'specially when he's bitchy," Ricartsen muttered. Then, rolling back his shoulders, the doctor sighed wearily. "Come on in in the morning, Will. We'll check you out."

Doris seemed to feel the tension and stirred as she had not in nearly an hour. "What is it, Mr. Minnick? Is it Freddy?" Grover patted her hand, unable to speak without clearing his throat.

"How about right now?" Will asked the doctor. "You weren't planning to ask my mother to dance, were you?"

With a look, Doc rose and waved for Will to follow him to the clinic. "Come on, then, Captain Minnick. It'll save you a trip back from the farm in the morning and there's no chance of my getting to sleep in my room any time soon with this festival you've all rained down upon us going on."

"Mr. Minnick?" Doris asked again, growing frightened.

"Our son is going away again," Grover told her.

"It is Freddy then."

"No, Mother. Freddy is planted where he's gonna stay. Forever. It's Will this time. His Army service…"

"Army? Are we at war?"

While the others shook their heads to try to reassure her, Nandria rose from her chair and faced her mother-in-law.

"Yes, yes, we are. We just do not want to admit it yet."

Float

CHAPTER TWENTY-EIGHT

No one looked over at her. No one faced Nandria after her affirmation of war. She sat, holding herself in check to say no more. Her point had been made. But gradually, as she realized no one at these small, clustered tables would challenge or agree with her, her shoulders sagged a bit in yet another momentary defeat as she watched Will and Dr. Ricartsen make their way inside the clinic.

"Excuse me," she said quietly. It was Eli who gladly took the sleeping baby from her as she rose.

"I'd wanna know for myself, too," he muttered to her. "You go on ahead, Miz Minnick. Doc won't mind, and, sure as fate, Will'll be glad to have you with him."

The Minnicks, Paislers and Ron Bean resumed their conversations. No one stared after her as Nandria walked with purpose toward Doc's house and entered.

A few people had slipped in the clinic to use the "facilities" but they were mostly folks Nandria had never met. They ignored her greeting and gave her wide berth as she knocked softly at Ricartsen's office door.

"Yeah? What?" the doctor called.

"It is I, Nandria Minnick, Dr. Ricartsen," she answered and in a moment Will, shirt unbuttoned, drew the door open for her.

"Glad you're here, love," he assured her. As Nandria slid into the far chair, Will sat again for Ricartsen to continue listening with his stethoscope to his chest.

"Slide your hips forward on that chair so I can get at your belly, Will."

Awkwardly, Will straightened his torso against the right angle of the chair. Doc listened and pressed, then turned him.

"Slide them pants down. Unless you got something you don't want your wife to see 'ceptin' when it's dark."

It was as close as Nandria had ever heard the awkward colt of a doctor come to an off-colored statement, but Ricartsen was deep in concentration in his examination and he paid her no mind. "In a way, this new assignment is gonna save you a lot of pain, Minnick."

"You, eh, you think so?"

"At least it'll give you a chance to finish healing—which you weren't giving yourself on that farm."

"So you will release my husband for active duty, then, Doctor?"

"How about I give you three a week or so to settle things before you go? Unless you wanna stay…?" Ricartsen straightened to peer into Will's face. "This could go either way, but not for long, by my reckoning."

"No," Will stood up to redress. "It's time. Greg has Pa's back and they both know it, though how they will work it out between them, who knows?" He shook his head.

"It will be just the three of us," Nandria said low. "And a half," she added, chuckling. "It will not take me long to pack and be ready."

Ricartsen, with his back turned, continued with his own thoughts. "Do you think Greg's gonna wanna take over from your father, Will? Is he thinking of matrimony? Who...?" He turned, startled to see Will sorrowfully shaking his head at Nandria.

"Just *my* clothes, Bunnyduck."

"Only your things? Not mine, or Rose's?"

"'Fraid not, love. Not this time."

"We will not be together? Will?"

The pain between them was too much for the doctor. "Do you know where you'll be assigned, Will?" he asked, desperate to break in.

"No, but I did get one letter," Will sighed. "Picked it up at Owens' store a couple days ago. Evidently someone wrote to tell the Army that I was fit enough to work on the farm..."

Nandria flared. "In pain! Did their missive happen to mention that fact?"

"...so why weren't you able then to perform your service for our country?" Doc completed the complaint for him. "Signed? No? Probably the same Mr. Anonymous who's been stirring up the War Department to hound me. Who wrote that poison pen letter, do you know?"

"I wonder if..." Nandria began, but Will cut her off with a gesture and a grin terrible to see.

"You may be right—probably are—about who comes to mind to blame it on, love, but since we'll never know for certain and it does more harm than good to suspect anybody —everybody..." He sighed and sat down again, pulling his chair over to her so he could take her hand. "Brooding, that's all it would be. So let's just drop it."

She knew he was right, but the betrayal was all the more reason she wanted to go with him. "How does that letter preclude our coming with you as a family?"

"Let me find out what is expected of me and whether or not the new area will be safe for you and Rose. Wherever it is, I want you safe. And here, at least, you have created a reputation worthy of respect. And Pa and Greg are here to keep an eye out for you. I want you and our daughter safe, Nandria."

Ricartsen turned away again.

Nandria half rose in her chair. "I want that for our children, as well, but..." She shuddered when Will only shook his head, his green eyes pleading.

* * * * * * * * * * * * * * * * * * * *

The party was breaking up. Farm folk rise early, and this shindig was already hours beyond the normal time for turning in. Few even noticed that Nandria stumbled as she followed Will out of the clinic front door.

The Minnicks were already nearly packed up. Grover Minnick stood impatiently beside Doris at the passenger window of his truck. Bodie, who'd slept through the entire party, lay in its bed with Rose comfortably splayed sound asleep across his chest.

Will helped Nandria up and around the supine figure to sit close behind the back window of the cab. His father came around the rear to raise the tailgate, and to question him with his eyes.

Will nodded. Minnick went close-lipped and continued around to get into the driver's seat.

Will covered his daughter and Bodie with the Great War blanket, then stepped past them to seat himself beside his wife.

"It is because of me, is it not?" she whispered. "It is because you married a Ne…"

Will pressed her lips gently with the tip of his finger and then drew her into his arms. As she wept against him, he looked out over the fading town and then countryside freckle-lit by a cloud-covered moon.

Ah, love, I wish I'd had an auntie in Japan I could have sent you to.

Float

CHAPTER TWENTY-NINE

On the Minnicks' back porch, Rose snorted once through her tiny clogged nose, then turned onto her tummy and laid her cheek on flannel sheeting that was soon wet with her drool. Will, with one hand draped by a rail of his baby's crib, slept heavily on his back. When Rose stirred, he, too, changed position, shifting onto his side with his back to Nandria, who lay eyes wide open and tearing. If she slept at all it was in fits that started up out of cloying dreams.

She caressed Will's shoulder as he turned away, almost wishing he would awaken to comfort her. But knowing he needed sleep to heal, she did not want to take from him what his body craved. Instead, she shifted closer into his warm back and huddled beneath the quilt his mother and her friends had made for him when he was confirmed at the church years ago. There was comfort in its muted, warm colors in the gently repetitive pattern locally called "Shannon." Merely touching him brought her a degree of peace. Sighing, she settled again to sleep.

The surroundings this time as she drifted into dreaming were fragrant with spring blossoms. Gradually she felt herself a little girl, running with abandon after her little brother Ned, who bent unexpectedly to grab a fistful of wild marguerites and lupine to fling at her. Laughing in a tinkling child's voice, she bent as well and scooped up wild flowers to toss at him, roots and all.

Float

Behind them, their father called gently for restraint. Instantly both children dropped what was in their hands and hid green-stained hands behind their backs. They moved slowly toward him at his call. But rather than scolding them, he, too, bent to pick up a white-petaled flower with its sunny yellow center. He crouched beside them as they came near, holding out in his huge, pink-palmed hand the fragile flower for them to inspect. In her dream, his deep voice sounded smudged to her ears the way the bass words on a record do when it is spun too slowly. "In America," his odd but still-comforting voice explained, "this is called a daisy."

Nandria slept contented as her father rose and led them through the field, interesting them in the different parts of the colorful flowers. But then Ned began to sob quietly in a shift which is accepted without analysis in a dream. Nandria, now larger, but still only a young adult, turned to face him. He huddled against a flowered sofa that she only gradually recognized as belonging in their diplomatic apartment in Spain. Brilliant flashes lit up the boy's face as he cowered, whimpering with each flash, and then lowering his hands from his face to gape up at her in the instants of darkness. No sound penetrated, but Nandria's breathing grew ragged as she felt the rumbling of the cannons being used to fire at their building.

Nandria reached out to touch her brother's cheek, to comfort him. To protect him. She had in Ethiopia. She could do less in Spain, only take his hand and draw him up to run with her to the back of the building and down clattering stairs to safety in the suddenly—inexplicably— soaked streets. Past garbage containers

212

twisted, demolished, spilled. Slipping on rotting cabbage heads with eyes staring at them as they approached and still staring directly at them as they fled beyond. Cabbage heads with hair outspread and matted. Panicked, Nandria hauled him, at times nearly faster than he could keep up, threatening to splay him in the filth. He fell. She turned, her mouth open but no scream emerged. Instead, the roar came down upon her and the road swelled in inky water, swallowing Ned as he implored her with raised arms and terrified, dark eyes.

Gasping, Nandria woke, and sat up, shaking and staring around her. Uncomprehending, she shuddered violently. Gradually she recognized Will. Clamping her mouth to suppress her gasps and sobs, she slid from beside her husband. Snatching up her robe as she huddled near the outside door, gradually quieting.

Will, now again on his back, snored a roaring blast that brought relief to Nandria's next exhalation. She realized finally the source of the cannon sound that had triggered the shift in her dream. But her shoulders dipped and her breath caught—her parents and brother were still dead. As so many friends in London and up the coast undoubtedly were, or wished they were.

They still want to hide, these Americans. They want to pretend this war in Europe is not theirs. Oh, Lord, protect them, but give them insight and strength to realize that England cannot do this alone, and the mainstays of Europe are being swallowed up one by one.

Shuddering, Nandria checked her precious daughter, who was sleeping soundly. She touched her husband's strong, rounded shoulder and drew comfort, then shuddered again, knowing how tenuous was their hold on the time they would be together, whether or not he took her with him when he left this family farm. Drawing her robe closed around her, she stepped out the porch door and stood looking at the heavens.

Stars arched over the farm. *Looking down, they arch over the countryside, the nation, the planet peopled by beings who tread on their own dreams.*

Ah, Loves! My brother—so young, missing so much of what he had no way to know was his to come. My parents, who knew, but could not protect him, either. Why? Why, Lord? Why do we follow the insane into war?

Hugging herself, Nandria wandered across the yard, away from the clothesline which tethered her to this earth. Off into the west field, beyond where Bodie's grandniece Emmy Lu had fallen as she came seeking help months before. Such a precious, helpless, battered young woman. *I could not save her, either.*

Breathless from sobbing, Nandria climbed to the top of a rounded hill and stood at its gentle peak, looking out at the surrounding farms, then lifting her eyes to the studded milky path thick with stars.

What is any human being, that Thou art mindful?

* * * * * * * * * * * * * * * * * * * *

Nandria's slipping back under the quilt beside him disturbed Will, but he woke slowly, not realizing she had been gone. He lay rigid in the darkness, his anguish at needing to hurt her yet again stiffening his limbs as well as his resolve. *I've given her nothing but pain. Isn't there one place in this whole blessed world where I could simply give her the love I feel?*

He raised his hands and felt her stir beside him. Gritting his teeth, he lowered them to his sides and held himself still until she went quiet, breathing regularly.

Oh, Precious Lord, watch out for her. Now she will have two little ones to look out for. Two little ones this country—and most any other—will condemn as soon as they look at them. It's my fault, and I won't be there to help them. Protect them. Isn't that what a man is supposed to do? Protect his family? Protect his little brother. His head. That's Freddy's…

He must have moved or moaned because Nandria stirred beside him.

"Darling?" she murmured and rolled near, careful of his hip and side. "Darling?"

"How can you call me that?"

"What?"

"How can you call me 'darling' when…when I'm about to leave you yet again?"

"Called back into the war? What else could you do but leave? Will, you so seldom speak of feelings. What…?"

"No point," he muttered, looking at her with hard eyes that made her hike up on one elbow to peer at him. Her gentle shaking of her head as her own dark eyes pleaded with him to speak brought the bitter words to his lips. Words he'd never spoken aloud, though he had groaned them over inwardly so many times in the past decade. Only with her had he found a peace that would allow him to forget, even for a little while. *And here I go, leaving her in pain again.*

"No point?" she questioned. "In speaking aloud?"

"What would it have done except get him to commit murder? And then what would have happened to Mother?"

"You were dreaming of your brother's death," she whispered. His devastation at her guess told her she was right. "Oh, my darling, that's over, finally. Your father knows now."

He wept. Perhaps now it could be over. "I...I'm sorr..."

"No, love, no. No 'sorrys.' None. Not between us. We agreed to take it as it comes, knowing full well it was coming..."

"....hard and fast," he finished for her. "But this hard? I cannot leave you—or our children—in a safe..."

He wouldn't be comforted. Rose stirred in her crib. Nandria touched his lips to quiet his words, then kissed him.

Despite the ache in his hip, he rolled toward her.

CHAPTER THIRTY

Greg and Bodie stood rubbing their arms in the chill of dawn, watching out from the corner near the open barn door as Minnick shifted the large picnic basket onto his other arm. Carefully, he closed the door to the porch behind him and huffed across the yard. The three men found seats on hay bales or horizontal areas of equipment with the basket open at their feet. Two unwrapped loaves of last night's bread bulged atop a crock of churned butter. Minnick had gathered them from the kitchen, but had not thought to bring knives, or drinks.

"Hope you had your coffee somewheres else," Minnick muttered. He broke a chunk off one of the long loaves and swiped it through the top of the bowl of churned butter. Eying the inside of his barn, he munched without looking at the others.

"Never you mind 'bout that, Mr. Minnick," Bodie assured him. "The missus still sleepin', is she?"

"Glad you give Will and Miz Nandria a minute to themselves, sir," Greg said over his crust of bread. Yellow butter dotted the insistent, unshaved spokes of hair on his upper lip.

For a moment, Minnick didn't know if he was offended by the Paisler boy mixing himself in the family's intimate affairs or amused by the gleam of delicious grease on what might yet someday grow to be a mustache. Sighing, he decided Greg Paisler had been too close a part of this family too long for there to remain many secrets. "Not sure they was truly sleepin', but I wasn't about to argue a few minutes from 'em, one way or t'other."

It was Bodie who grew red-faced. Both the others chuckled to see his embarrassment.

"Any luck with that tractor?" Minnick demanded, changing the subject.

"Well, not sure," Greg answered, still smiling. "Mebbe best for you to see for yourself. She's a proper lady hound, that one."

This time it was Minnick and Bodie who laughed aloud. Greg grinned. The tractor was every bit of that, they knew from experience.

Still munching bread, they shuffled deeper into the barn where, as Greg fiddled, they heard sounds of the tractor moaning, coughing, grinding, giving up.

"Ratsunflankel!" Minnick cussed loudly. "Paisler, you're no handier than the rest of us!"

* * * * * * * * * * * * * * * * * * *

Will awoke into daylight. It startled him to have slept so late until he remembered last night's party at Doc's. And before that, the long drive back from the ill-fated family reunion. He grimaced at that, until he remembered his father's comment about not needing to be bothered with Doris's meddlesome family again for a while. Will had smiled, then frowned, aching to realize how much he and Nandria would give to be "bothered" by his own in-laws. He turned and felt Nandria beside him. She was trembling.

"Darling?" he whispered.

She shook her head, wiping at her eyes. "It is nothing," she said, but he knew that wasn't so. He drew her toward him.

"Go ahead and cry, love. You'll feel better."

She lifted her head, inhaling deeply and pulling away to start to rise from their bed. "If I once open myself to tears, I shall surely drown. I will drown."

"Ratsunflankel!" they heard, clear from the barn.

"What?" Nandria looked stunned.

"Pa," Will chuckled, and when her face softened to a bewildered smile, he sat up to hold her. She clung to him.

* * * * * * * * * * * * * *

With baby Levitt at her feet, Cynthia Paisler scrubbed the last of the breakfast pans and the skillet in the deep sink. At Levitt's squeal, she bent to see that he was all right and missed her third-born son entering the kitchen through the back door.

"Top 'o the mornin', Ma," he told her low from behind as he caught her around the waist.

"Gregor! Oh, my Lord! I was fearin' I'd never get to feed that hungry mouth again. Sit down and I'll rustle up some…"

"Never mind, Ma," he said as he bent down to scoop up his youngest brother. "I ate with the Minnicks." *Kinda.*

"Are you done with us, then?"

"Done with you? Of course not! I'll always be close, Ma. Always."

"Will you have a fried egg on that welcome promise?"

"Well, sure. But I come to see if I could use your phone." At his mother's nod, Greg tucked the youngest Paisler in the crook of his arm and crossed to the wall phone.

"Trouble?"

"Nah, not really. It's just Mr. Minnick deciding finally there ain't no gettin' 'round his needin' a real mechanic to keep that blamed tractor of his workin'. He says I'm no more use to him than the rest of them." As Levitt poked and giggled at the greasy bristle above his lip, Greg cranked the handle of the phone, so he was laughing when the operator answered.

"That's gotta be Greg," she chuckled. "I ain't heard that laugh for a while now, and I've missed it. How are things at the Paislers, Greg?"

"We're fine, Mrs. Johnston, and how are you and yours, ma'am?"

"Doin' well, Greg. Please give my best to your mama."

"She's right here, ma'am, if you'd like to…"

"Oh, no, not today, thank you kindly. This board has been lighting up like fireworks on the Fourth. Just give her my best. And what number was you wanting?"

"Jim's Auto, in Fox Haven, if you please."

"Jim, the mechanic? Ain't he just the best, but so busy, it's hard to get him to come at times."

"Oh, yes, he's top notch," Greg laughed, finally needing to put his little brother on the floor so he could concentrate on his conversation.

Levitt pouted for a moment and probably would have raised a howl if his mother had not distracted him with two grapes, one purple and the other green. He crawled over to her chair and pulled himself up to receive the only "candy" his family would let him have.

"Uh, hello, Mrs. Austin," he greeted his nebby neighbor as she came on the party line. "Greg. Yes, Greg Paisler. No, no trouble. I was just gettin' connected with Fox Haven, if you don't mind. No, it shouldn't take long at all. Yes, thank you," he added, as she said she would hang up and try her call again in a couple minutes. "Uh, thank you for connecting us, Mrs. Johnston. Yes. Jim? It's Greg Paisler, sir, calling from my folks'. Yes, thank you, the whole clan's doin' just fine. And Mrs. Weakly? I hear that summer cold thing has been goin' around. Terrible to get a cold in the summer. Don't seem right somehow. Please tell your missus that Ma hopes she'll be feelin' right as rain in no time. Say, I'm callin' for Mr. Minnick. Yes, sir, that blamed tractor again. Been workin' and workin' on it, but what we need is a real mechanic. You think you could send somebody over to the Minnicks'? You'll come yourself...? Well, thank you. That's mighty fine. Mr. Minnick will be so...Owe you? I'll tell him, I guess, but...You'll tell him yourself? Oh, yeah, that would be lots easier on m...Tomorrow, early aftern...? Oh, yes, that will be...Well, that will be...Thank you again, sir. We'll see you then."

As Jim hung up, finished with his conversation, Greg grinned as he set the long, black ear piece into its cradle. On second thought, he picked it up again, cranked the handle and rang Mrs.

Austin's seven to tell her the phone was free for her, but her line buzzed "busy."

"She was listening, wasn't she?" His mom smiled over the sizzling bacon.

Shrugging, Greg lifted his baby brother in his arms. He sat down with Levitt on his lap, drool and grape skin-faced though he was. He hadn't realized when he'd struck out on his own how much he'd miss the kids, especially this little boy with the thatch of dark golden-brown hair.

"Ready?" their mother queried and both looked up at her, wide-eyed. She set down before them a huge plate of thick bacon, pancakes, fluffy scrambled eggs and cottage fries sporting colorful bits of green, yellow and red peppers, and sautéed onions. She sat to watch her sons dig in and devour. Satisfied that Greg would be doing the breakfast justice, she rose to fetch them glasses of fresh milk with foam still bubbling at the rims.

After he had downed five pancakes at record speed, Greg again studied the little fellow on his thigh. "You sure are growin', littlest man."

"Ain't he, though? And just you wait 'til you see the twins, especially Travis. You been sleepin' over at the Minnicks'?"

"How's Twig?" Greg changed the subject without answering her question.

"Our Todd stays scrawny. He misses you, son. But he don't say nothing. Just runs around with a long face. But there's a boy about his age that's been fishin' our creek."

"A boy Twig's age? Who?"

"Emmy Lu's little brother, evidently. Says his name's 'Situs.' Never heard that name before."

"He's a swell kid. Yeah, I'm the one who told him to come on up here to fish. I hope that was okay? I thought it'd be good for both those boys."

"Good to have him. Todd is surely one caught in the middle of you brothers. Good to have his own friend," she said, leaning automatically to wipe the baby's face with the hem of her apron. "And speaking of new faces, have you met the young man distributing for GEM now? Comes in a brown painted-over milk delivery van like Ron Bean's. Polite young'n, I'll give him that."

"You say that like you don't mean it's a good thing."

Sinking into Greg's lap, Levitt swung his left arm listlessly toward his mother.

"Oh, I don't know," Cyn protested, picking up Levitt and tucking him into her own lap to give him nurse. "Just somethin' about him."

"Too polite to be believable? What's his name?"

Cyn laughed. "I guess I'm just not used to such glitterin' charm. Stewman? Something like that, I think he said."

"Struan? A little shorter'n me? Slender? Yeah, I know him, but just to talk to and not that often."

"So he's not a friend y…?"

"…yet," Greg finished with her, knowing how his mother treated people and what she would expect of him. "Yeah, Ma, I'll work on that acquaintanceship. But you won't be so glad to hear about the Minnicks—Will and Miz Nandria."

"So Will is getting called back into service? We all wondered when Mr. Owens gave Doc that telegram," Cynthia sighed. "I'll sure miss them. Was just gettin' to know his wife."

"Not 'them,' Ma. Just 'him.'"

"Will's leaving without them? Oh, sweet savior Lord, that poor girl."

Levitt had fallen asleep in her lap, so Greg brought over the bowl of string beans from the sink and a separate clean bowl for his mother to snap them into. She took a rare moment of quiet for her youngest and herself. Greg brushed her cheek with his lips and, with a rub of his tummy and a grin of thanks, slipped out the back door.

It felt strange to know all his family was somewhere busy on the farm, but to see no one, and not to know where anyone was at the moment. Greg strolled toward to barn, hoping to have a quiet word with Eli if he could find him. The last time the brothers had talked alone together had not gone well, Greg remembered. He was surprised at how angry the older siblings still were that he was giving his muscle and sweat to the Minnicks instead of the Paisler farm. He had just stepped into the shadow and redolence of fresh manure of the huge barn when he was tackled and nearly taken to the ground. On one knee, Greg twisted to swing at his assailant, only to pull back his fist when he realized it was Todd hitting him.

The boy pounded him furiously with fists, his face red with anger and hurt.

"Hey, Twig, it's me!" Greg cried as he peeled the boy off him and held him away so his blows were spent on air.

Greg peered at his little brother's grimace; Todd obviously knew exactly who it was.

"Todd," Greg murmured. "Twig!" Greg crouched beside the boy, drawing him close so the blows landed on his torso and face. He let go and let the boy do what he would. And then, as Todd's fury gradually died, he drew his scrawny brother in to hug him close.

The boy was in tears and angry now with himself for crying.

"I'm not going far, little man. I'll always be around right where you can reach me."

"Oh, yeah?" the boy sniffed.

"Yeah." Greg tugged out his own shirt tail and used it to wipe the kid's nose.

"When?"

"Whenever you want me. Or need me."

Todd's face told him when that would be.

"Especially if you're ever scared, Twig. Always then, little brother. Just come, and, whatever it is, we'll look it right in the eye together. The two of us. Now what could stare down the both of us?"

"N-nothin'," Todd stammered, and Greg nodded solemnly

"Not one gol-darned thing. Not against both of us together. Hey, I think that's Pa coming."

Swiping at his eyes and nose with his sleeve, Todd whispered, "Promise?"

"Promise."

Nodding, but not wanting his father to see that he'd been crying, Todd scurried away out of the barn and out of sight just as Zeb Paisler approached his third son, pitchfork in hand and straw bits glued to his boots with manure.

"Gregor."

"G'morning, Pa."

"You're makin' it permanent, then?"

"No, sir. Just settin' up a little on my own. Mr. Minnick's give a section to Will, and Will's hired me to work it for him 'til he comes back from that war."

"And, thinkin' about the needs of that wee gal of Will's, you'll want a cow, I reckon."

"Thinkin' hard about what's gonna come at the missus—both of them, and maybe another—how are they gonna handle things when Will goes?"

"Well, I guess Will was smart, hiring you away from us. They'll need you close. I was thinkin' Glorianna might do for the gal."

"But Glory is your best milker."

"Take her or leave her. If'n you want a cow…"

Nodding, Greg's face expressed his thanks, but for once he said it aloud anyway. "Yes, thank you, sir, Pa. I surely do."

CHAPTER THIRTY-ONE

"Come on down to supper, Greg," Will insisted against his young neighbor's gestures of refusal. "You've worked hard all day without that stubborn mule of a tractor." Will threw his hands up and chuckled; Greg stared, wiping his brow. "Did you know it was a church group, I think, once gave a basic tractor to some group of peasants somewhere to help their economy? They loved it; used it from dawn to full dark. But when it ran out of gas, the whole village gathered around it and beat it with sticks to make it go again as they'd always done to their donkeys. They hadn't a clue how an engine works."

Bending over with laughter, Greg joined in with Will's weary humor. "Maybe we should try that. Nothing else works." He strode to the edge of the field and back, picked up a broken branch and used it to swat and then thrash the tractor's cowl.

Will's laughter rang, and he waved Greg toward the house. "Come on, will you? Nandria'll have plenty of supper and she will be glad to see you. Come on, Paisler."

Tossing the branch aside, Greg shrugged and followed Will down the slope toward the Minnick farmhouse. "Okay to leave the old girl out here?"

"We've got most of the same neighbors you do. Most are honest as the day is long, but, come to think, I do have my doubts about that third Paisler…"

Greg picked up a clod of hand-turned earth and hurled it at the back of Will's boot, then strode forward to catch up and walk with him. "That Bean gal still comin' for lessons at your house?" he asked casually.

"Ronda?" Will slowed to let him come alongside so he could grin into his face, but then he frowned. "Ain't seen her today," he started, and then nodded. "But didn't Nandria tell me this morning that she had a class today with her professor from Fox Haven at some farmhouse between the two towns? Sorry, young man, you'll have to pine away this day," he added, chuckling.

Greg gave him the satisfaction of reddening before he stooped to pick up another clod of dirt to hurl.

* * * * * * * * * * * * * * * * * * *

Nandria approached the oak table with the coffee pot to refill her father-in-law's cup, then Doris's. Will took it from her to reach to the wall side of the table to pour warm-ups for Greg and Bodie.

"Great supper, Miz Minnick," Greg told Nandria. "Loved the biscuits—near as light as my mother's, and that's saying something."

Smiling her thank you, Nandria took back the pot and set it on her empty plate. Little Rose's eyelids were drooping. With a rhythm of her own, she rocked forward, forehead closer and closer to resting on the tray of her high chair. Will lifted her onto his lap, then settled her against his shoulder where she snuggled drowsily.

"Do you play cards, Mr. Paisler?" Doris asked, wiping her lips with the square of the discarded shirts she had hemmed as napkins.

"Please, Mrs. Minnick, do call me Greg. When you use 'Mr.', I look around for my pa."

Giggling, Doris tugged at the scarf tied loosely around her neck. "All right, Mr. Greg Paisler, I wondered if'n you played cards? When I was a girl up near the Canada border, we'd deal a hand or two of pinochle. Made the evening melt right into a good night's sleep."

"You don't do that now?" Greg asked, surprised.

Minnick stirred to tilt his chair back against the alcove wall by the door to the living room. "Used to."

"Years ago," Bodie added. He shook his head, remembering.

"The reverend don't approve," Doris frowned. "Guess we still could, but it takes the fun, knowing you're doing wrong."

Minnick dropped his chair onto its front legs with a crash that made Rose stir and cry once against her father's shoulder. "That Kylie fella don't approve nothing what'd give a man ease."

"Allergic to laughter," Nandria commented with a smile.

"'Allergic to laughter'? Is that what you said, girl?" Minnick stared at that end of the table where his son was comforting his pickaninny. "If that don't beat all."

"It was my mother's way of dealing with some of the sourpuss dons from other colleges in London she had to work with."

"What's a 'don'?" Minnick wanted to know. "Sure it couldn't be that everybody at any college is all named Donald."

Nandria's smile widened with the general laughter. "No, not all of them. It is a term we Brits use for a professor, especially at Oxford or Cambridge."

"Those are prestigious universities in England," Will explained. "Getting in as a student is a big thing, let alone teaching there."

"And your mama worked with them, girl?"

"Not there, except at conferences, where she was often asked to speak. My mother taught at the London School of Economics," Nandria explained, then went pensive before speaking again, softly. "Mother knew a long time ago that Germany's desperation after World War I would lead the world back into conflict."

Minnick snorted. "Them Krauts brung it on themselves—and the rest of us. What right've they got bringin' war on us again?"

As Doris turned to placate her husband's anger, she jumped, startled by a sharp rapping on the porch door. Rose's head lifted from her drool on her father's neck; she cried out. Handing the baby to Nandria, Will climbed over both of them to go to answer the knocking. They could hear him cross the porch.

"Frank Paisler, come on in," he welcomed, then added, "yeah, Greg's here."

Greg rose quickly; Minnick hiked his chair flat and then closer under the table to let him squeeze behind him. Greg was already in the open part of the kitchen when Will led Frank, a slender, older version of his brother Greg, into the warm area where the family was gathered. A quick, low wave of Frank's hand reassured

Greg that it wasn't a pressing emergency which had brought him. Greg held, but his breath was tight as he stood waiting while Will introduced Frank to his parents.

"Mama, you remember Frank Paisler, don't you?"

"I watched you boys grow up. Not that I can tell you one from the other now that you're men. Come in, Frank. Sit with us a spell."

"G'evenin', Mrs. Minnick. Sorry to barge in on you folks this way."

Greg couldn't stand it any longer. "What's wrong?" he asked outright.

Frank sat down sideways in the chair beside Doris, nodding to thank her, then turned to look back at his brother. "Not for sure anything's wrong as such. It's just Mrs. Bean is up in arms. Can't find anybody's seen her gal Ronda and she was wondering maybe the girl was here with Miz Minnick working on her school lessons?"

"Ronda's missing?" Greg demanded.

"Please, just sit with us, both Mr. Paislers," Nandria coaxed as she scooted over into Will's seat so Will could offer his chair to Greg, but the anxious young man refused with a quick shake of his head. "No, we have not seen Miss Bean this day," she said, looking to the others for confirmation.

"How long's she been missing?" Will asked.

"Evidently Sadie's been all over town asking. Finally called our farm from the doc's office. I had Ma tell her that I was closer, that I'd come here to ask and let her know."

"All your pa's sons make a prosperous farm, right enough," Minnick observed. The Paislers looked at him, and then, puzzled, at each other, but said nothing. They were relieved when Nandria spoke up.

"We should get in touch with Mrs. Bean."

"Yeah," Will agreed. "If the girl hasn't turned up, we should offer to help in the search."

Greg nodded vigorously. Bodie rose quietly to take the baby from Nandria.

"I'll settle her for the night, Miz Minnick, and stay with 'er," he offered. Nandria murmured her thanks. She was fond of her pupil and very much wanted to be with the group looking for her.

"Pa," Will turned to Minnick, silent and stricken at the head of his table, "Pa, may we take the truck?"

The man shook himself. "'Course," he agreed. "That's one thing farm life's got right. We all help when there's need."

CHAPTER THIRTY-TWO

In the cooling evening, Doris, agitated, struggled in Grover's arms as they stood at the porch stairs. Nandria glanced back as Will handed her up into the passenger seat of the truck.

"They look so…" Nandria cried, but Will only nodded without looking at his parents.

"Probably remembering my brother Freddy," he muttered, and Nandria knew to go still. There was nothing for it. Nothing that she could say or do would comfort them. They had known the anxiety of their younger son missing, and then found dead. They had each other, and the only thing Nandria could give them would be privacy.

"Greg and Frank went on to their farm first," Will said, "so Mrs. Paisler will call Doc's office to let the Beans know we hadn't seen Ronda all day. I wonder where that girl could be."

"They must be out of their minds with worry."

Will shifted gears, his face drawn tight. But when the truck was finally in running gear along the paved road toward town, he rested his right palm gently on his wife's knee. His mind had been rehearsing the often-heard dialog between his mother and father: *"There's something wrong, Mr. Minnick, dear,"* his mother would say fearfully. *"Is it Freddy?"*

"No, Mother," Grover would answer gently, *"our boy is finally just right. No trouble for him, no more."*

"Really and true? You promise?"

And then his father would enfold his beloved in his arms and whisper, "With all my heart." There would be tears in his eyes. Even when the man's foot had been all but crushed by the thresher, Will had not seen tears in his father's eyes. Only then, when he was comforting his wife. It had been one of the compelling reasons he'd enlisted in the army, those tears for something they both blamed their remaining son for. And now, this homecoming marred by ever more often episodes of Doris unsure, lost in their grief. And Grover's gentleness in holding her with what comfort he could give. *Please, Lord, spare the Beans the anguish of the loss of their only child.*

Hearing his sigh, Nandria gathered his right hand in both of her own.

* * * * * * * * * * * * * * * * * *

Boonetown bustled with mothers holding tight to small children while fathers, bachelors and old maids scoured every conceivable yard, shed and garden for Ronda Bean. Sheriff Yakes, ever more pot-bellied and sour of disposition and expression, caught sight of the Minnick truck pulling in nearly a block east of the Owens' general store. Clutching his abdomen, he scurried up as Will opened his door to get out.

"You got her?"

From down the street, someone had pulled Ron Bean by the shirt to see that the Minnick truck had come. Bean and half a dozen neighbors and friends scrambled toward them but slowed when Will shook his head in answer to Yakes' question. They moved ahead then, hesitantly, with more exchanging of opinions between them. Ron Bean arrived in time to help Will hand Nandria out of the truck.

"No?" Bean asked quietly.

"We are so sorry," Nandria began, but Bean couldn't handle the sympathy in her voice or her eyes. He turned to Will.

"Your gal didn't show up at our place this day, Ron," Will told him.

Bean nodded to say he'd taken in the news, but he couldn't speak, and all those gathering around them understood. For several moments there was murmuring as others arrived at their small clutch, but no one spoke outright.

"Well, it was a hope anyway, but it's gone," Ron finally lifted his chin to say. "So I guess we'd better get set to drive out there while we got some light, anyhow."

"Out there?" Nandria looked up at Will to explain.

The Paislers—Frank, Greg, and their father Zeb and oldest brother Eli, followed by young Sam —emerged from two trucks and joined the group.

"Ma stayed home with the little boys," Sam explained to Mrs. Owens.

"Of course," the patient store man's wife nodded. "Best be gettin' back to the store in case anyone else wants a lantern or rope. Been quite a run, and I guess now we'll be needin' all the mister's got." She scurried away.

"No sign of her mare?" Greg asked. "Surely the horse at least would make her way home by this time." He looked as anxious as he felt. Several women noted his fear and nodded to one another, suspecting an attachment they had not known about.

"No sign of her mare," Yakes said, but Bean, shaking his head in wonderment, disagreed.

"It's a fact the mare's been in the barn all along. Since before noon."

"I thought your gal always rode that nag."

"Not this time," Bean shrugged. "Sadie says Ronnie ain't felt good all day. Missed class. That professor fella said she showed up, but he sent her home because she looked so peaked."

"She's sick?" Greg demanded.

"Not really sick, Sadie says, just kind of wastey-like."

But Nandria was concerned. "Feverish?" she asked. "Delirious?"

Greg caught her anxiety immediately and in his own mind elaborated on it. "Mebbe she's out of her head. She could'a been wanderin' not knowin' where she is."

"I take it you have already covered the town thoroughly, Sheriff Yakes," Nandria said, but with the edge of question that made the paunchy man stiffen and bristle.

"'Course!" he snapped. *Uppity nigger! I know how to do my job!*

Will was aware of the man's anger at the perceived slight before Nandria, who had spoken with her focus on the problem of the missing girl, unmindful that a Negro seeming to criticize a white man would be far out of line in this small town.

"You've had kids go missing before, Sheriff Yakes," Will coaxed with a smile. "So of course you've searched all their regular holing-up places." Aware suddenly of her error, Nandria smiled and nodded as well.

"Of course the sheriff has done all that already," she scolded Will gently. "I was trying to think from the point of view of an imaginative child of somewhere else she might hide. You know how impish children can be. But our sheriff would have thought of that as well." Will nodded with relief. She'd gotten his message. Yakes' sloping shoulders relaxed. He seemed mollified. Nandria squeezed Will's hand in thank you.

"Not much gets by you, Yakes," Will said aloud.

"Thorough job of the place. More'n half the town checkin' everywhere," the sheriff explained with the superior graciousness of someone who has forgiven another's error. "Not a rag to show for it and now you say she ain't been out to your place." Sighing, he turned toward Ron Bean, who hung his head and looked keenly at the ground at his feet.

"Time, I guess," the father murmured. "Best while there's some light left."

"We'll need more trucks 'n' lights…"

"The Bogs," Bean whispered. *Oh, God…*

"That's treacherous ground," Greg protested, not wanting even the possibility of Ronda being there to be true. "Ronda'd know to stay away from there." Both Bean and Greg blanched as Nandria swiped her forehead to remind them that Ronda might have a fever. Frank stepped closer to his brother, realizing finally how much the girl's safety mattered to him.

"Whichever, it is the next logical place to check in whatever daylight is left to us," Zeb stated quietly.

"So we best be gettin' started," the sheriff squared his shoulders. "I'll gather the men and let 'em know."

"I'll tell my missus," Ron Bean sighed.

"Would you like me to tell her, Mr. Bean?" Nandria offered, knowing how much he would want to be to getting underway. "If I am not intruding to ask, sir."

"Intruding? Hardly," Bean told her, relieved. "Obliged, ma'am."

"Well, come on then," Yakes growled. "We need a passel of men and lanterns. Gotta come up with a plan. No place to lose track of nobody."

Nandria pressed Will's arm as the others started toward the center of town. "It is dangerous then?"

He patted her hand, but his eyes told her what she feared to know. "Half this town's lost a dog or a horse or cow. Some even a son or a nephew. More quicksand there than any other place in a hundred mile radius. But don't worry about us. We'll rope together and stay as long as we can in the shine of the headlights."

"That is why the sheriff wanted more trucks, then. I gather everyone was hoping she had come out to us."

"We wish that, too. But now we deal with what's left," Will nodded, touched her shoulder and turned to hurry toward the gathering posse.

Float

CHAPTER THIRTY-THREE

Kylie sipped the last of the tea from Mrs. Struan's dainty cup and set it carefully in its translucent saucer, feeling like an elephant handling crystal goblets. It had been years since he'd felt less than the master of any social situation. He had worked with such boors for so long a time in his rural exile. But this woman…

"Cucumber sandwiches with formal, delicious, fine tea," he commented, smiling, hoping his facial expression would convey what at the moment he had no words for. The muscles, particularly around his mouth, felt awkwardly moved. *How long has it been since I've fumbled for words in a social situation? Even longer since I've felt cowered by the presence of a lady? An elephant, indeed. Me? Dean Frederick Kylie, unsure. But she is a lovely woman. Kept her figure. Slender. Graceful. Gracious in her movements. Ladylike. Even cut the crusts off that white bread for the sandwiches. Now I just hope my stomach does not betray me, grumbling.* With his napkin, he tapped his upper lip; he'd seen it glistening with sweat reflected in the surface of the tea. "How delightful it has been, dear lady, but I truly must be getting back to my flock."

"I am so relieved by your assurance that Sheriff Yakes was merely asking for my son's help, not accusing him of any wrong doing. Your counsel has been exceptional, kind pastor. Your flock is indeed privileged to have such an insightful gentleman as its shepherd."

He felt himself blush. *How very strange. This woman is wielding far too much influence. I must get hold of myself.*

"I do attempt to be a bastion to my people." Whatever a bastion is? *I must get out of here while I am still a smidgen above blithering idiot!*

"I am sure that you fulfill your role admirably. Let me help you with your coat, Pastor."

"Oh, no, thank you. I believe I will carry it on my arm. The weather has turned dark."

She looked at him. He shook his head. She had him. *It wasn't the weather that had turned dark. Only the afternoon that had turned to evening while I've been inside here panting, positively drooling. Get out of here—now!*

"Thank you for your hospitality. I will indeed endeavor to continue to aid your son in any way that I am able," he pronounced and turned without another word to seek shelter in his Chevy.

* * * * * * * * * * * * * * * * * * *

Nandria slowed a moment, her hand resting on the smoothly opening front gate, to admire the welcoming white picket fence surrounding the Beans' corner lot. There was love and warmth here. Not a place to make one think of tragedy. We must find Ronda. Please, Lord. Swallowing, Nandria approached the steps to the porch and climbed to knock at the front door. Surprisingly, it was Sadie Bean herself who opened it.

"Mrs. Minnick!" she cried expectantly. Looking past her, Sadie seemed to grasp that Ronda was not with her. "Ah."

"Will and I came to help, Mrs. Bean. Your husband wanted me to let you know they will be proceeding now to…"

"...the Bogs," Sadie finished for her. Her broad face paled. She closed her eyes. Nandria could see them roll beneath the covering lids. And then Sadie sank as though deflated.

"Mrs. Bean!" Nandria cried aloud. She lunged forward, but the woman was simply too large for Nandria to be able to hold up alone.

"Sadie!" Cries came from deep within the house. Someone was at Sadie's back helping Nandria ease the woman to the floor. Nandria crouched to rest Sadie's head in her lap. Women crowded close; many murmured or muttered. One screamed but was quickly hushed.

"Leave it to a nigger to deliver a blow like that instead of breaking the news gently like any civilized person would've."

There were quiet gasps, and then a silence amid the hubbub of ineffectual chattering of the cluster of women.

"Here, try this on her forehead," Mrs. Drangler directed those crowded closest to the door. They passed the cold, wrung cloth forward until Nandria was able to wipe Sadie's face gently with it and settle it on her forehead. Sadie stirred.

Stirring, Sadie murmured, "Ah!" as she opened her eyes. She looked around wildly at first, then took comfort and orientation from Nandria's presence with her on the floor. "Ah, Mrs. Minnick, you—you don't have Ronda with you, do you?"

Her own tears welling, Nandria slowly shook her head. "Not this day, Mrs. Bean. She had told us she would be in class..."

"Yes, she had class," Sadie explained as she insisted on sitting up. She rested her back a moment against her own front door frame, still talking sadly with Nandria. "The professor said he'd sent her on home when she showed up this afternoon, she looked so poorly." She started to try to rise, but Nandria persuaded her to take a few more minutes.

"I am sorry she was ill."

"Not ill so much as something eatin' at her, I think." This time Sadie had her own way. She pulled herself up to stand against the door frame, shaking, but on her own feet. She bent close to say the last few words to Nandria alone while her bulk gave the two privacy from the ministrations of the townswomen behind them in the vestibule. "I was so sure, even when my Ron told me Ronnie's mare was in the barn. I hoped mebbe that Paisler boy had picked her up in his truck. He's brought her home a time or two, you know."

Nandria nodded.

Sadie had turned before she was quite finished speaking, and Claudia Freshstalk gasped behind her, having heard her final words.

"Are you saying Mr. Paisler has been out to see the Minnicks?" she demanded of Sadie. That she was ignoring Nandria's presence was obvious to both.

"Out helpin' on their farm, what with Will hurt like he was in the war."

"Oh, and your daughter was helping as well, Mrs. Bean? I understand Mrs. Minnick has, er, lost some capacity."

Mrs. Drangler had wriggled her way to the front of the gaggle of ladies. She twisted to look back, nearly scraping Mrs. Claudia

Freshstalk's arm with the pins on her wide lapel. "Doris can still hold the love of the family," she snorted, and Claudia huffed and retired to the living room, sweeping her closest allies in with her.

"Make room now," Mrs. Drangler crowed. "Let's get Sadie here to the sofa to lie down and recover her wits." Enlisting several farmers' wives accustomed to moving heavy loads, Drangler directed a support system that landed the moving crew in the living room. Mrs. Freshstalk and one of her friends needed to vacate the sofa at the last minute or be sat upon. But soon Sadie was protesting the supine position Drangler had dictated for her.

"Lemme up, Ella Mae," Sadie demanded. "I gotta think what to do next for my gal." Her color was now nearly as feisty as her tone, Drangler realized to her own satisfaction.

"Up, then, if you insist on being in on everything that goes on, just like always." But Ella Mae Drangler was smiling to see her recovering her spirit. "So, what are you thinking?"

Sadie looked from one face to the other, seeing bewilderment, resignation, and even encouragement on a few—including Ella Mae's and Nandria's.

"Well, the men are goin' to the Bogs. That's what Nandria here come to tell me."

Claudia Freshstalk looked shocked. "She can't be thinkin'..."

"You grew up out that way," Mrs. Drangler pointed out. "You know them Bogs as good as anybody."

"You can't go out there!" Mrs. Freshstalk protested.

"We'll be here in case your gal wanders back," Mrs. Drangler assured her.

"But—but it is the woman's place to…"

Sadie looked at Claudia Freshstalk as though she had newly arrived from somewhere foreign and did not know anything about how things were done in rural southwest Missouri in 1940. "A woman's place is to be lookin' out for her own," she explained patiently. "I'm goin'. Miz Minnick, will you come with me?"

Glancing around, Nandria felt, as well as saw, the women's glares of blame, but they rolled off her as unheeded as rain off the sleek back of a beaver. "If I can help you," she answered quietly. She offered her hand to help Sadie to a stand.

Sadie swayed, then spread her feet for a wider stance to steady herself. "We ought'a have boots, I reckon. In the mud room at the back," she called to one of the younger women who looked ready to assist. "See if'n there's an extra pair for Miz Minnick, will you, Cora?"

Young Cora ran to look. Sadie was still weak as she shuffled toward the front door, but she was obviously growing stronger with purpose. That determined look spread over her face that made even towering, grown men do exactly as she told them in the doctor's examining room where 'yes'm' was the only acceptable response.

"These are all I could find, Mrs. Bean," Cora apologized as she returned from the back of the house carrying three well-worn pairs of boots.

"Ah, exactly, Cora. Thank you." Sadie slipped on her own pair as Cora offered the other two for Nandria's choice. Both pairs were too large, but Nandria tried on each and decided on the smaller.

Taking them off again, she hauled a large, men's handkerchief from her pocket to stuff into the toe of one boot. Cora patted her own pockets, but it was Mrs. Drangler who supplied a large square of cloth for Nandria to use in the other.

"Good for you, gal," the seamstress whispered.

With a brief nod of acknowledgment, Nandria stood tall and stomped her feet to adjust the wadding. "These are fine," she stated. "All set." She had never been welcomed to take off her coat, so she was ready.

Sadie, slipping on her own heavy coat from the peg near the bottom of the stairs, checked for her gloves and scarf in the ample pockets. "Ready." She led the way out onto the porch. Far down the side street they could see the posse intent upon the sheriff's words, though they could not hear any of them from here. At the edge of the crowd, Sadie spotted her Ron, his anguish visible to her in the set of his shoulders. And hovering near her husband, Sadie could make out the tall figure that had to be Greg Paisler, close and attentive as a bodyguard. "Well, come on then," Sadie declared as the two women started down the porch stairs.

"She's actually going!" Claudia Freshstalk crowed behind them. "Well, I never!"

"Yeah," sniped Mrs. Drangler. "We know."

Float

CHAPTER THIRTY-FOUR

As the convoy of pickup trucks filed away, Boonetown shimmered in its recent agitation through a silent fog of dust settling in sunlight. But the sunlight was already beginning to slant from the west. Nandria prayed that what was left would suffice to allow the men find Ronda.

Lord, please let her be found somewhere else. There are fields of green, farms where she could be. The men are only going out there to that monstrous place now because they are afraid not to while there is still light. The Lord would hear. But she knew that whatever happened had more to do with decisions made long ago this day by others than herself. She could only pray for the girl's safe return to her loving family.

Sadie stopped in the road in front of Owens' store. Mrs. Owens hustled out and took her hands in both of her own.

"They've only just gone, Sadie, dear."

"I can see their taillights," the determined mother nodded. "I'm going after them."

"Oh, my dear, you can't!"

"I grew up there, remember? I know the ins and outs of that place better'n anyone in that herd, I'd be willing to bet," Sadie declared, then added under her breath as Nandria joined her. "Though the only thing anybody knows about the Bogs is that they shift and change most every day. Rain, no rain, even wind."

"Then it isn't a lake of some sort?" Nandria asked. The whole idea of quicksand was foreign to her, thank the Lord.

"More of an ox-bow lake that went bad," Sadie told her, but that information did little to enlighten the Englishwoman.

"A change in the bend of a river that leaves an area about the shape of the gear that oxen can be hitched to," Mrs. Owens told her.

"Well," Nandria responded, though she was only beginning to imagine that shape in relation to ground. Her thoughts were going back quickly to her time in the African "outback" with her father that she had been avoiding remembering for months now.

"Well? That sounds deep, Miz Minnick," Mr. Owens teased wearily as he exited his store, closing the double entrance door behind him.

"Oh, Isaac," Mrs. Owens called softly, stepping toward him on the boardwalk. "Don't lock it, dear, in case someone needs something and they can't find either of us to help."

"You're right," he sighed, pushing the keys on their crowded ring back into the pocket of his pants. He walked awkwardly a few steps until they settled. Glancing over at Sadie, he grinned foolishly with weariness.

"You aren't going out there now, are you, Isaac?" Mrs. Owens knew he had worn himself out seeking, selling, loaning, and giving needed supplies to the searchers since early that afternoon. "Why don't you take an hour to rest and eat a supper I'll put together for you right this minute. Come home, dear."

Shaking his head, he descended the few steps to the roadway and approached, with Mrs. Owens close beside and behind him, her arm in his.

"Mrs. Bean, Miz Minnick," he nodded in greeting. "Your menfolk just left."

"We seen the last of the taillights of their trucks."

"I cleaned out my rope and lanterns from the store. Was just goin' to check what I might have at the house or shed, and then I'll be goin' to join 'em."

Mrs. Owens shook her head, frowning, but knew better than to plead her case any longer once her man had made up his mind.

"Might be an even better helper-neighbor if'n you had a bite to eat before you go, Mr. Owens," Sadie told him. "You got sharp eyes, and they'll be doin' a heap more good for the men if'n they're clear and sharp rather than blurry with over-tired."

"I'll grab a bite," he assured them, "but then I got to get out there to see what else might be needed."

"In that case," Nandria drew a breath to ask a great favor, "is there any chance that Mrs. Bean and I could ride with you, sir?"

"What?"

"They want to go out to the Bogs, Isaac," Mrs. Owens explained.

"What? Sadie Bean, Lord Almighty, you don't want to go out there! It's tough enough for those poor men. And your husband, especially, if'n he needs to be worrying himself about you, too."

"I'll walk, if I have to."

"You're going, no matter what?"

"I'm going," she stated, and Mr. Owens lifted his bloody, soiled apron to wipe his forehead and face. He blew his nose, at which Mrs. Owens did her best not to show her revulsion, knowing it was his way to indicate his displeasure that he could never put into words to another man's wife.

When he looked over at this hulking nurse, she was still staring at him with fixed determination. Nandria's expression was no help as she had donned a mask of non-commitment. His wife looked at him pleadingly, but what she was pleading for, he wasn't at all sure. Nor would he ask her—now or any time in the near future.

"All right, then," Owens finally surrendered. "Come along. I think I got a couple lanterns at the house I mean to take with us."

He turned without looking again at any of them. They followed, with only Sadie striding erect.

* * * * * * * * * * * * * * * * * * * *

Pastor Dean Kylie drove slowly since he was really not seeing the road. But there was little traffic this far from Fox Haven, and all he needed to do was to keep between the vague green strips at each side of the crumpling macadam. He twitched with discomfort. *Must be gettin' the hives. Though I had cucumbers just this past Sunday in that bitter salad Mrs. Zorn brought me. They didn't bother me none then. Surely cuttin' crusts off white bread don't change the chemistry to bring on an allergic reaction.*

You blamed fool! Of course cuttin' off crusts doesn't bring on hives. You are smitten. And she's—she's been married. Had a man. More than likely, more than one, Dean Kylie, if you are going to be honest with yourself. And? That's her past. It was probably legitimate. Marriage. Loss. Widowhood. How can you hold that against her? She did not even know you existed at that time. Still...

He sat up and focused on the road when the pavement went rough under his tires, but it was only a series of pot holes, probably caused by heavy farm machinery and then the stiff winter ice and snow storms. He was still driving reasonably well. He sighed and settled again into his driver's section of the bench seat. His hand went to his mid-section to try to calm his stomach, only now, thank goodness, beginning to growl aloud in protest of the scant meal. He looked into his rearview mirror to judge the time from the western horizon. *I wonder if Mrs. Owens is still in her store that she could make me a couple hearty sandwiches with that beef Owens slices so thin. And pickles and sweet onion? No appointments with parishioners scheduled tonight so I can for once indulge myself in that crisp, sweet, off-putting-smelly treat?*

Will you look there! Two, no, three sets of headlights heading south. More, even! But there's nothing down there but that Lord-forsaken area of quicksand and rattlesnakes. He shuddered. *Don't think I've ever seen that much traffic goin' down that way before. Hmmm.*

* * * * * * * * * * * * * * * * * *

Behind his house, Owens shuffled out of the shed, juggling three lanterns, with a large coil of rope dangling from his shoulder. He dropped the mass onto the rest of the supplies in the bed of his pick-up. Mrs. Owens hurried out of their house with Sadie and Nandria, each carrying a large basket, presumably of food, for the men. They hurried to set the baskets among the gear in the truck bed.

"See what the neighbors been settin' up for you to take out there with you, Isaac," Mrs. Owens burbled, trying to ease her husband's funk.

"Get in," was all he said, and Sadie climbed into the passenger side of the truck without a word.

"I'll stay to make more food and keep an eye on the store if anything else is needed, Isaac," Mrs. Owens said meekly. Her willingness to follow what he felt was the right path for a woman would mollify him somewhat—and make their relationship gentler after all this was over. Besides, she hated snakes; shuddered at the sight of one, and she knew the Bogs slithered and crawled with those critters cursed by God Himself. Owens humphed low but nodded once as he went to close the tailgate. And then he looked embarrassed.

"I will be fine in the back of the truck," Nandria assured him, climbing up and in. She settled surprisingly gracefully among the coils of rope and smiled up at him.

"Sorry," he muttered. He hadn't thought about where the colored woman would sit and had not wanted to be the one to tell her that that was the only possibility. But she had seen for herself and saved him the humiliation of needing to say that to her. For a moment he was grateful, then slipped quickly back into his pique that either one of them was insisting to go where no woman had any business.

"Thank you for all your help," the dark woman told him as he raised the tailgate. He blinked, too surprised at her civility to be able to answer directly.

And yet, Sadie was right, he thought as he stalked around to get in behind the steering wheel, she had grown up on a hard-scrabble farm not far from there. She did know the area better than anyone else. She had been out before to help the crew search, years ago. For the Pilford's nephew, if he remembered right. And glad they had been for her help in finding the foolish lad. A broken leg, but that would have mended long ago, though, as he recalled the young man walked with a limp. Still, he was alive, and Sadie was partly to be credited with his being upright and walking at all. Stupid kid.

Owens settled behind the wheel and started the truck without speaking. He didn't want Sadie Bean to think he'd softened.

Bernice Owens let her eyes follow her husband's taillights until they faded into the landscape west and south. She lifted her own apron to wipe the tears from her eyes. With one last look at the diminishing cloud of dust they had raised, she blew her nose into the apron, and stripped it off all but defiantly.

Float

CHAPTER THIRTY-FIVE

As Mr. Owens pulled into what was probably the last solid earth field at the edge of the Bogs, he parked his truck at one end of the semi-circle of pick-ups that concentrated their headlamps beams toward the entrance of an eerie forest of living and skeletal trees.

Sheriff Yakes stalked up near the arc of ghastly limbs to raise his hands in the intense light. Gradually the gathered men quieted in their efforts to wrap their waists bands of hemp to several others of their acquaintance. They were hooking up as best they could with those they would be trusting with their lives. They turned to look as the sheriff cupped his mouth to megaphone his words to all of them.

"Might as well save them truck lights for now," he hollered. One by one, men returned to switch off the headlamps at his words of wisdom. Yakes was right. It made little sense to beam the lights now when there was enough sun to see by, at least for a while. Most of them swallowed the realization that that meant as the sun set, they would be too deep in the treacherous swampy area for the light from the trucks to penetrate. They'd be alone with the snakes and quicksand, in the stinking dark. Most turned back to their tasks without looking anyone else in the eyes.

Sheriff Yakes stood, arms at his sides, staring at Owens getting out of his truck and moving to the bed, where he lowered the tailgate and lifted a hand to help Nandria down. The rest of the men stopped what they were doing and twisted to stare as well. Nandria flushed. Aside from glancing around for Will, she kept her eyes down, hopefully forestalling comments.

And then Sadie Bean emerged from the truck cab and stood, feet apart, chin up, meeting the stare of each of the men closest to her.

Murmurs rose, which Nandria could not interpret. Guessing their significance, she bent to help Mr. Owens lift out and organize the lanterns and ropes. Nandria then took charge of the baskets of food, which, she was glad to see, the men recognized. Their expressions mostly changed as they saw sustenance. A few wandered over. They'd come to help without taking time to eat. Nandria set the baskets to one side and began setting the sandwiches from one onto a chipped platter on the blanket she'd spread under a thick-trunked elm.

"Thanks," a few men murmured, but she quickly told them that the food was courtesy of Mrs. Owens and the women of Boonetown. She was merely setting it out for them.

"Still," one slender youth told her as he took the offered sandwich with long, tapered fingers. His hands were not as calloused as she had come to expect of the farmers in this area. His pale eyes appeared green, but as he turned away, from the side they seemed to flash golden. "Glad you came. Thank you, ma'am," he told Nandria. "You're Will Minnick's, aren't you?"

"Yes. And you are Mr. Struan, if I remember correctly. From the G.E.M. company."

He grinned and nodded, impressed. "How's the missus enjoying her brooch?"

Mr. Struan was the picture of politeness, but Nandria found herself feeling a discomfort that ate at any trust she might have had. Under other circumstances, she might have tried to question him about that brooch. *You've spent too much time among diplomats and their double-meaning cronies,* she scolded herself. *Too quick to see ulterior motives. He seems a nice enough young man...* But any further consideration of him was lost when she caught sight of Will approaching. All thought of the soft-fingered youth swept away as she lifted a large ham sandwich for her husband.

Will shook his head, the beginnings of a proud smile on his lips. "Thank you for thinking of us."

"It was Mrs. Owens' and the ladies' doing. I merely came out when Sadie Bean asked me."

"Ah, Mrs. Bean," Will exclaimed aloud as the large woman came up. "I, for one, am glad you're here. Any edge you can give us will certainly help."

"Will Minnick," Sadie nodded as she gathered her rope and began to wrap it around her waist.

"Are you figurin' to go in there?" the sheriff demanded, striding near.

"You'll be glad I come, Yakes."

"So they tell me, but we'll let your man decide that, I guess."

The four turned as Ron Bean hurried up, a tail of rope trailing behind him. He reached for Sadie's hand, and they exchanged a look that made the others turn away without comment to give them a moment together.

"Are you sure, angel?"

"I need to be here."

"I know. Thanks, Mr. Owens, for bringing her," Ron called, and Owens nodded but busied himself distributing the last of his lanterns. "And thank you, Miz Minnick, for not lettin' my lady come out here alone. Stick close to her, please. No, Sadie, you can't be out front with me. Just stay back where we can count on your wisdom when we need you. Please?"

He was just over half her size; she could have crushed him, and they both knew it. But she respected her husband, and, for now, at least, she was going to do as he bid her. Heaving a deep sigh, she nodded and reached to untie the knot of rope at her waist. She stood beside the middle basket of food, watching after him as he and the sheriff left again for the center of the gathering line. Yakes lifted his hand to start the broad line forward into the weird murkiness of whole and broken trees.

Will cupped Nandria's elbow. "Left over from an ancient bend in the river, evidently. Nasty even in what daylight that penetrates. Love, this is going to be tough." At Nandria's nod of understanding, Will trotted over to hook up with Greg and Frank Paisler. Their father and young Sam were in another group just to their right.

"Nandria," Will called back, "you can drive a truck. Would you take a driver's place?"

She nodded as Sadie peered at her. "So that man can take another place in the line," Sadie reasoned, nodding gratefully. "Come on, Miz Minnick. At least we can be that useful."

Glad to be of real help, Nandria and Sadie found the Minnick truck and persuaded the driver that they would follow directions and drive forward only when the men around them had said it would be safe. Reluctantly—for himself as well as for the two women—the driver let them take over. He hustled back to the elm tree to pick out one of the last of the rope lines and then, tying as he moved, shuffled to the edge of the half-circle of men.

Nandria climbed up behind the wheel and Sadie got in, shoving the cardboard box of tools into Nandria's hip as she settled on the passenger side.

The line had started forward jaggedly but found its cohesion as the men realized the best techniques to stay within sight and sound of the others.

Nandria shifted the truck to be as near behind Will as she could manage. No one knew how far any of the trucks would able to maneuver. It would depend on how long solid ground remained beneath their tires, and that would be a gamble at best. Sadie studied the textures of the ground in front of them; both the women watched the men for signals. Nandria did not turn on the headlamps yet, but she wanted to. It amazed her how dense the gloom had become in only these few yards into the morass of grotesque trees silvered in their death throes by what light filtered to them. Gloom descended to hover over her. A gloom that threatened to penetrate the thin barrier of her clothes and skin and pierce into her muscles, and finally into her vital organs, stealing her own vitality before killing her.

Nandria shuddered, then, glancing over at Sadie Bean to see if she had noted her cowardly reaction to this ungodly setting, shifted more abruptly than she would have normally. In low gear again, she crept forward inches, but it was enough for several of the men in front of the truck to look back at them anxiously.

"They're as afraid as we are, God bless 'em all," Sadie gasped. "But they gotta pretend they ain't. We women get to say—at least a little—that our goosebumps've got goosebumps."

"You like being a woman," Nandria all but chuckled. She hadn't thought about the advantages of her sex in quite that way before.

"A huge woman," Sadie laughed, but her voice strangled high before it slid to its normal range. "This way I got the edge of bein' able to pulverize someone who threatens physical assault, and they know it before they get into it, too, so I seldom've had to."

Nandria laughed outright, but quickly subdued her outburst behind her hand. The truck lurched a little but was quickly reined in.

"I like you, Miz Minnick, always have." Sadie turned to peer at her.

"I am not merely a 'nigger' to you?"

"You?" Sadie snorted. "Too refined to be one of them. But there are such, don't let yourself be fooled to thinkin' there ain't. Just like there's plenty and enough of white trash. Don't let nobody tell you there ain't that, too."

Nandria set both hands at the top of the steering wheel and inhaled slowly, then, even more slowly, exhaled through her nostrils.

"My point exactly," Sadie told her. "Rather 'n fight me outright while you got a slow burn on, you take a minute to pull yourself together so you've got all your forces on your own side. My Ron does that, too. And I admires it in both of you. Makes you bigger 'n me and bigger 'n most people I know who just snap out with cuttin' words and think they're gonna win by bein' loud and obnoxious."

The truck stopped its inching. The men were unhitching into smaller groups to go around ghostly gray trunks of dead and dying trees, then re-hitching to one another to stay more or less in a wide single line on the far side of each obstacle. The two women watched the process. With their windows cranked open, they could hear Sheriff Yakes yelling encouragement to hurry forward—that the sunlight wouldn't last a lot longer to help the deeper they got—best take advantage of it while they had it.

The men did hurry perceptibly, but progress was still slow.

"Probably dreading every step," Nandria murmured, unaware at first that she was speaking out loud.

"Can't blame 'em none," Sadie agreed. "I'd rather be here with you in the bit of safety of the truck, then out there."

"I as well," Nandria whispered. Again they giggled, two girls against a malevolent world they were coming to know.

"In cahoots, are we?"

"In cahoots," Nandria lisped carefully to luxuriate in the wonderfully odd sounds. "Such a wonderful idiom. A delightful expression," she rephrased in answer to Sadie's frown. "I love languages. Always have."

"You know a lot of them, don't you?"

"My father was a British diplomat. I traveled a great deal with my parents, to many countries. Mostly in Africa, of course, since that is where the powers that be decided a Negro diplomat would do Britain's interests the most good."

"Dark on dark. I can see where that might make a guy feel more trusting, like he was talkin' to someone who knew what he'd seen and had done to him."

Nandria twisted to face this insightful country woman. Her smile came slowly, in recognition and honor. Sadie blushed, but nodded in acceptance of her due.

"Ronda has some of your strengths, and some of your husband's. She will be a beautiful young woman."

"If we find her," Sadie sat forward suddenly, resting her forehead on the dashboard.

Nandria let her sob.

CHAPTER THIRTY-SIX

The Chevy was running mostly on fumes, though Pastor Kylie was only aware when it bucked as he turned toward the rectory. His first reaction was surprise, then annoyance that a mechanical problem would interrupt his deep thoughts. Only as he recognized—to his chagrin—that he might well be left on his own in the dark in this, he realized finally, deserted town, only then did he feel the beginnings of panic. He'd never been good with machinery. And he was not quite yet near enough to the church or to the small, dilapidated frame house his congregation saw fit to "give" him as part of his inadequate compensation for him to feel comfortable walking in the growing darkness. How many times had the Council talked about putting in street lamps, but had found the cost prohibitive? Kylie did not like the dark. His boyhood and his study of the Bible had reinforced his inclination to believe in a merger of darkness and evil.

The Chevy sputtered. Kylie pressed the brake, and belatedly the clutch, and let the car coast to a stop in his lane.

"Lord, look down—please!" he breathed. After sitting for a moment with his eyes closed and his lips beseeching, he was startled by a timid knocking at his window. Hiking over toward the center of the bench seat, he opened his eyes and looked wildly at the figure leaning in at the driver's window. "Mrs. Owens! Oh, you startled me."

"Dear pastor, forgive me. I didn't mean to. We were just anxious to hear any news about our young Miss Ronda."

"Miss Ronda? Bean?" He stared at her blankly, his mouth dropping open to reveal that blamed lower incisor of his that was turning gray. Hurriedly, he snapped his mouth shut.

"Oh, yes," Mrs. Owens cried, her wailing concern being echoed now by three women who had joined her beside the pastor's Chevy, also anxious for news. "Do you mean you aren't coming from the Bogs?"

"Ronda Bean is at the Bogs? Great heavens! It's dark!" He hitched to his left and cranked down his window fully. "What in the world is the child doing in a place like that?"

"We ain't sure that's where she is," added that nebby Mrs. Drangler, shuddering so the deadly pins and needles in her collar glistened in what little light reached them. "Just that the menfolk felt they ought'a get a look-see before full dark. Hoping she's somewhere else entirely."

At last the full import of Kylie's sighting of the headlights going south toward the Bogs and now the emptiness of the town sank into his consciousness. "Ronda Bean is missing?"

If it had been any one of the other men, the women might have laughed, or at least giggled behind lifted hands. But this was the pastor. The gathering women spoke low to one another, but not one dared smile.

It was Mrs. Owens who answered kindly. "Yes. Sadie started the alarm at noon or thereabouts. We combed the town. No sign of her Ronda. When the Minnicks came in and had not seen her this day..."

"We all had fervently hoped that she was out at the Minnick place getting help with her mathematics course from Will Minnick..." Mrs. Freshstalk interrupted, only to be interrupted by Mrs. Drangler.

"Not Will. It's Nandria Minnick that's learnin' her."

Mrs. Freshstalk gathered her skirts close and stepped away from the little seamstress in a huff.

"But you ain't seen the town's menfolk then?" Mrs. Zorn demanded. "No word?"

"I was tending to a distant parishioner. In Fox Haven." Kylie stumbled over his explanation, unsure that was truly a definition of his relationship with Mrs. Constance Struan. But it sounded official. It would do, for now. "I have not eaten..."

"Oh, we have baskets of food ready to go out to our menfolk."

"Will you cart them out for us, Pastor, please?"

"If that is where pastoral care is needed, of course I will go. Only..."

"Only?"

"My Chevrolet seems to be choking on me. Ordinarily I would have Daniel check it for me..."

"He's out at the Bogs with the others."

"Naturally," Kylie admitted, raising his hands as though in surrender.

Mrs. Owens glanced at Mrs. Drangler, both having seen the car's behavior just before it sputtered to a stop. Mrs. Drangler hiked up to poke her head deep in at the driver's window. Cowering to his right, Kylie did his best to avoid those murderous pins and needles.

"Ah," Mrs. Drangler sighed. "Just like I thought. I think I know what you'll need," she assured him as she withdrew. "Your gas is…"

"In need of fresh," Mrs. Owens supplied quickly.

"Yeah," Drangler agreed. "Fresh'll do it, I imagine. I'll fetch it right now."

The women dispersed even more quickly than they had gathered. Blinking, Kylie sat a moment, then got out and stretched beside the car, unsure what was about to happen, but sure the women of the town would be sending him out to ministerial duties and emotional upheavals he was not anxious to encounter. He would so much rather be snuggling in his spacious bed, considering the attributes of one fine city lady.

CHAPTER THIRTY-SEVEN

The beseeching branches of the half-drowned trees writhed in the tilted beams of the Minnick truck headlamps. Nandria's breath caught, remembering childhood terror of near-naked dancers, their sweating, muscular bodies glistening in leaping firelight. Her father sat beside her, long legs crossed, large head thrust forward, rhythmically darting forward in time with drumbeats like those skinny-legged birds jerking forward along sandy beaches. He was fully drawn into the tribal cadence and took no notice of his small, skinny-legged daughter beside him shaking in fear for her life and limb. She gasped; Sadie Bean looked over at her.

"They do look bad, don't they? Them trees," she commented kindly. "Not full dead, most of 'em. But not alive in health neither. Gives me the creeps. Can you imagine how them menfolk must feel with them branches dangling all around them as they slosh with that muck grabbin' at their feet?" She shuddered, perhaps a slight bit more intensely than Nandria would have expected.

"What a thoughtful and compassionate woman you are," Nandria whispered. "What a treasure you are to your Boonetown. I wonder if the residents fully recognize what they have."

"What?" Sadie reacted in surprise. "What brought that on?"

Nodding rather than replying or explaining, Nandria sat up to peer out at Will's insistent hand signals pointing out just where Nandria was to try to drive forward. They felt as well as heard a schmlucking tug at the left wheels of the truck. They held their breath and Nandria pressed harder on the gas pedal in response to Will's urging waves. The truck lurched, but settled, rocking on its elderly springs as they slowed and stopped on thankfully still solid ground. But again, the rounded hillock left the truck tipped, this time to Sadie's side. The headlamps again pierced the gloom at an odd angle that made even eerier their glare on the twisted trees.

"You done good," Sadie murmured. "And here comes your Will to tell you so."

He looked ashen, but then everything and everyone in this hideous environment appeared covered in ash and soot and gray slime. He rested one hand on the open window frame on the driver's side. Nandria covered it with her own. It was so cold she had to fight her urge to jerk away her hand from over his.

"Ahhh, that was a close one," Will told her, exhaling. He grinned with pride at her, and Nandria smiled from deep within herself.

"Good directions," she murmured. "I was only doing what you told me to."

He withdrew his hand to caress her cheek.

"You are so cold, Will."

"And I'm afraid you will be, too, sitting here waiting for us. This is as far as you dare go. I don't want to be the one to tell my father than I lost his truck in quicksand. I wish we could spare someone to lead you two women back to where it is safe. I will, if it gets worse, but for now your headlamps are a big help and we will leave it at that."

Ducking to nod quickly at Sadie Bean, Will touched his wife's cheek once more and mouthed the words, "Stay, please." He turned to slog back to the other men in his center section. Nandria watched as he gathered up the dangling partial line to rope in with Frank Paisler. Greg handed Will his lantern, and the three skirted a hulking tree. The women glimpsed them re-form the line of about seven men carrying forward into the deepening darkness. The play of the lanterns quickly became their only way of following their progress. The flashes of bared tree limbs diminished. Both women went silent, listening.

The sounds in the growing darkness grew eerier for having no discernible source. Night birds swooping, yes. That was at least familiar, although even at home, the underbelly of a near-silently soaring owl intent upon a scurrying rodent was enough to make one's skin crawl. Whatever belief in invulnerability an individual might have had was dispelled by the sounds of the night. Calls as of longing, of fear, of horror, of dying. That was reality, not the oblivious chatter around a wood stove with steaming mug of tea or chocolate in hand to warm one's soul. Grunts. Screams. The low swearing of the men fighting mud and slime and their own fear.

To his right, Will again heard Ron Bean call his daughter's name. All around him, the men stood silent, listening, longing, praying that the girl would answer. Then they would know she was alive, know where to go to find her. Nothing. Far up and down the line, knots of men separated now by the layout of this inhospitable land would set up their own cries of Ronda's name. Each member of the rescue posse breathed his own curse or prayed fervent wish to be done with this nightmare.

Will had sunk so deep within himself that he started when Greg spoke aloud just behind him.

"…if this d-don't w-wake up the town to what she's w-worth…"

"What?" Will twisted to look back. Greg's whole left side was coated with drying greenish-gray slime from the fall he'd taken testing the ground to their left at the base of a vine-choked stump. The vines had tendrils he hadn't seen. He was lucky that both his brother and Will had been tight beside him to yank him up. He had been lucky, but the staccato blips in his voice gave away the chill he'd sustained. He was shivering, though Will knew he would never admit to being cold. What he'd said came back to Will's mind, so he answered. "This town already knows what the Beans are worth."

"I-I meant-t your N-Nandria," Greg corrected him, then clamped his mouth to keep from stammering.

"Maybe," Will nodded his thanks, wishing even more than he longed to be done with this night, that that could be true. He looked back over young Paisler's shoulder toward the headlights of his father's truck where his wife sat, probably shivering as well. So like her to be right where she was needed most. He'd seen again and again the Brown family honor upheld by that dark, slender girl, often to her own discomfort or even danger. He wanted to send her home, but there was no home for them. Perhaps there never would be. So many saw only the color of her skin and missed the courage and integrity in that slight figure.

They blamed her in light of their own shortcomings. And they blamed him because he would not leave her but admired and loved her.

For a moment he stared at the fragmented headlamp light, beams shattered into streaks that glistened against rotting bark, then shifted as the growing wind tossed leaves and branches in irregular patterns and rhythms.

"Who…?" Greg cried.

"Shit!" his brother Frank swore aloud. "Them flittin' shadows about made me soil the one clean spot on my pants' behind."

"It's Yakes," Eli Paisler declared. "Know that pot belly of his anywhere."

"What's the sheriff doing, crossing between groups like that? He could step…" Will stopped without describing the image in his head of Yakes sinking in a pond of mire deeper than the bent man was tall.

"How you makin' out, Sheriff?" Eli greeted him as he slogged up to them.

"Any word on Miss Bean?" Greg wanted to know.

"Nah," the sheriff hawked and spat. "It's that woman of yours, Will Minnick."

"What? Is she all right?"

"Right as rain this time," he hawked again and looked at this man who'd married Negro. *She is somethin', all right, but still ain't sure just exactly what. Only now when she says something I listen. Didn't promise to act on it, mind you. But I listen and that's more'n I've done for a darky since I was a boy of eight. Mebbe ten.* "Your woman come sloggin' up bold as you please and said that Mrs. Sadie Bean recognized where they were—though how in tarnation she could, is beyond reckonin'—still, Sadie said she did, and to tell everybody that this here is the higher mass her folks called Snake Island. Mocs here, and throughout, she says. And rattlers. That don't make sense to me, but I guess I take Sadie Bean at her word. Anyway, your woman was walking all over like she owned the place to warn all the men. I told her to get back into that truck of your'n and to do it mighty quick. She did," he added with a glimmer of surprise in his expression.

"Water moccasins?" Frank cried. "Hate 'em worse'n pythons."

"Pythons? Around here? You crazy, Frank?"

"Whatever they are, they aren't going to be happy with us tromping on them, that's for sure," Will summed up.

"Rattlers like the dry, don't they? And mocs love the wet. So what're they both doin' here?"

"Not quite as simple as that, I guess, but Sadie Bean says there's patches of hot 'n' dry and wet pools and slow streams in and around the island, so you keep an eye out for both."

"And watch for what might look like vines hangin' down," Zeb Paisler cautioned. "My pa's told me he's seen more'n one what looked like a vine turn out to have a head with real nasty tiny eyes and fangs."

"J-just what we need," Greg sighed, and Will chuckled.

274

It was the break in the tension that they needed, and the men laughed, sketchily, but laughter nonetheless. After a moment, Greg joined in.

"What we really need is to find the girl," Will brought them back to reality. "No sound in answer to the calls of her name?"

Yakes shook his head, hawked again and this time spat a glistening wad against the nearest tree trunk. He watched it stick, then separate of its own weight and begin a slow slide.

"You're sure Nandria got back to the truck all right, Sheriff?" Will bent close to ask quietly.

"Took her myself, Will. Sadie'll keep hold of her from now on. Promised. Don't want nobody wanderin' out here. We'll be plumb lucky if we only lose one this night."

Greg straightened, erect and tense, but there was nothing to be said, even in protest. He rolled back his shoulders, lifting his chin to open his mouth to bellow at the sky. "Ronda! Miss Ronda Bean, you hear me? ANSWER ME, RONDA!"

Rustling noises and slithering close by startled them all. Then silence.

They looked at one another, and then away. Each man picked at the knots of his ropes rather than let his fellows see the anguish in his face.

And then, from the left, a cry. Excited voices. "Oh, God!"

Float

CHAPTER THIRTY-EIGHT

Greg bent, still as a sucker-punched statue. Frank Paisler thumped his younger brother on the back. "Hear that?"

"What do you hear?" Will demanded. He heard the excited voices as well, but he wanted to know if what he was reading into the clamorous sounds was what the others were hearing, too.

"They found her?" Greg asked, incredulous. He straightened slowly, head cocked, working to suppress the smile that threatened to take over his face.

"They heard something, that's fer sure," Yakes stated. "Couldn't be the girl. Couldn't be. Prob'ly a coyote. They can sound mighty human in the dark. I know."

Will put a hand out to ask the sheriff to be quiet. "They heard something. That's Isaac Owens' voice. It goes up an octave when he's really excited. I remember from when I was a kid."

They heard a high squeak: "She's answering!"

"Can't be," the sheriff insisted, but quietly.

"Use your whistle, Sheriff," Eli demanded. "Make everybody go still."

Yakes fingered in his pants pocket, then dug deeper under his paunch to extract his whistle. "Can't hurt to be sure," he muttered, not giving in that they could possibly have found the girl. He was doing this only to satisfy the urgings of the men around him, not that he believed it was so. He huffed, took another deep breath, and let loose a long, piercing whistle that reverberated off stunned and stunted trees. Shudderings and slitherings close by, then silence. The gray and black had seemed to shimmer in the sound, and then went dead.

The men held their breath. One truck engine they had not been aware of distinctly shut off, and the stillness crept into them with the cold.

Silence.

Long silence before a bird screamed, whether as predator or as prey, they could not tell. More than one man gasped at the cry.

And then men called from their right. Will and several others lifted their lanterns and flashlights to brighten the way for what emerged to be Dr. Ricartsen and Ron Bean picking their way over. Ron grabbed the sheriff's arm.

"Did they find her?"

"Now, it's too soon to get excited, Bean," the sheriff warned him. "Just some gibberish from over yonder there to our left, thinking they heard her answer Paisler's bellow. I think it was louder than my whistle. Swear it was."

"Was it Ronda?" her father demanded

"Nah, prob'ly not. You know how people-like coyotes can sound," Yakes coaxed him not to get his hopes up.

"But they did hear something?" Ricartsen demanded.

The sheriff shrugged. "Think they did."

"More likely a critter gettin' himself ate up in the night," Eli said, shaking his head.

"You know how much we all wanted any sound to be Ronda answering..." Will tempered their hopes with reality.

"Why don't you go on over there so you can hear for yourself?" Zeb suggested. "Nothin' less'll ever satisfy you."

"Will, you go with them," the sheriff directed. "You got training in rescue strategy, ain't you? And you, Greg. You got the penetratin'est call of any human in this county."

"We'll let you know to use the whistle," Greg promised, already manipulating his rope to include the doctor and Ron to his team with Will.

"Oh, I'll be along. Just my legs are tired of this muckin' along. Don't wanna slow you down."

"Frank, you go along with the sheriff," Zeb commanded his son. "Nobody ought to be moving alone in this."

"Right," Ron Bean settled their plans. "Come on, let's go."

"The good Lord be with you," Zeb told him quietly.

"It's gotta be R..." Ron murmured, then stopped himself as Will led their knot of men on what looked the most likely solid path he could guess.

The farther they strained to the left, the more the tired men in line were at least open to the possibility it had been Ronda answering Greg's call. Ron Bean found his breath choking at the back of his throat. He dared not hope. *But what if...?*

It was old man Nickleberg who stepped in front of the errant crew, commanding, "Call her, Ron Bean. She'll know your voice."

Ron stopped where he was and glanced at Will and the sheriff with Frank coming up behind them. Both nodded, neither with hope in his expression, but more of, "It couldn't hurt."

"Ronda!" her father bellowed. "Ronnie! It's Dad. Answer me, please!" Listening as though his life depended on it, he still added under his breath another, fainter, "please."

It seemed the entire forest of broken, eerie trees went silent. The men held their collective breath. Even the skitterings nearby went still. A shrill cry high, swooping above them was Ron's only answer. He looked up, and staggered. Will, next to him, slid a hand under his elbow to keep him upright. Ron glanced up at him with the devastation Will had only seen before on the face of his father.

"We'll find her," Will found himself saying low, although it defied all logic and probability. "We will."

"Yeah," Ron whispered finally. But his heart was no longer in this fight. Only his longing. He would keep going, but Will could see that he no longer believed that his Ronda would be found. The anguish in his eyes made Will step to one side to keep himself upright.

"With all due respect, sir," Greg was saying. Will looked over at the half-gray-green, shivering young man, grateful for the distraction. But Greg wanted Ron Bean's attention. "I know she'd answer if she could hear you. But that's just it, isn't it? I mean, I'm louder."

"You're younger, and a mite broader in the chest, I'll give you that, son," Bean agreed. "Holler. Make her hear."

Greg stood upright, lifting his shoulders and expanding his chest. He let out a piercing yell that scared the predators and prey that had only just settled in. "RONDA! YOU HEAR ME? ANSWER! WHERE ARE YOU, GAL?"

They held their breath.

It was as though the penetrating sound of his voice reverberated in tones of gray and green-black. "RONDA BEAN, ANSWER ME!" Then silence. And then a murmur and chaos of cries to Ron's left and forward, so deep in darkness beyond him it sounded like echoes from within a watery cave—or grave.

"What?" Ron looked over, his pale face drained now of all color, but his eyes bright again with hope that he knew was beyond reason.

"Sounds like the guys over there think they might'a heard somethin'," Sheriff Yakes allowed, though he was reluctant to credit it as a possibility. "Once more, you young bull, you!" he commanded Greg Paisler.

Greg inflated and bellowed so loud he seemed to send his soul out with his voice. Again silence, and then again, agitation from their left. Ron was already pulling on the rope at his waist to get the others to follow him there. They slogged, met and followed the excited voices. Yakes whistled and raised his arms up over his head. "SHIFT LEFT, EVERYBODY. SHIFT LEFT!"

They could hear the instructions being passed again and again down the line. Even as the men shifted awkwardly beside and behind them, Ron and his crew slogged on impatiently. Will quietly exerted pull on their rope to keep Ron more left than forward on his own until they got to someone who had actually heard a response.

Ahead was a knot of men surrounding a young man covered from head to toe with muck. He was wiping his face so his startling eyes gleamed golden from the side, even in this dim light. Ben Struan swiped again at his mouth and faced Ron Bean. "Heard somethin' for sure, that time," he yelled, spitting out mud.

Mr. Owens, who had been helping brush the crud off the youth, stepped back and held his lantern high as Ron approached.

"What'd ya hear?" Ron demanded. "How about you, Isaac? You hear my gal?"

"Young Struan here is sure, but me...Mebbe," Mr. Owens shrugged, unwilling to raise his friend's hopes. "Something, but not sure it was your gal, Ron."

"Prob'ly some cat form crying in the night," Yakes put in.

"Sure it was a girl," the slime-covered Struan insisted. "You're her dah, ain't ya?"

"Bean. Ron Bean." Ron lifted hands to both sides as though ready to introduce the others as well, but Struan waved impatiently. Niceties of introductions could wait.

"Look, Mr. Bean, I may be from all the way in Fox Haven, but I do understand English."

"English? You heard words?" Ron demanded.

"No cat form I know yells, 'Help!'"

"Oh, God!" Bean cried, and went suddenly quiet, gulping.

"You heard the word 'help'?" Will wanted to know. Some of the men nodded; others were not positive.

"Well, I heard it," the filthy youth insisted. "I started in after her but it drops off just about there," he explained, pointing. "If it hadn't been for these guys…"

"That's what the ropes are for, you young fool," Sheriff Yakes chided, but the tone was one of praise.

"Thank you!" Ron Bean breathed, then cleared his throat and mustered his strength to get things rolling forward toward his girl. "Glad you men were able to pull him out safe," he muttered, almost as an after-thought.

"How far in do you think she is?" Will asked, searching for practical clues to help direct their next step.

Bean cupped filthy hands to his mouth and hollered into the weird darkness. "RONDA! RONDA GIRL, do you hear me?"

As from a nightmare, a quavering wisp of sound came toward them. "Daaaddy? Daaaddy!"

"Cat forms don't yell 'Daddy' neither," the muddy youth smirked.

"How far in, you reckon, Will?" Yakes asked.

"My guess, near a hundred yards," Will figured. "But if it drops off there, we'll need to go around."

The men looked up, startled when a small group stumbled toward them. Sadie led, pulling along Nandria behind her and followed by Dr. Ricartsen. The men muttered, looking down or away. Women shouldn't be out here, not with things the way they were. But Ron Bean slogged joyfully toward his huge wife. "We heard her voice, Sade! She's alive!"

CHAPTER THIRTY-NINE

In the finally coming-into-focus chaos of men scrambling now to do what they'd been striving for without hope, the entire line bunched and shifted to concentrate behind the area where Ronda's "H-hurry, please, Daaaddy" was best heard. The stark skeletons of drowned trees seemed a brighter, stark gray, if only from the multiple gathered lanterns. Excited, still the men held themselves subdued so they wouldn't miss the girl answering her father's or Greg Paisler's repeated calls of encouragement. Shaking with miserable, penetrating cold, they shuffled in to stand on what solid ground they could find. Wide-eyed and slowly shaking their heads in dissent, they looked to the sheriff, who turned to Will.

"They don't wanna go 'round, Will," the sheriff put it to him. "You heard that gal; she sounds cold, and we gotta get to her quick. How we gonna do that?"

"Yeah, Will," someone called from the edge of the coven of men moving and slapping themselves simply to keep their circulation going. "You're Army. How we gonna do this?"

"She is sounding very cold and is probably badly dehydrated," Ricartsen conjectured quietly. "I'm not at all sure how long she can hold out."

Exhaling, Will glanced at Nandria for focus, but he was looking deep within his training, sorting between possible but bad options for the one most likely to work here with the fewest would-be rescuers maimed or lost. Nandria bit her lip and met his eyes, willing him to find the best solution. Praying for the safety of the girl she had come to admire and even love.

Anchor, Will thought. *Anchor the best we can and float a team willing to swim in this. Not Ron Bean. Much as he'll want to, he's too light to lead this parade. And we'll need floats. Yeah, wood. Fair-sized branches to cling to when you do step off. The wood'll hold us up for a while, even if it is quicksand we bungle into.*

"All right, then, we'll need double roping—and wood, branches, whatever will float—though I still say it's safer to find a way around. We don't know how far this deep spot extends. Maybe all the way to her. It'll be tiring—hell, it'll be exhausting— to swim out to her. Still want it that way?"

The men murmured, nodding, but looking at each other and then either down or out at the stricken trees. The thought of immersing in that cold muck was putting the damper on the enthusiasm of a number of them. Several dropped away to look for broken branches and wood.

"If that's the fastest…" Ron said aloud. Greg lined up beside and slightly behind him, nodding.

"Hell, I'm already acquainted with the slimy bitch," the mud-caked Struan cried, joining them. "Er, excuse me, ma'ams, for the French, if that's what it was. Never been to Paree, but I been in there," he pointed with vehemence at the murk, "and it names it pretty good, I'm thinking."

"Indeed it does," Sadie agreed, stepping forward also. "I'm one strong swimmer. Raised out here. No surprises for me, so count me in, Will Minnick." She stood tall beside her diminutive husband, ignoring his protests with a face granite with determination.

"Sadie," Nandria approached her to remark softly, "she will need you. After. Warm, comforting. She will need to be held close in your arms."

The granite face drew down, not so much softening as considering and growing unsure.

"She's right, Sade," Ron looked up to tell her. "Our gal is gonna need what only you can give her to be well again. Please?"

"Would you be willing to stay in reserve, Sadie Bean?" Will started, not wanting to spell out what might happen that would call for her to step in later. Reluctantly, Sadie peered at Ron, then nodded, face distorted with anguish. "Good, we'll need strong-backed, weak-minded men out front and even stronger-backed anchors and haulers behind them—all double roped, you hear me? Everyone. Double roped. No telling how much pull down there is in that muck."

"Might be a current down there we don't know about," Yakes called, and the men sobered considerably. That was not something most of them had contemplated. This wasn't going to be pleasant; probably even more unpleasant than they had thought about. With few words, they helped each other rope up—double—into a single line with small crews of four or five to one side and the other behind them for fast maneuvering and reinforcement if necessary. All were tied and retied, anchored to broad-beamed trees—several of them. Every man or pair held wood of some kind. At last, Will was satisfied, and nodded to the sheriff. Yakes raised his arms above his head and the main body moved forward.

Greg shouldered by Ron slowing to touch Sadie's arm as he jostled forward to be first in line.

"Think I can go ahead of you, Mr. Bean? I'm taller."

"And younger," Sadie pointed out.

"And stronger," Ron chuckled. "It's a fact. All right, go ahead. But let me warn you now, if I have to choose between doin' for my gal or you…"

"Better be Ronda, sir."

"As long as you know," Ron said low, nodding at the rightness of the young man's answer.

Sadie stepped back, almost into Nandria's arms, but standing stiff so her friend knew not to touch her, only to be there.

Greg started into the watery muck where the men were pointing. Sadie suddenly went limber and called out in strained voice. "Thank you! THANK YOU, ALL OF YOU!" She choked; the men, nodding, looked away.

Slogging, chilled, Greg led, followed closely by Ron Bean, then Will, Yakes, Struan, Frank and others. Will had started them out a bit left of where Struan had stepped over the drop off, so they'd only gone down to mid-calf but each was expecting with every step to be pulled deeper. Only the repeated calls to Ronda and her eerie whine-screech answers gave them the heart to keep laboring forward. Many grew peeved trying to manage their branch, until they stepped into the oblivion of nothing solid beneath their feet. Then they were glad for the buoyancy while they floundered and were hauled back by their companions. Greg, Ron and Will were swimming now, though their strokes were less than graceful. Doggy-paddle with their branch ahead and strong legs pumping. One by one, the men behind them went reluctantly horizontal as each came to the point where the bottom of the morass was far below his feet. More and more the job of calling to Ronda was left to the men still slogging as those deep in the cold mud and water were drained by their efforts to keep moving.

The growing shakiness of Ronda's answers spurred them on.

A snake slithered by on the surface of the water parallel to the line of men. Each gasped; many sputtered as he took an unexpected coughing swallow of muck. Progress slowed, then sped a little again as Struan doubled the front ranks, taking the lead with exhausted Greg Paisler. It was Struan and Will who spotted the bedraggled girl clinging to the stub of a branch on a splintered gray tree trunk.

"Oh, God!"

"Praise Heaven!"

"Ronda-gal! Ronnie, Ronnie, are you all right?"

"D-d-d-d-d-," she stammered, shaking violently as she was pulled into her father's arms.

Between their own chill and Ronda's near-frozen state, the men had quite a time unclawing her hands for her to let go of the splintered tree. She went limp in Ron's arms long before they'd freed her. As soon as she was tied securely to a makeshift raft and secured between them, they signaled back to be hauled in. Ronda knew none of it.

Float

Nandria and three men had been able to maneuver their trucks at least somewhat closer, so the exhausted rescuers were able to land the raft in the kaleidoscopically scattered beams of their headlamps.

Farther back, others had built a bonfire near the main body of trucks. It was there that they lowered the raft they were using as a stretcher and Ricartsen and Sadie took charge. Ron sat cross-legged on the ground holding Ronda's head in his lap. Nandria had water on to boil and had gathered as many blankets as she could scrounge.

The men huddled close for a while, but as no one was cheering and the girl did not sit up to give them the sight of her grateful smile, they began to tend to their own misery. Weary men stumbled back toward the edge of the bog to claim their own comfort and warmth and begin reloading their trucks to make their way home.

Above them, a bird of prey shrieked as though angry at having been cheated of the bounty that should have been his.

CHAPTER FORTY

Every electric light and hanging bulb in the lower floor of Doc Ricartsen's house blazed so the stark white walls menaced with a weird, artificial light much as the dying trees of the Bogs had. Most of the men were so mud-covered and filthy that they were ashamed to enter the doctor's house. They stood, wrapped in blankets, outside on the walk and lawn with their wives and families, talking together in small groups. Such a change from the festive groups who had chattered at Doc's party only the night before.

Truth be told, it was mostly the women doing the talking; the men swayed on their feet with fatigue. But none of the townsfolk would leave until they'd had word of Ronda's condition. They wanted a happy ending to this monumental effort and seeing the girl pale and still beside the bonfire had not promised that. The murmuring stopped and every person turned to look as Sheriff Yakes grumbled through their midst and up onto the porch stoop. No one greeted him; all merely stared.

Inside the house, Yakes glanced up at the eerily shining walls and shuddered, looking immediately down at the worn carpet his muddy boots were staining. Not that his were the first. Tracks and trails of glopped green-brown muck traced from the front door directly across the room to the exam room hallway. But the thought of his adding to the mess was enough to justify his stopping where he was. He pulled over the chair with the creaking arms and lowered himself into it to take off his boots.

But he'd slouched and stretched his legs out in front of him; the effort to draw them up to lean to unlace his boots simply took more energy than he had left once he was seated. His hips slid forward; he laid his head on back of the chair and was, almost immediately, snoring.

He never heard the few who had dared follow him into the house, even when, at their spouses' insistence, they took or kicked off their own filthy boots to kick them against the wall beside the front door. Both Mrs. and Mr. Owens, and the elder Paislers were among the crowd waiting. The oldest Paisler sons leaned against the wall. Young Sam sat beside his mother and fell to sleep against her shoulder as soon as they sat down. Yakes didn't stir even when Will Minnick and Greg Paisler shuffled in from the exam hallway. Will brought extra chairs from Dr. Ricartsen's office to accommodate the overflow crowd. Pastor Kylie strode in, newly arriving after taking the time to serve the women's food to the rescuers as they emerged from the bog. Kylie sank into the doctor's desk chair as it was the most comfortable of those available. The room buzzed for brief moments with murmurs between those waiting, then seeped in that dreadful hush usually heard at the entry to Fox Haven's hospital or Quail's Fine Funerals Parlor.

Snorting, Yakes startled awake at the stir caused by Ron Bean leading Nandria into the waiting room. Will stood and stepped forward to take his exhausted wife into his arms. The Owens rose as well, anxious to hear how Ronda was doing. Ron looked at the waking sheriff and his crusted, weary face nearly broke into a smile. He glanced around the room at these people who had worked so desperately to save his daughter. His eyes glistened with tears, but the turn-up at the corners of his mouth remained.

"Everyone, thank you," Ron rasped, his voice raw with fatigue.

"Your gal is doing all right then?" Mrs. Owens asked.

His head jerked in a nod. "Sleepin' now. She got a bad chill, Doc says. But he's pretty sure she'll pull through. And Sadie and me have you folks, and so many more, to thank for that. I—I don't know what to say..."

"Don't say anything at all, Ron Bean. That's all we wanted was to hear; that she's safe and on the mend."

He nodded again, and, head down, exhaled.

His neighbors and friends began to get to their feet and find their boots, many simply allowing their wives to carry the muddy weights rather than be bothered trying again to put them on, such was their weariness.

"Go back to them, Ron Bean," Cynthia Paisler counseled. "We'll tell the rest waiting outside. Time we were headin' home."

He nodded once more, convulsively, and turned on the ball of his right foot back toward the hallway and exam room where Sadie held their daughter while she slept.

At the doorway, the others stood aside to let the sheriff give the good news. "You done good, folks," he said, one hand on his belly and one lifted as though in benediction.

"The gal's good then, Sheriff?"

"Sound asleep," Yakes nodded vigorously, then waved the crowd away. No more needed to be said, and no one had the energy to question further for this night. Behind him, Pastor Kylie reached out to lay a meaty hand on the sheriff's drooping shoulder.

"So?"

"Huh?" Yakes turned to ask.

"So, what is the story? What was the girl doing in the Bogs in the first place? Why was such a young girl out by herself on such a night?"

"Where you been?"

Kylie drew himself up, forcing Yakes to step down from the door sill so the pastor towered even more above him. It took too much energy for Yakes to keep twisted, looking up and back. He lumbered down from the porch stoop, caring only that the clergyman had not been there to help in the swamp although he made much of himself delving into those baskets of food and handing it out as though he'd made every sandwich himself. Yakes lifted his free hand once more in a wave of dismissal as he stumbled down the walk toward home and, finally blissfully, hopefully, bed.

The crowd had already pretty much dispersed. Mrs. Drangler waited at the end of Ricartsen's walkway to help the stumbling sheriff toward home.

"Good night, Sheriff," Nandria said low as they passed. "Excellent leadership."

He hesitated a moment, then let himself be led on.

Will looked at her, eyes bright with appreciation. Frank Paisler patted him on the shoulder to say farewell.

"We'll take the hero home with us for the night. He can't drop into Fox Haven smellin' like he does now."

Struan grinned, further cracking the mud mask that still cling to most of his face. "I don't see why not. I told 'em I was comin' to Boonetown."

Laughing, Frank punched him on the arm, laughing again when he staggered. "Come on," he said, and Struan got up into the middle of the bench seat of the Paisler truck with Greg crawling in after him.

"Come, love," Will told Nandria gently. "You've done all anyone could do, and more." Nandria climbed zombie-like up onto the once-blue Minnick pickup. As he drove, Nandria slumped against him, weeping bitterly. Not until he'd reached the end of their farm lane did she pull herself up, drying her face.

"I am sorry, Will."

"For crying like a woman? I was waiting for you to, so I wouldn't have to. Don't you know how much I depend on your courage during the crisis and then on your being a woman afterwards?"

She moved closer again, both hands encircling his arms, head on his shoulder. As they passed under the overarching trees at the dip, he could hear her breathing go slow and regular. He carried her sound asleep in to their brass bed.

Float

CHAPTER FORTY-ONE

Another dry day. The wind hustled and bent the weeds under Minnick's hoe. He couldn't simply sit around waiting for who knew what now until Jim could get out to work on that blamed tractor. He stopped his rhythmic hacking at the clods that crumpled into dust that rose to clog his nose and stuff his sinuses. Swearing under his breath, he rubbed at the small of his back and glanced over at his son. His remaining son.

No use dwellin' on what never was gonna be anyhow, he scolded himself silently. But the grim set of Will's lips when his hacking with own hoe hit something hard and unexpected reminded Minnick that this young man with the widest stubborn streak he'd ever known was hurt more than he was saying. *But what to do about that? Telling him to ease off did nothing and earned nothing more than a scowl. The boy wants this farm sold and his father to move his mother into town. Doris wants it, too.*

Give up? Never!

But Minnick straightened, looking around at the rolling acres that had cost him his sons, his health—and hers—their lives. *We should have had more sons. Like them Paislers.* He glared at Greg Paisler. *This young buck ain't nowhere near ready to take on a farm this size. Sure, he's young and healthy and cock-sure he can handle whatever comes his way. But he don't know. Can't know. Any more 'n I did.* He hacked angrily at the indifference of the universe, no matter what they said about every sparrow falling to the ground being reckoned.

Sons. But I did have two. My part givin' both up's bigger 'n most ev'rybody else's...

It was Bodie who interrupted the goin' nowhere thoughts that had been plaguing Minnick for weeks. *For months, goin' on years, if truth be told.*

"Will ya lookee here now? Here comes the missus again, swingin' that there basket like she was a schoolgirl off on a lark with her friends."

Minnick twisted and lifted his hand to resettle his battered felt hat so the brim better shaded his eyes. Also to hide his profound reaction to seeing his gal now looking joyful as she had in those early days when they'd come to the farm. Full of hope. Full of surety of the fineness of the future. Never doubting the hard work, but so confident that it would pay off in prosperity. *We just didn't know that you don't own a farm; a farm owns you.*

But now here she was again, Doris Rose delighting in her pickaninny granddaughter and helping swing the picnic lunch basket with her dark-skinned daughter-in-law. Who would have thought?

Will and Greg hustled down the slope to greet and take the basket from them. Nandria touched Will's arm affectionately, then let him take Rose so she could spread the blanket out under the tree at the edge of the field.

"Seems so dry," she commented.

Will grimaced, nodding. "Won't be a profitable summer, most likely."

"What about all the farmers here who planted cotton?"

He shook his head and raised his eyebrows to warn her not to say anything in front of Greg, but Paisler had heard them. Shrugging, he, too, grimaced at Nandria, but said nothing rather than what had to be on the tip of his tongue: "I tried to tell them."

"Seems like we could use a good rain or two, Mr. Minnick," Doris observed as her husband helped her to sit down on one corner of the blanket near the basket.

"That we could, Mother."

Will helped Nandria sit on the other corner to assist with distributing the food. He settled in the grass and dirt with Rose on his lap. She reached up with small, pudgy hands to pull at his nose and earlobe, frowning at the sharp edge of the stubble of beard on his chin.

"Black dots," he told her. "And if you aren't a good girl, Daddy will give you those black dots," he play-threatened, jutting his jaw at her. She ducked and giggled. The adults laughed, Minnick, in particular, at the happy tittering of his wife. After all the years of her declining health, his whole being rejoiced in seeing her this way, but fortunately he was able to disguise that in the moments they bowed their heads while she said grace. "…this food to our use and thus to thine service. Amen."

They leaned in to take baked chicken parts and set chipped plates of potato salad on any flat surface. They would need to eat quickly before the ants took possession. When everyone had been served and conversation had stopped because of full mouths, Nandria reached into the basket for the thermos. She poured fresh-squeezed lemonade into each cup, many missing a handle or showing a faint beginning of a crack. But they were still lemonade-tight and needed to be used out here in the field, as there was no money to replace them with better cups. Each man took the drink gratefully. As Nandria finished pouring, she studied Bodie—another stubborn member of the family who was obviously hurting more than he was saying. He would do his share, no matter the cost to himself.

Is this farm worth that? The health and lives of each of these obstinate people? She shook her head as she stoppered the thermos and set it beside the basket. *But the British are not that much different, are they? They are probably the ones who taught these colonists the "stiff upper lip." If only now they could teach these Americans that they are going to be part of this war the Nazis have brought upon us. Sooner, rather than later, if they are to be most effective in their assistance.*

Swallowing the irony of her chiding Americans for not playing their part when she was here in Missouri rather than England, Nandria glanced at Rose content in her father's strong arms. He'd given her bread to gnaw on, and the mash of crumbs and drool coated her lower face like a pasted-on beard.

Without the child to protect, Nandria had no doubt that she would return to England once Will had been deployed again. But now? Nandria startled from her own thoughts as Doris wiped her hands on her oversized cotton napkin and asked, "How is the girl doing? Sadie Bean's gal."

Chapter Forty-One

"Your folks hear any news?" Minnick asked Greg.

"How would they hear, Mr. Minnick?" Doris giggled. "Must have awful good ears."

"We got a phone on the party line," Greg explained once more. "Pa said it was cheaper to do that than to let his boys sneak off into town to check up on their fancies and be missin' work so much."

"But do you know anything about Ronda's condition this morning?" Nandria questioned.

Sheepishly, Greg lowered his chin to answer. "Well, yeah. I had Ma call Sadie at Doc's office before I come over here." He blushed as the Minnicks and Bodie chuckled at his embarrassing admission. It would be early in the morning for such a call, even for Sadie Bean.

"You talked to thet gal yet, Greg Paisler?" Bodie taunted.

"Well, yeah, sure. You seen me."

"Thet's not the talk what I'm talkin' 'bout, and you knows it."

"So how is Ronda doing this morning?" Will interrupted.

"Well, Ma says Sadie says Doc thinks she might be headin' into p-neumonia. Her chest's rattlin' some, and I guess that's no surprise to nobody considerin' how cold and miserable she was for so long."

Doris put her hands to her face. "Oh, my, that's too bad."

"Yeah, but Sadie told Ma that her gal is strong and'll come out of it good."

"And how is Sadie?" Nandria asked.

"You know Sadie. She'd never tell you if she was walking around on a broke leg."

"You admire a strong woman, Paisler," Will commented, looking at his Nandria.

"Yeah. Woman or man," Greg answered.

* * * * * * * * * * * * * * * * * * *

That evening, the sun was just dropping the last gleaming arc below the horizon as the Minnick pickup parked beside the Paislers' near the end of Doc Ricartsen's property. As the family started up the walk, the older Minnicks were greeted by neighbors clustered on Doc's lawn. Sheriff Yakes, in consultation with a group near Doc's front stoop, saw them coming and broke away from those men to hurry toward them, his right hand outstretched to Minnick and then to Will.

"This town done good, working together," the sheriff exclaimed.

"Always has," Minnick replied.

Under his breath, Will murmured, "Uh, oh," and Nandria took Rose from him and slipped behind him as Pastor Kylie approached.

"He wears that there turned collar like a king wears a crown," Minnick muttered. "Like we should be bowin' down before him or somethin'."

"Oh, look, Mr. Minnick," Doris chirped. "It's our minister comin'."

"So I see."

"Evenin', Reverend," the sheriff bellowed, still in expansive mood. "Heard about our gal? I didn't see ya out at the Bogs, don't think, 'cept handin' out food."

Kylie stiffened. "I had just returned from Fox Haven. I regret not being there sooner to help find the girl. Such a tragedy."

"Tragedy?" Doris clutched Minnick's arm. "I thought you said she was gettin' better, Mr. Minnick?"

"Only thanks to the Lord for saving wayward children," Kylie pronounced.

"Humph," Minnick cleared his throat. "I thought this here town had somethin' to do with that there savin'."

"Well, naturally, man can act as instruments of His mercy. I prayed about it."

"That would make a difference," Will said low.

"Thank you, Brother Willard. I suspect it is not often in your line of work that you see the power of prayer."

"Mebbe it matters who's doin' the prayin' and how," Bodie suggested with innocence written from his receding hairline to his boney jaw.

Nodding at the praise he took from an unexpected source, Kylie could only murmur, "I'm sure the Lord sees m..." when Dr. Ricartsen's door opened from the inside. Everyone stopped and turned to look.

Ron Bean was talking to Mr. Owens right behind him as he stepped onto the stoop. He turned to look out as Owens halted, mouth dropping open.

"Why, folks!" Bean exclaimed. "So many of you. I—I thank you. She's sleeping sound now, and I…" But he could say no more, so he hurried down the steps and out onto the lawn to shake the hand of every man there, excepting that something seemed to deflect his path each time he neared Kylie. Other townsfolk crowded close, forcing him to stop. "Ah, folks, so glad you come so me and the missus could thank you. Everybody get that slime washed off okay?"

"The Lord," the pastor began low, but audibly. As people quieted and half-turned toward him, his resonant voice increased in volume. "The good Lord truly washes his saints even of their hidden sins, if only they will confess and beg his forgiveness."

Ron Bean widened his stance and stood gaping at the minister.

"Hidden sin?" Yakes questioned, confused. "What hidden sin, Reverend?"

With a long glance at Ron Bean, Kylie shook his head slowly. "Of course, I know of no particulars."

Bean's mouth closed. His hands clenched and lowered straight down his sides, but he kept his voice edging on civil. "You thinkin' of my Ronda, Mr. Kylie?"

The pastor lifted his chins and looked down his nose at the diminutive man. "I am saying nothing against the girl," he started, and Ron visibly began to relax until Kylie, looking around at the gathered neighbors, continued. "Only just wonderin' with the rest of us here, what might a young girl be doing in the Bogs alone at night?"

Most of the gathered crowd twisted so they could see Ron Bean's reaction. Ron's mouth dropped open in quick retort and his hands re-clenched into fists. He swallowed then and lifted his own chin in defiance. "I hear tell that wonderin' is good for the digestion." Closing his mouth but not opening his fists, Bean stalked past Pastor Kylie and around the crowd on the walkway and on down the street toward his home without another word.

At the murmured responses of the townsfolk, Kylie raised his hands as though in blessing. "Charity, Christian neighbors," he intoned. "Charity." Touching the turned collar to ease his chins settling against it, Kylie strode to the door and, knocking low but not waiting for an answer, entered Ricartsen's house. In his wake gathered neighbors stared at each other and murmured among themselves.

Doris pulled on Minnick's arm. "Pastor didn't pray for us."

"Pastor best pray fer hisself," Bodie said under his breath. "Didja see Greg Paisler's face just now?"

Float

CHAPTER FORTY-TWO

"Is we still goin' in, Mr. Minnick?" Bodie asked as they hesitated awkwardly near the front door to Dr. Ricartsen's house and clinic.

Minnick looked ready to lead Doris to the truck and go home, but Will knew how much Nandria wanted to be sure that her young math student was recovering.

"Nandria, why don't you slip in and see if Sadie is there?" Will asked, but she turned to him, shaking her head gently. "Well, no, maybe that isn't the best idea, seeing as how we Minnicks seldom bring out the best in the good pastor."

"Especially you," Minnick agreed with her gruffly, ignoring his own effect on Kylie. "Lemme step in. You folks wait by the truck."

As Minnick bulled his way to the front door and inside, the rest of the Minnicks moved to one side of the walkway. They stood, Doris fussing with her skirt and wringing her hands. Bodie sidled even farther toward the street. Mrs. Drangler emerged from the crowd of people, the shortest of whom, except for the youngest children, was half a head taller than herself. She hustled up to Doris.

"Evenin', Doris Minnick," she murmured as she settled in beside her. "Got your family warm and dry again by now? That was some town undertaking, wasn't it?"

"Why, Mrs. Drangler, so good to see you. I hear you took good care of our Sadie Bean and her home for 'em. Thank you kindly for that."

The woman chuckled until the pins in her collar glittered. She raised a sore-fingered hand in deprecation of her efforts.

Doris frowned. "My mister went on inside. You think he'll come back?"

"For you, Doris, always. He's just checkin' on the Beans, most like."

"But that was Mr. Ron Bean just stalkin' past a minute ago, wasn't it?" She gaped at Mrs. Drangler, beginning to be frightened in her bewilderment.

"Well, so it was," Mrs. Drangler said, but Will and Nandria saw her expression and drew in close.

"He may need a word from a friend about now," Will said quietly. "Do you think we should walk over to his place and sit with him a while?"

Nandria, her eyes glistening with tears, brushed her cheek against his shoulder. "Do you hear what is being murmured?"

Will concentrated on the words from knots of townsfolk: "What was she doin' out thet way?" "Such a young gal out there all by herself." "That's the question, ain't it? Was she all by herself?" "We was asking ourselfs that back home at the kitchen table." "That Ronda Bean's always been a feisty one." "Such a big gal." "No grace at all…"

Nandria bent forward to whisper. "No one was voicing such derogatory remarks…"

"...until the good pastor brought up the subject and put doubt into their minds."

"Oh, Will, nothing will be the same for Ronda in this town regardless of whether or not she recovers from her physical challenges from her long chill exposure. Gossip and rumor can be so devastating."

At the corner of Ricartsen's walkway and the edge of the road, Mr. Owens' scowl grew deeper as he shook his head, listening. He cleared his throat and said rather loudly to his wife standing close beside him, "The Bean family has always been steady neighbors, don't you think, Bernice?"

"Oh, yes, Isaac, steady and true. Always."

A few in the crowd looked over and then down, shame-faced. All startled as Ricartsen's door opened; they looked up expectantly. After a moment, the doctor showed the unruly hair of the back of his head as though he were about to back out when called by someone in his lobby. The brown hair disappeared, but a moment later, the doctor's long face appeared. "Oh!" He startled as though fearful another party was gathering in his yard. "Ah!" he exhaled, spotting Will and Nandria. He beckoned them to him. "Will, Sadie'd like to have your missus come in," he declared, and then, without a word to the rest of the crowd, face and long, lanky body disappeared inside again.

Doris Minnick questioned, "Did he say how the girl is doin'?"

Will took his mother's hand and settled it on his arm as Nandria hurried toward the front door. Inside, Nandria slipped behind the pastor and the sheriff sitting close with their elbows resting on their bent legs, talking intently with red-faced, frowning Grover Minnick. Grateful for the distraction of their argument, she angled through the lobby to the back hallway and into Ronda's room. Sadie sat in a straight-backed chair close beside her daughter. She looked up; her frown turned to relief when she saw who had entered.

"Ah, Miz Minnick, it's you. The gal is asleep again now, but she was awake a bit ago. She knew us both. Her mind is good."

There was such deep relief in the statement, that Nandria realized how anxious Sadie had been on that point. She nodded, smiling, and, at Sadie's gesture, sat carefully on what had evidently been Ron Bean's chair in the corner.

"My Ron went on home for some sleep. Too worn. I worry about him. Always givin' of himself way past what he ought'a be doin' for his own sake. I made him go. Ah, my gal's stirrin'... I was sure she'd wake up pretty soon again."

Ronda's head twisted on the pillow at the sound of her mother's voice. Ricartsen must have been hovering just outside the doorway. His haggard face studied Ronda a moment before he leaned back into the hallway.

"Sheriff, I think she's comin' around again," he called and then entered to lean over to examine his patient.

Nandria heard chairs scraping on the wooden floor as the men evidently rose to come to Ronda's room. Ricartsen bent to listen with his stethoscope. He frowned and shook his head. Sadie stiffened.

"Now, Miz Bean, it still rattles, but no worse than last night, I'd say. Nothin' more'n we expected."

Sadie bent close over her daughter's chest and listened for herself. She straightened again, nodding, but obviously not satisfied that the errant lung sounds were no worse than they had been. She shook her head at the noise the men were making as they shuffled into the hallway to look in.

Sheriff Yakes peeked, nodded to Sadie and stepped to one side against the door frame. Minnick backed against the far wall where he could glimpse inside the room, but Kylie brushed past the sheriff and entered as far as his bulk would allow. Sadie shifted in her chair so her leg blocked any further progress unless he was willing to bump her. She wasn't sure whether or not he would, but she braced herself, ready. Only Nandria, from her corner, seemed to recognize when Minnick left the hall.

"Mama?" Ronda whispered and all attention focused on the awakening girl. Sadie leaned to gather her child in her arms.

"Good," the doctor exclaimed. "Hold her up a second while I listen at her back, will you, Mrs. Bean?"

"Here, pretty chirrup," Sadie whispered, holding her.

Ronda blushed at seeing how many people were there to hear her mother call her the childhood endearment. "Oh, Ma," she whimpered, then saw Nandria's gentle smile and focused on that until the doctor had finished his poking and listening.

"Well, Dr. Ricartsen?" Sadie demanded as he stood up, folding the tubes of his stethoscope. Everyone's attention swiveled to the hallway as Minnick returned with his wife and son, carrying Rose, and Bodie at the last, ducking to be able to see in at all.

"Why didn'tcha just open the front door and let in the whole town?" Yakes complained. "How'm I supposed to question the gal with everybody snoopin' in on our conversation?"

"Just come to see she was all right," Doris placated. "We'll leave this here minute once we're sure the gal is right as rain, won't we, Mr. Minnick?"

"Come in, come in, Mrs. Minnick," Ronda invited, growing quickly breathless. "So sorry—I caused you s-such a—lot of bother." Her face flushed when she saw Greg Paisler slide in behind Will Minnick in the hallway.

"No trouble, now that you're pink-cheeked and smilin'," Doris protested kindly. "'Sides, it wasn't us who pulled you out'n that mud. It was my boy, here."

Ronda leaned into her mother to be able to stay upright in the bed. She nodded at Will, then turned again to Nandria. "Oh, Miz Minnick, I hear you drove truck for Mama up there, and everything."

Caressing Ronda's bare forearm a moment, Nandria answered quietly. "A great number of people worked hard to be sure you were found safe."

"The Lord is merciful and kind," Kylie intoned, and heads bowed as though on command. His droning prayer was cut short, however, when Ronda coughed and could not stop coughing. Something stirred within her when she could glance up and see the stricken look on Greg Paisler's face.

"Amen," Will interjected when Kylie slowed to inhale. "Amen," the others dutifully echoed and raised their heads. Minnick nodded at his son and herded his wife and handyman to leave the hallway.

"So glad she's safe," Doris called back to Sadie.

"Thank the Lord," Sadie breathed in answer, laying her girl gently back onto the bed to rest.

Sheriff Yakes pushed his way around the preacher, who was forced then to step back to the hall. Ricartsen eased his way to the door sill but stood there to watch.

"Glad you're awake and able to talk, little lady," the sheriff huffed. "You sure you want all these people here while I ask ya a few questions?"

"Just wish Papa was close."

"He's sleeping, child. But we can send for him, if you want."

"Oh, no, Mama, don't let anybody wake him. He looked so tired…before," she finished lamely, evidently confused as to the time of day, or night. She turned her head to the sheriff. "Why can't they stay, Mr. Yakes? Papa says they were all there to help me."

"Folks come all the way from Fox Haven to help look. What was thet boy's name? The one covered with mud like some statue of wet clay?"

"Stru. Ben-something Struan, I think," Greg offered when no one else could supply the name.

"He swallowed just about half the Bogs stepping right out for you when they first heard you answer Greg's bellows," Will chuckled. "Went completely under before they could haul him back."

"Was he hurt?" Ronda and Sadie demanded in unison.

"Nah, just slimy," Greg laughed. "We hosed him off good before Ma'd let him in our house for the night."

"But the one who worked hardest to rescue was this young man here," Will stated, much to Greg's embarrassment.

"You helped?" Ronda gasped, in tears, watching him confirm his part by the tightening of his lips.

"A lot of people helped," Sadie said. "Your pa's earned us Beans a lot of respect over the years, Ronnie." Hearing footsteps in the hall, she blushed to realize her Ron might well have heard her praising him as he entered.

Yakes shifted to let Ron in to crowd against his wife.

"You're awake, my girl. How are you feeling?"

"Lucky, Pa. I don't think I'll ever feel clean again, though." She coughed, and Ron looked pained to hear the rattle from deep within her.

"Sure you will," Sadie soothed. "Soon as the doc here says your lungs are strong enough, I'm gonna take you home and scrub you harder 'n that time you got into the molasses when you were a tyke."

"That was some mess," Bean nodded with a strained smile.

"Well, all right then," the sheriff broke in, seeing the girl visibly tiring. "You up to tellin' what happened last night?"

"I'm sorry, Mama. I didn't feel good," Ronda whispered, glancing at Greg Paisler.

"We knew you was under the weather all day," Bean said. "That professor told us he sent you on home, you looked so bad, so we thought you went on to the Minnicks."

"I didn't want baby Rose to catch nothing, so I went for a walk," Ronda stated, then coughed. She stopped to look at the incredulity on the faces around her. "Out in the country where there wasn't nobody to make sick."

"To the Bogs?" Yakes questioned.

"No, no. I don't go there. Snakes."

"But that's where we found you," Sadie reminded her softly.

"I seen Pastor Kylie's horse running loose. He sets a store by that mare, so I thought I couldn't just let her run away like that."

"Your mare loose, Preacher?" Yakes demanded.

"I—I don't know. I'm just back from pastoral duties in… around."

"You ain't checked your animal? Even today?"

Kylie looked so drained that Sadie took a brief moment of pity for him and urged Ronda on with her story to divert the sheriff's attention. "Go on, Ronnie."

"S-she's fast. I couldn't begin to catch up until she was already in the Bogs, and gettin' deeper."

"You went in after the animal?" Yakes was aghast.

"She was so scared. I tried to lead her..." Ronda coughed again. This time she lay back against the pillow for some minutes before she could continue. "She wouldn't come. Then I felt we was sinkin'," Ronda whispered, shuddering.

Everyone waited quietly until she could continue.

"Oh, Mama, I was s-scared. Tried to climb a tree. But it broke. I climbed on that mare. On her back to try to reach higher, but that branch broke, too. Oh, Mama," she cried. Sadie held her as she wept.

The others glanced at Kylie, and then away. Except Ron Bean who stared at the pastor full face. "Brave gal; fool owner of a horse," he said low before turning to comfort his wife and daughter.

Ricartsen motioned the others out. Kylie stormed through the front door, leaving it ajar behind him. Ricartsen closed it and slipped into his office. He sank into his desk chair to fiddle with his radio dial. The others stood in a numb circle in the lobby, listening to the plaintive voice telling them: "...days now of every craft that floats crossing the English Channel to ferry home our brave but desperate troops. French forces remain in place to cover...monstrous losses..."

"Most of the men saved, thank God," Dr. Ricartsen moaned. "But all that gear and equipment. How are the Brits going to fight now? With their bare hands?"

"If we need to," Nandria murmured.

CHAPTER FORTY-THREE

Greg Paisler strolled up Dr. Ricartsen's walk just as Ron Bean was escorting Nandria from the clinic to the battered blue truck. "Miz Minnick," Greg lifted his cap and held it in two hands. His stricken expression was nearly more than Nandria could cope with.

"Greg," she managed, and then fled to the vehicle and away.

Silent, the two men watched the truck disappear. It was more than a minute before Greg reset his cap and took a lungful of air before facing the diminutive man he admired.

"Think she'll be up to goin' home soon, Mr. Bean?"

"Ronda? Well, I don't know, Greg. The p-neumonia is slow clearing up. It's like she ain't thawed yet, but she is some better. I'm gonna have to go back to my milk route startin' tomorrow. The guys at the dairy have been terrific about splittin' up my deliveries for me, but there comes a time..." Ron Bean stopped to look at the young man who had given so much of himself to find Ronda. *It's a wonder he wasn't laid up with p-neumonia himself. Now why was he so...?* "You'd like to see her, wouldn't you? Why don't you go on in?" *Ronda was tickled pink to have you bring her home from studying at Minnick's. At least for while there. Lately she's been all but rude. There comes a time when whatever it was went wrong between these two got to be talked out.* "Go on, young man. She's strong enough now, I reckon."

Float

Greg hesitated before steeling himself to knock on the doorframe of Ronda's room. He could hear Sadie washing up dishes or surgery tools in the back kitchen. And he could hear—without understanding the words—the drone of Doc's radio behind his office door. News of the war, no doubt, but Greg was wrapped up in his own war. He dreaded the girl's rejection, but he needed soon to find out exactly what he'd done to make her so anxious to keep him out of her life. He knocked and stepped into the doorway so she'd know who it was.

"Hello, Ronda. How are you feeling?"

She smiled first, then scowled, he saw. He frowned and entered though she hadn't invited him.

"You're lookin' stronger. That's good."

Her sharp response made him step back and blink.

"Ida Jane give you permission to come here, did she?"

"Why would Ida Jane give me permission to do anything?"

"I can't exactly picture Miss Freshstalk letting her fiancé loose to go call on another gal."

"Her fiancé?"

"I know she's engaged to young Mr. Paisler," Ronda snooted.

"Oh," Greg laughed, but quieted, smiling, when she glared at him. "She is. But I'm not that young Mr. Paisler. My brother Frank is the lucky guy. Not me."

"Oh!" Her stricken face told him all he needed to know.

* * * * * * * * * * * * * * * * * * * *

Nandria did not look up from her slow swinging under the elm. Neither did she resist Will's effort to lift her into his arms to dance with her in her anguish. After a few moments, he tried to speak. "We knew it was coming."

"I know," she murmured.

"Ever since the courage of those French troops and resistance fighters who stayed to cover the Dunkirk escape, there simply isn't enough left to them to defend themselves. Paris is going to fall. If I can do anything to help, I have to go, love."

"Yes." She lifted tear-glistened eyes to peer at him. "But I am here."

"What?" He took her face in his hands and lifted it to study. It wasn't until he recognized her guilt that he understood. "You are here, my darling, because I need you to protect my little Rose, and her little…brother, do you think?"

"But…"

"No, love, no 'buts.' You've heard your own parents say it. We must protect the next generation. We fight, but we also find whatever safety we can for the children. Ned would have been here, too, and he'd have needed you, even more. That's for sure. A young Negro male in Boonetown? All the uncomprehending white faces he'd have had to deal with hereabouts…"

"I know," she whispered, shaking her head, allowing the tears to flow unheeded down her cheeks. "But…" She shook her head, then leaned it against his chest and he drew her to him, hugging her in a swaying dance as the retiring sun lingered a moment, then disappeared behind the west hill.

* * * * * * * * * * * * * * * * * *

The soft dark just before sunrise was stricken by the sudden glare of the bulb hanging over the kitchen table. Minnick glared at his son working at the stove.

"You here? Whatcha doin' working in the dark?"

"It's not that dark," Will said, turning the sizzling bacon. "I guess I have good rods in my eyes for dark vision."

"Huh? Sounds painful."

"No, Pa, it just means the light receptors in the back of my eyes are better for distinguishing light than for, say, colors."

Minnick frowned; Will shrugged.

"Anyway, I was seeing well enough to get breakfast started. Have a seat, if you're brave enough to try my cooking."

Seating himself under the glare of the still-swaying bulb, Minnick drew a knife and a fork from the piles beside the stack of plates Will had left on the center of the table.

"Coffee's ready," Will sang. He left the bacon hissing angrily and carried over two mugs and the tall pot. He poured for his father and then himself. "Eggs over easy?"

Minnick nodded, sipping to taste the hot coffee. Again he frowned, but was careful to have his expression bland when Will looked over again from the stove. They listened to the egg protein protest at being suddenly dropped into searing hot bacon grease. Will stood poised over the skillet with the metal pancake turner.

"So where's...?"

"I let her sleep," Will answered, keeping their fragmented conversation low.

Minnick held out his plate as Will approached with the skillet in his left hand and flipping the eggs with the other. Miraculously, both eggs and five strips of bacon landed on the plate without introduction to the linoleum floor. But as Will returned to the stove to dish up his own plateful, Minnick rose to carry his portion over and flop it back into the skillet.

"Sorry, Pa."

"The gal does it better, but you're all right. Just a mite in a hurry to get done with the job." Minnick stirred and flipped. He reached into the icebox for the pancake batter and poured out four large ones onto the bacon grease as well. "Glad you let her sleep. She's been lookin' peaked. So," he said, flipping one pancake toward Will, who had to catch it on his plate or do without. Minnick settled the rest of the food onto his own platter and set the skillet to the edge of the stovetop away from the heat. "So," Minnick repeated as he came back to his place at the table, "what are your plans? You gonna stay and help rebuild this here farm?"

"That was never a possibility," Will stated without emphasis, knowing that his father had understood that all along.

"It'll rot here without you," Minnick stated around a mouthful of pancake and egg. "You know that."

Will nodded.

"Army calling you back, is it? Doc gonna let you go?"

"Any time now." Will laid down his fork and knife on the edge of his plate. "Pa, I'm sorry, but my farming here was never going to be. At least," he added when he saw his father's expression cloud, "at least not since—not since Winfred's death. There's no sense in going over that again. What we need now is to figure out the best way to go from here—without me."

"They sendin' you anywheres you can take the gal? And that pickaninny? Now, don't you go gettin' riled with me. That's your own doin'. You chose. You live with it. And that's what it is."

"That pickaninny is my daughter."

"I know it. Already showing some of the stubborn streak you had growing down your back since you wasn't much higher than she is now. That ain't the issue. She's only part white, and that puts her in deep manure for a lot of folks around here. It's a fact you gotta deal with."

Will let out his breath slowly. Finally, he nodded. "Worst part," Will said low, "there's a good chance I won't be around to help her face it."

"They're sending you back out to get shot at again," Minnick stared at him. "You knew that was comin'."

Pressing his lips into a straight line, Will nodded. "From what's happening across the Pond, I'd say most likely."

"Which brings us back around. You're plannin' to leave the gal here, with the pickaninny?"

"Lord, Pa, I don't know. I honestly don't know what's best to do. When I was fairly sure I'd get assigned just outside of D.C.—Washington, D.C.—then, even knowing the prejudice there, Nandria and Rose would have come with me. But if I'm going back to Europe…"

"So it depends on the Army."

Chapter Forty-Three

"Pretty much, I guess."

"And if you're right and this country is gonna get dragged in, how am I gonna support your ma, let alone your wife and child if I don't have the cows and the chickens and the garden here on this farm?"

"And how can you keep all that going alone?" He'd thought about that; he had. But the enormity of the problem from his father's perspective only now swept over him.

"You're gonna say somethin' about the Paisler boy, ain't ya?" Minnick questioned.

"He is interested in buying in, if not outright."

"How long will he last?"

"Greg Paisler will keep his word, Pa. If he agrees to something—to help you on whatever terms you agree on—then he'll stick to it as long as he has breath."

"I know he'd mean to, Willard. He'll be a fine man. But he's young. Got ideals. How long you suppose he'd be able to stay out of signin' up like you done? Now Winfred, on the other hand, that boy was born to run a farm."

Will went silent. *The old accusation that I got Freddy killed. Or not. Pa knows better now, finally. That it was a ghoulish accident.* But Will sat absorbing the guilt he'd borne all his adult life and only recently laid down, however briefly. He looked up to see his father peering at him.

"You know I'm right, Willard. For a decade this section of Missouri'd clobber anybody even bring up the subject of this country lookin' cozy at Europe. After the Great War, and that

323

greater Depression we're still fightin', nobody wanted to even think about bein' part of the world." Grover reached for the coffee pot, poured, and then thought better of drinking what was in his mug. That gal was far the better cook in Will's family.

Grover heard his son exhale slowly as Will realized his father had not been accusing him again of Fred's death. Minnick shook his head and went on with his train of thought. "Far as I'm concerned, we'd be better off just forgettin' that any land or peoples beyond our oceans even exist, so you know I'm in a stew when more 'n more I hear people right here in Boonetown and farms between here 'n Fox Haven talking like we ought'a get in this here war they got goin'—again. Now, I know your gal feels for her England. But nobody in Europe is a concern of mine. Got enough right here where I'm at. With my farm dying under my feet. Wife—who knows what's wrong?" He shrugged with a sigh that would have broken her heart, had Doris heard and understood.

"I know, Pa."

"You bringin' home that radio…"

"It's your home. You didn't want to know…"

"But you gotta."

Will nodded.

"You'll be goin' back into that whole blamed mess, and I'm like to lose you, too. Your gay Paree ain't the only one fallin'."

"So what do we do for Nandria and Rose?"

"And the new one comin'," Minnick reminded him.

Each lifted his mug of now-cold coffee and sipped without tasting it.

CHAPTER FORTY–FOUR

The heat of the day had sapped them to the point that Minnick had to order Bodie to go home. Without the tractor, the work was pure drudgery with hoe and spade and sweat heading toward heat exhaustion, though neither Will nor Greg would admit to Minnick how near he was to falling down. And neither admitted that he heard the older man groaning under his breath.

The myth of male invincibility, Will all but chuckled. *I wonder how many boys and men that had killed, each proud to go under in silence.* He stood a moment, leaning on his hoe. "Now, why isn't that sad rather than a thing of pride?" he muttered.

"Huh?" Greg took a grateful moment to stop and question. "You see them?"

"What?"

"I didn't catch what you said."

Will gaped at him, unaware he'd spoken aloud. Shaking his head, he looked away down the field and saw his saving grace in the form of his mother and wife, with child strapped to her chest. They were trudging up the hillock carrying the huge picnic basket between them. He only hoped they had remembered water—and salt tablets. The faintness he was sure his father and Greg were feeling as much as himself, was not merely nauseating. It could prove humiliating, and Will had hoped to end this home sojourn with his father's respect.

"Ah, the myth of male invincibility," he muttered in a raspy voice. At Greg's odd expression, he laughed again, jerking his thumb toward his womenfolk. "I'm ready for a rescue by the ladies. Aren't you?"

Greg lifted his hand to the visor of his cap. "So there they are. Looks like they could use a hand on this slope." He loped down the hill to help them with the basket, proving to Will once again that even a few years younger meant a great deal when it came to strength and endurance.

Minnick glanced over at his son, followed his gaze down the field to the women and staggered over to stand panting in scraggly shade. Will joined him.

"Isn't she beautiful?" Minnick murmured, and Will studied the slender figure of his wife. "I never get over the wonder, just looking at her."

Will's eyebrows raised of themselves, surprised to hear his father sing the praises of his colored daughter-in-law. Not that he didn't agree completely with the assessment. And then it dawned on him that Minnick was speaking of his own wife.

Studying his mother for a moment with his father's prejudice, Will said, "They are that, and so much more," he added low.

Greg had Doris giggling as he sat her beside Minnick in what shade there was. He poured out a goodly portion of water to everyone while Will helped Nandria spread the lunch.

Doris rummaged in the pocket of her printed cotton dress. "I remembered these salt tablets, Mr. Minnick," she said as she handed them to him. "Though it seems to me that this summer we are faster runnin' low on 'em then usual."

"We'll need to get more. Remind me, will you?" he said automatically, and then wondered whether she would be able to do that. She was doin' better this spring and summer than she had for some years. He glanced over at Will and his woman. *It's that girl's doin', taking the stress off Doris so she can function with the best she still has in her. A darky, but not like no other darky I ever heard tell of.* Shaking his head, Minnick took another long swallow of the blessed water with his salt tablet. He passed the bottle over to Will. "All packed for this after, Willard? We'll only get another couple hours in now before we need to leave for that train."

"Yes, sir." Will nodded, handing a tablet to Nandria and passing the bottle on from her to Greg.

Wiping the last of the potato salad from his lips, Minnick turned to his son. "So, what's the arrangement with young Paisler here, Willard? He's to manage the section you're buyin' from me?"

It was Greg who answered. "I'll be working it, sir, but I'll leave the overall decisions to you unless Will has told me different."

"And if'n he has? Told you different?"

"I guess we talk."

Having known the boy to be straightforward these past months, Minnick reached to put his arm around his wife's shoulders. "That might just work." Twisting to get a good look at Nandria, he spoke again with the same matter-of-factness.

"So, how about your woman, Willard? Takin' her with you, or plannin' to leave her here with us?"

Nandria went very still.

"Well, sir, until I get settled someplace where Nandria and little Rose…"

"Seems like she's a help for your mother. Just like to know ahead of time what's expected."

Seeing Will's discomfort as he exchanged eye messages with Nandria, Greg intervened. "I like to know what I'm expected to be doing, too, Mr. Minnick. Appreciate your bringin' it out in the open. I'll be helpin' on your part of the farm…"

"I can't pay ya."

"Greg and I have an understanding," Will broke in.

"Umm," Minnick looked between them, apparently satisfied, then eyed the thick slices of cake, but reached instead for his third pasty. All three men glanced up, startled by Doris's questions.

"Is Willard buying this farm, Mr. Minnick? Or is this young man? Will we be leaving?" Then, reaching an understanding from her husband's expression and body language, she needed no verbal confirmation. "Ah," she sighed. "We'll be staying, I see. Ah, well."

For a minute or so, everyone brought explanations to the tip of his tongue, but stayed silent. It was up to Minnick himself to answer. Eventually he did, as he shoveled a slice of the carrot cake onto his plate with his warped tine fork. Scraping up a bit of the vanilla icing that someone had left behind on the cake plate, he spoke without looking at his wife. "Well, now, Mother, I doubt either of them boys has got enough in his pocket to begin to buy. But it looks like they's both a-tryin.'" Licking the icing directly from his fork, he did not dispute her conclusion that he and she would be remaining on the farm, at least for now.

Nandria, sad-eyed, stiffened as Will reached to hold her. It was all she could manage not to fling herself to the earth to dissolve in sobs.

* * * * * * * * * * * * * * * * * * *

The scorching sun hung bright belly down halfway beyond its zenith over them as Greg and Bodie helped Minnick load Will's bags into the bed of the truck. Holding her sleeping baby close against herself to shield her from the sun, Nandria sat stiff with self-control even when Will, in uniform, climbed up and settled himself beside her with his back against the cab's rear window. He touched her hair and caressed the side of her face until, finally, she yielded enough to lean against him, still unable to speak. But she did unstrap Rose so they could hold their beloved child between them.

Bodie kept his side to them as he looked steadily out the back of the truck at the rising and falling dust they were disturbing in this dry world.

* * * * * * * * * * * * * * * * * * *

At the paved street through Boonetown, Minnick eased up beyond Owens' store and parked. With Doris at his side, he checked his pocket watch rather than trust himself to help Will give a hand to Bodie and then to Nandria down out of the bed of the truck. But he did then grab one of Will's bags. Bodie insisted on shifting the other close to the tailgate.

"We made good time comin' in. Got a few minutes yet before we'll hear that train chuggin' in," Minnick announced.

"Assumin' that there train is even close to bein' on time," Bodie chuckled in strained tones. "Whaddaya say, Missus?" Bodie offered. "Whyn't we take the wee miss here into Owens' and show her the purdies?"

"I'll carry the gal, Bodie," Minnick told him. "You're still weak. Don't want nobody to drop her."

Will nodded with gratitude to his father for leading them away into the store.   "Bunnyduck," he murmured, "would you care to escort a lonely soldier on a stroll through your fair town?"

"Fair?" she recoiled but bit her lip to say nothing as Will set her hand on his forearm. They walked together away from the boardwalk. They passed the cluster of shops and moved toward the railroad tracks. Will stood a moment between the blindingly shiny rails, staring far into the distance where the two dissolved into one and then a mere speck in the haze of far away. Nandria kept her eyes staring, much as she had when she arrived in Boonetown those months ago, at the rusted vehicles in the field beyond the tracks. She shared their abandonment.

Suddenly she bent in toward her husband, willing herself not to lose these last few moments with him.

"Should we bring up your bags?" she asked and immediately chided herself. *What difference did they make? Why can I not find words to tell him what I so want to tell him?*

"We'll hear the train whistle with plenty of time to do that," Will answered her words. "Besides, Pa and Bodie'll want to help."

Bitter, Nandria rasped, "I hope we never do! I hope I never to hear that train whistle again."

"Spoken like the wife of many a military man," he chuckled.

"I married a fine man. His choice of the military was his own long before I met him. But at least that choice allowed me to meet him."

"It might be we'd never have known each other without it," Will speculated. 'I hadn't thought of that.' He turned her shoulders to face him. "I am so glad, then, for that choice. So very glad," he added low, drinking in the sight of his wife. He drew her against him as they stood looking together out beyond the fields at the edge of the town.

"As am I, my dearest love," she whispered.

They stood a long time, holding each other.

* * * * * * * * * * * * * * * * * *

Inside Owens' store, Cynthia Paisler handed Rose to an eager Ella Mae Drangler, who smiled with peace and contentment to hold the sleepy-eyed child in her arms. Doris giggled with pride to see the honey-colored little girl snuggle under that murderous collar of pins to lay her head on the woman's shoulder.

"Smart!" Cynthia and Doris remarked at the same time. Reaching to hook little fingers and make a wish in acknowledgement of their unplanned chorus, Cyn chuckled at the foolishness. Bewildered, Doris frowned at her unexpected joy. Growing disoriented, she began gaping around for her husband or that dark girl who always seemed to know where she was and what to say to help her know she was all right. Gladly, Doris looked over, distracted as Sadie Bean entered with her pale daughter—*the one who'd come as a little one to the quilting days with her mother long ago. Oh, and the one that got lost in the Bogs, too, wasn't she? So much happens all around us, though we never seem to go nowhere. But wasn't that why we're here now? Somebody going somewhere? Now who…?*

"Good afternoon, Mrs. Minnick," Sadie greeted her kindly, seeing her confusion. "How are you doing?"

Sadie stepped around her Ronda, rooted as she was staring at the far corner of the store where the sheriff was introducing a handsome, if slight, young man to Mr. Owens. Greg Paisler looked over at Ronda's growing interest with growing concern of his own.

"Ben Struan," Sadie told the women as she realized they did not seem to know who the stranger was. "With G.E.M."

"Drives that brown milk truck," Doris grunted, triumphant.

"They say he near drowned in the Bogs," Cynthia added, "but he claims it was worth it to save such a pretty gal," she added with a rolling of her eyes against the blarney until she saw Ronda blush under her grin of satisfaction and wonder.

But everyone stopped, listening.

"Time, I reckon," Minnick announced, acknowledging the nearing whistle of the train.

* * * * * * * * * * * * * * * * * *

On the boardwalk and patches of discontinuous sidewalk, people had stopped to stare at the unlikely—and for some, unholy—pair. No one spoke whatever he was thinking, each assuming the others were mulling their same conclusion about the marriage of white and Negro. How surprised many would have been to know of the true variety of opinions.

All startled at the mournful sound of the approaching train.

"I'm so sorry, Bunnyduck," Will murmured into Nandria's hair as he clutched her to him. "So sorry to leave you. I hadn't counted on doing that. But with Paris…"

"It's the war. And your mother still needs…And did you see? It was your father who took Rose in his arms," Nandria whispered all but frantically. "We'll be fine, Will. It is you we shall be concerned about. Write often. Please, my darling. The children and I will come at a moment's notice as soon as you find a place for us."

— RECIPES —

Doris's SWEET LEMONADE

Ingredients:

3 oranges

6 lemons

2½ cups water

2 cups sugar

Heat 2 ½ cups water with 2 cups sugar until sugar dissolves. Grate 2 Tbsp. orange peel. Squeeze lemons and oranges (about 1 ½ cups of juice each). Add peel and juices to cooled syrup. Cover and steep 1 hour. Strain in jars. Refrigerate. To serve, mix equal parts water and fruit syrup and pour over ice. Garnish with fruit slices or mint, as desired. Makes about 6 cups concentrate.

1940's Meal Cookbook

Mrs. Zorn's CARROT GLAZE

Slice 4 new carrots into long, thin strips and bring to near tenderness in boiling, salty water. Coat with glaze. Sprinkle with mint or parsley, as desired.

Glaze:

2 Tbsp. butter   2 Tbsp. corn syrup
2 Tbsp. water   ¼ cup brown sugar

Cook together until color is clear, attending constantly.

Mrs. Nickleberg's APPLE JELLY GLAZE

2 Tbsp. water   1/3 cup apple jelly

Cook water and jelly until smooth. Spoon over cooked vegetables; or dribble over meat loaf ten minutes before end of roasting time and return to oven for final ten minutes and re-glaze while cooling.
(Orange slices make a nice garnish under the final glazing)

Cornish Pasty Pastry

3 cups King Arthur unbleached all-purpose flour

¾ tsp salt

½ cup lard (traditional), 8 Tbsp. unsalted butter, or

½ cup vegetable shortening

1 large egg, beaten

3 to 5 Tbsp. water

2 tsp vinegar

Egg wash: 1 large egg beaten with 1 Tbsp. water

In a large bowl, whisk together the flour and salt. Cut the fat into small pieces and distribute over the flour. Cut the fat into the flour until the mixture resembles coarse crumbs.

In a small bowl, beat the egg with the water and vinegar. Drizzle this over the flour mixture while tossing everything together with a fork. Gather the dough together, folding it over on itself until it becomes cohesive. Sprinkle any dry or crumbly bits with water, a tablespoon at a time, until the dough comes together.

Divide into six pieces, shape into discs, wrap and chill while preparing the filling.

To assemble and bake: Preheat oven to 400 degrees.

Line a large baking sheet with parchment.

(continued next page)

Roll each piece of chilled pastry into an 8" circle.

Place ½ cup of filling in the center of each circle. Brush
the edge of each circle with water, fold over the filling
and pinch to enclose. Flute edges.

—*King Arthur Flour – since 1790*

Nandria's Basic PASTIES

Fill 16 to 20 cm (~6 ½ inches) pastry circle with Meat
Filling; fold in half and crimp edges. Bake at 425 degrees
about 30 minutes.

MEAT FILLING: Melt ¼ cup drippings, add 3 Tbsp. flour and
1 cup milk. Cook until thickened. Season with ½ tsp. salt.
  Add: 2 Tbsp. diced onion
  ¼ cup chopped green pepper
  ¼ cup chopped celery
  ¼ cup sun-dried tomato
  1 ½ cup cubed leftover cooked beef,
        veal, pork or lamb

  Makes 6 to 8 pasties (have fun varying the ingredients)

Sadie Bean's BISCUIT ROLL-UPS

Melt 3 Tbsp. drippings in a frying pan. Add ½ cup chopped onion,

½ cup chopped green pepper, 2 cups ground meat (beef, pork or lamb) and brown lightly. Season to taste.

Make soft biscuit dough and roll out to ¼ inch rectangle.

Spread with meat drippings and meat mixture. Roll like a jelly roll.

Cut in 1 ½ inch slices. Bake with cut side up on greased baking pan at 425 degrees for 15 minutes.

May be served with brown gravy or mushroom sauce.

Mary Jane Nordgren, D.O., a retired family practice physician, was raised in the Midwest, the daughter, granddaughter and niece of a family who had struggled through the Great Depression and comprised the "Greatest Generation." MJ lives in the Pacific Northwest on a hill overlooking three snow-capped Cascade peaks. She is the author of *EARLY: Logging Tales Too Human to be Fiction* and other non-fiction works. *FLOAT* is the second novel in her Nandria Series, which began with *NANDRIA'S WAR*. The series is dedicated to that Greatest Generation, who found themselves called to respond to the extraordinary challenges of World War II with tremendous courage.

Float

Made in the USA
Columbia, SC
29 May 2021

38604644R00192